License Notes.

This book is licensed for your personal enjoyment only. This book may not be re-sold or given away to other people. If you would like to share this book with another person, please purchase an additional copy for each person you share it with. If you're reading this book and did not purchase it, or it was not purchased for your use only, then you should return to the vendor of your choice and purchase your own copy. Thank you for respecting the hard work of this author.

This is a work of fiction. Names, characters, businesses, places, events, locales, and incidents are either the products of the author's imagination or used in a fictitious manner. Any resemblance to actual persons, living or dead, or actual events is purely coincidental.

ISBN 9781687174482

Rogues… Rakes… Smugglers…
Vikings… Highlanders… Pirates…

Other books by Shehanne Moore

Black Wolf Books –
Splendor – London Jewel Thieves
Loving Lady Lazuli – London Jewel Thieves
His Judas Bride
The Unraveling of Lady Fury
*

Soul Mate Publishing -
The Writer and The Rake – Time Mutants
The Viking and The Courtesan –Time Mutants

*

Meet the Author…

When not cuddling inn signs in her beloved Scottish mountains alongside Mr. Shey, or spending time with their family, Shehanne Moore writes dark and smexy historical romance, featuring bad boys who need a bad girl to sort them out. She firmly believes everyone deserves a little love, forgiveness and a second chance in life.

Shehanne caused general apoplexy when she penned her first story, The Hore House Mystery—aged seven. From there she progressed to writing plays for her classmates, stories for her classmates, plays for real, comic book libraries for girls, various newspaper articles, ghost writing, nonfiction writing, and magazine editing. Stories for real were what she really wanted to write though and, having met with every rejection going; she sat down one day to write a romance, her way.

http://shehannemoore.wordpress.com/
https://www.facebook.com/ShehanneMoore
http://shehannemooreweeblycom.weebly.com/
https://twitter.com/ShehanneMoore

Acclaim for Shehanne Moore

'There are many reasons I enjoyed this story but like the other Moore books I've read, I can narrow it down to…
1. The folksy idioms threaded throughout the story
2. The female characters who are so independent, a man is an accessory
3. Strong men who deserve to be felled by a good woman
4. Laughing, laughter and more laughing
5. Sensory scenes that will make you sigh or shake your head in astonishment
6. An ending that satisfies.'

Author—Ann Fields

'Her characters are real: gritty, decent and flawed as the rest of us. And ultimately, as redeemable by love we all are. Though it's bloody hard work for them sometimes!'

Author--Paul Andruss

'I'm becoming a big fan of Ms. Moore's work as I discover more and more of her unique scenes and roguish but loveable characters.'

Author—Carolee Croft

'Talented author Shehanne Moore never disappoints me with her books with a touch of darkness.'

Book Reviewer—Nicole Laverdure

'Ms Moore's books are always everything but ordinary.'

Author—Erin Moore

O'Roarke's Destiny

By Shehanne Moore

Black Wolf Books.
Kara imprint
Copyright © 2019 Shehanne Moore

CORNISH ROGUES

'*We are the life we live. Its graces and its pain.*'

DEDICATION

To Amara Patricia Pow, when it comes to destiny, may life always give you the best.

With special thanks to writing buddies everywhere--you know who you are--and most of all to you, dear reader.

CHAPTER ONE

Cornwall 1801--For every smuggler, there is an exciseman who will hunt him down ...

Destiny Rhodes was used to losing everything in one stroke. She'd just never thought it would be this stroke.

"A Gull Wrysen, here, you say?"

"I does, ma-am." Lizzie's voice tolled as befitted someone who was in the running to win the grand prize in the *looking most like your surname* competition at Penvellyn Fair. So, *Here Lies Lizzie Tooms, Loyal Servant of the Rhodes, Now Gone as Them, Probably unto Hell*, could have been etched into her forehead.

Ignoring the rattle of the chimney pots crashing onto the lawn outside, Destiny stared harder at her reflection in the mirror above the fireplace.

"And?"

"And quoth I, seein' as you be a' askin' *and* me havin' spoken to him, far worse bells could be a'tollin' for them what be cursed."

"Do you know, I'm very glad you think so, Lizzie? After all, here was me thinking it could well be the man who did the cursing. So why don't we all just look on the bright side and say a prayer of joy and thankfulness? I mean, it's not like we haven't got anything better to do, now is it? Where's the captain by the way?"

"Busy."

"Lying drunk on the stable floor, you mean? Having managed to get here on his sodding horse but not off it properly? Oh, that's busy, I suppose, if you can call such things busy." She clasped the mantelshelf tighter in her mittened fingers, the image of Orwell meandering home beneath frozen stars, flickering through the flames. If only she was such a frozen star, instead of standing here, staring as the straw end of this place disappeared down a dark rabbit hole. *Doom Bar Hall*. The only thing in her life still standing. The bricks and mortar she'd poured herself into. Every flower, painting, tuck on every cushion, even her pine cone garlands that made this room a work of art at Christmas. Gone. *On the turn of a card*. "Yes, a fine thing to be as busy as that."

"I can only reports what t'es my sacred duty to report, ma-am."

"Well, it's something of a pity you felt it was your sacred duty to come in here and report this."

Maybe she should just fall down now on the fender and be done with it? Then at least she might be buried along with her garlands.

"Anyways, I be sure your brother's done his sacred best."

"You know, for once you and I couldn't agree more. His *level* best, or should that be *epic*, to get drunk? His *very* best to lose this place. As for everything in it--?"

Yet, despite what she'd thought a moment ago, was this really so unexpected when Orwell inhabited the drinks cabinet the way fish did the ocean and would be sure to win the empty cider barrel in *the drinking it dry* competition at Penvellyn Fair. In fact, there was no *might* about it. The miracle was it had taken him this long. As for what she could do about it? Apart from winning first prize in the *breaking her hand by punching a wall* competition?

"Ma-am, I be sure that despite everythin', he has this in hand."

"Really? Well? That's a first. A second first, I must say. You thinking and him having this in hand."

"If he does not have it in hand, the Lord shall. You watch this. He will be our salvation, ma-am."

"Oh, please do spare me. Truly. Unless you think a sermon to match the one on the Mount, is something I can stand tonight? Wait around for the Lord being me salvation, and first prize in *the look at all them moldering bones* competition is what I'll win."

"Then what do you require, ma-am?"

"Right now?" She pushed her hand through her hair. "Apart from a sodding great dose of arsenic, you mean?"

The strength to deal with this but that didn't look like it was coming unless that sodding, great albatross that had just careered inside her velvet gown--a triple-weighted blind one at that—found some other gown to career into. Finally, ashes existed she couldn't rise from, despite everyone always saying she should have been named Phoenix. Imagine that, when Lizzie was sure to have it broadcast all over Penvellyn by this time tomorrow, if not before, how Destiny had collapsed in the library fireplace and lain there, *cursed*, like all who'd passed down the long, dusty road to the charnel house before her, too? Certainly she'd leaned her forehead on the mantelshelf. Clutched it for five minutes too.

"Ma-am, I know we have had our differences ..."

Mostly on the subject of accents. Destiny sounded like her mother who had come from up north. Yorkshire somewhere. And Lizzie only took instructions from those who didn't, which made it even more ridiculous she took them from Orwell who was more refined than a glass of malt whiskey. Orwell who probably reeked worse than one right now and was in no fit state to open his mouth, let alone let an order fall out of it.

As for Lizzie's pity? Another lecture on the Lord? Lizzie producing a bible from her apron pocket in another minute or so, in all probability, *and* asking Destiny to read from it? Well, Destiny wouldn't want first prize for making *the heavens fall down*. Now, would she? Especially not when she'd already won the one for *having her head panned in with the meat mallet*. After all, it was vital she at least try to raise her chin, though what she was lifting it for she'd no idea.

"Differences? You can say that again. No. *Don't*." Lizzie parted her lips and Destiny hurried on. "Once is quite enough. Look, just send in this ... this *man*. Me brother may be lying on the stable floor too drunk to deal with him. I'm not. Go on."

Yes. Let those who thrived on the pantomime of her life, say her black heart dripped something so common as blood? Over her burned and beaten body. *That* would be death, not this, even if all of it was death now. How could Orwell do this?

"If it is yore wish and yore command, ma'am?"

"I'd hardly put it that strongly. But what else can I do? Still, fear not Lizzie," she lowered her gaze from the mirror as Lizzie nodded. "Whatever happens, I'm sure the servants' places will be guaranteed. After all, in my humble experience, everyone needs servants. Even a death knell one like you."

Well? Everybody did. How very lucky to be one. Suppose she said she was? Found a mob cap, claimed to be the housekeeper? Bit an arsenal of bullets, swallowed them too, suffered the laughter, the snide remarks, the fact Orwell wasn't the only one to drag the family through the gutter? Endure the servants too? The ones who had so recently been hers?

How far a falling from a heaven too high.

What? Have it round the county that she qualified for entering the *best servants* competition because she cleaned boots and changed beds for her new master, fetched him his pipe and slippers, dusted his little ornamental vases?

No. It was better to starve. After all, she wasn't exactly likely to win it.

My God, if only Chancery had lived. Actually, if everyone who had ever touched her sorry life had damn well lived, she'd not be in this mess. But Chancery's death, over that sodding Rose O'Roarke had started an endless procession to the charnel house. All beneath the winding sheet of one certainty. The hollow toll of another death would shortly follow.

Until the moment Chancery took up with Rose O'Roarke, he'd been heir to Doom Bar Hall, not sodding Orwell and sodding Orwell's brandy bottles. Captain Rhodes, if you pleased, seeing as he, and them, commanded the local militia. Then the curse uttered by Rose's grey-eyed brother, Divers O'Roarke, across her marble-veined corpse had come true. They were all rotting in hell. Destiny most of all.

Her shoulders sagged. She glanced back in the gilt framed mirror, wreathed in ornamental cherubs on their way to heaven—

lucky them--the mirror she'd found in the attic and spent weeks cleaning, mending and wiping dead flies off. Gull sodding Wrysen's mirror now. Well?

Unless?

Unless she took it down, of course. Took it with her. It was heavy as an elephant. That much was obvious the second she reached forward to wrench it free. Not that she'd ever won any prizes for *wrenching an elephant*. No. There weren't exactly many of them about in Cornwall. And any there were, were hardly likely to be nailed to the wall, the half of which she'd be trying to get out of the door next if any more plaster showered onto her fingers. And where would she put that?

No. This was over. Over. *Over.* The words ticked like the grandfather clock in the hall outside. All she could do was go with her head held high. Let the locals have their farthing's worth. Well?

Unless?

She fingered her throat. It *was* an idea. Even if she wasn't quite sure where it came from.

"Dstny ... "

The French doors banged open in the gale howling over the cliff face. Orwell, staggering in here with wet boots and slurred apologies for losing her pine cone garlands, was the last thing she needed. Certainly, *if* she was really considering *that* idea. She slipped her gaze from her—*actually, some might say, edifying as a dead viper's*--reflection. And they would be right. Some things had to be faced when it came to ideas.

"Goodness me. Orwell. Sit down, why don't you? Preferably not in here, before your wet feet take first prize for ruining the rug, when it's no longer ours to ruin either. At least I hope that's from your wet feet."

The spindle chair nearly went over beneath his backside as he collapsed into it. She braced for the crash. It would certainly be one thing less for Gull Wrysen to claim if it smashed.

Unless?

Orwell sank his head with its untidy chestnut quiff on his chest and tried pulling his coat-tails from beneath his backside. "I say, old gril, l mean girl ... *I'll need* ... that is, I'll nleed to ... I'll need ver' much to ... to ... "

"What? Sober up? Stop drinking? Get Doom Bar Hall back? Likely as a chocolate doily surviving in hell that is, if you must know."

"Mulst know? Well, I... I sullpose, I sullpose I do. I mean ... Do you know, it's the damndest thing ... but I don't klnow what I mean ..."

"Oh, I think we can all see that, Orwell. Maybe we should hang a sign in Truro, saying, 'This is Orwell Rhodes. He doesn't know what he means but one thing's for certain, he has lost Doom Bar Hall. Throw him a farthing someone, so he can maybe buy it back.'"

Unless?

Hearing footsteps marching along the hall, she raised her chin.

"Yes Lizzie, what is it?"

"Milord Wrysen, ma'am." Lizzie's bobbed curtsy was probably the lowest the man towering in the doorway had ever seen. It was certainly the lowest Destiny had ever seen it. Start as you mean to go on her father had always said. Lizzie was starting well. Destiny should take a leaf out of that book.

"Should I fetch tea, ma-am?"

A good question. But no amount of tea in the best china cups Destiny had found moldering in the stables would sort this.

Unless?

She flicked her gaze over the man opposite. About thirty? Black haired—not her preferred color--a dusting of stubble on his chin. Eyes like gleaming black bullets. A plain, if not inelegant greatcoat, and leather boots, flecked with mud. No wedding ring. It didn't mean he wasn't married.

In that moment she decided.

"No. I am sure His Grace here would prefer something stronger, Lizzie."

Like herself.

She pinched her cheeks, although this Gull Wrysen could take her as she was. So long as he did take her.

It could be worse. Orwell could have lost the wager to Divers O'Roarke. Then she'd really be in trouble. It was common knowledge he regularly gambled the fortune he'd amassed designing houses and gardens in London.

Hadn't the sun's rays shone on him since he'd sworn that oath? Shone to the extent his chestnut hair must be burnt black while she looked more of a corpse than his sister, Rose.

This was the hand she'd been dealt. This was the hand she'd play though.

Smiles were beyond her. Gull Wrysen would see what he was getting and what he was getting was someone young enough at twenty five, to be thought attractive, despite her cropped hair and-- all right--the fact she'd give a dead viper a run for its money in the looks' stakes. But really, some might say, that was all.

As for what she was getting? Well? Doom Bar Hall was what she was getting. Very nice it was too. When nothing else mattered, she wouldn't be the first, or last, to manage a few ecstatic moans where required.

Only think of the fuel for the fires of all these little effigies the locals liked to make of her. The fires that had been dying of malnutrition lately.

She settled her gaze on his face.

"Well, Your Grace? Do allow me."

She meant a drink. Orwell was sitting there, after all. Besides Gull Wrysen was standing as if she was Medusa and he'd been turned to stone. But hopefully this was purely temporary.

"Thank you, Lizzie," she added, seeing that only Lizzie's jaw had moved and that was in the direction of the floor. "Yes. As you can see, I will deal with this. And please shut your mouth while you're about it. It's wholly bad enough *you* look like a tombstone. We don't want you adding trout to the mix. Not when Mr. Wrysen and I have things to discuss, regarding the house."

She waited for Lizzie to win every prize going in the *collecting her jaw and sailing like a doom-ridden ship away* competition, before setting out two glasses. Gold rimmed ones from the set that added perfection to her Christmas Eve when she finally sat before the fire in the cavernous, leather armchair and treated herself to a measure of port. Glasses she'd be keeping now if this went her way. Why shouldn't it? She was cursed, not incapable.

Yes. This man wasn't so bad. Fair hair would have reminded her of Ennis, who some might say, was probably birling ten times in his coffin. Not the man to think of and face this one standing in the candlelit shadows in his mud-spattered boots and greatcoat, holding his hat beneath his arm as if he'd no idea what to do with it.

Well, she knew, she knew exactly. She slipped the top off the decanter, inhaled the rich ruby scent. If it came right down to it here, she could cook and dust, if need be. If he wanted to bring in a woman, *if need be*, she'd say nothing. After all, there would be nothing to say anything about on her part. No jealousy. Nothing. She wouldn't insult Ennis's memory with that kind of thing that betrayed low moral fiber.

"But perhaps I am being presumptuous with your drink and your servants, now Doom Bar Hall has fallen to you, Lord ... Lord ...?"

"Me?" He shifted uncertainly, the ghost of a smile hanging to his lips. Totally unnerved. No bad sign. "Oh, good God, no. Miss ... Miss Rhodes, isn't it?"

"Well, it's not the devil incarnate, though there's plenty round here certainly say so."

"Good .. I mean ... No, I mean I think there's been some kind of mistake."

She nearly clattered the decanter top onto the sideboard. *Some kind of mistake?* My God. Damn Orwell. And yet, Lord love him. A mistake. *It was all a mistake.* Thank God she'd had enough moral fiber not to open her mouth.

"I mean ... *You mean* you're not Gull Wrysen? And you're not here to take Doom Bar Hall from me? Well, I never." Especially given how close she'd been to offering herself. "You know, I just can't believe how I—well, never mind, have the drink anyway."

"Gull?" Gull Wrysen lips twitched as he reached for the glass. "I'm not *Gull* Wrysen. Not that I know of anyway, unless I've been re-christened. I'm not Wrysen either. My name, so far as I know my name anyway, is Gil. Gil Wryson. And I'm not a gentleman either. Well ... again... Not that I know of."

"I see."

Damn Lizzie. As ever, *she* won first prize in the *being spat on by the Fates* competition. After they fell about the floor laughing at her first. Why hadn't she known no man would be called Gull? And Wrysen was a Cornish pronounciation? Still, she could surely weather a blob or two of spittle seeing as this was all a mistake?

"Although that's not the mistake," he added.

Damn the Fates to hell. Still, one mercy in a drought dropping from the heavens? She hadn't danced about the floor waving her drawers in the air. Whether he was a gentleman or not, was neither here, nor there, when it came to getting him to agree to this. And she would, so long as her own name was Destiny Rhodes, she would. *Now.* She'd have to. Just swallow what rose in her throat, forget about the fact that when everything she touched turned to dust, the pity was he didn't drop at her feet, and do it. Pray God the smile she dragged from God knew where, was warm, earthy.

"Then ... let's get straight to the point. I've always been a frank talking kind of girl."

"The point, Miss Rhodes?"

"Doom Bar Hall is not just my home, as well as my brother, Orwell's, it has been my whole life since my husband, Ennis, died. You look surprised?"

"Only in that—"

"I seem young to be a widow? Well, I was and I am, I suppose. Of course I could have lived at Pangbury, the family home but we were guests there ourselves, him having a younger brother with family. So I put the money he left me into Doom Bar Hall, because it has been in the Rhodes family for generations. I returned to my maiden name too. I think you'll find I'm quite a woman of the world, however."

It was the most tactful way to put what she was about to propose, which was why she turned away. Not before she saw Gil Wryson's gleaming black eyes were searching her face, with its warm, earthy smile hopefully still attached, in bemusement. But perhaps he simply couldn't believe his luck? She knew she couldn't. Believe *her* luck that was. Certainly at having got this far.

"I suppose what I am trying to say to you, is that I am in this house," she added. "Yes. It is in me even though you may have won it from my brother, Orwell."

"I think you're mistaken there, Miss Rhodes."

"Really? Well I don't. You did win it. I'm not going to argue about that, or how easy it probably was, knowing Orwell's drinking habits, to diddle him of his left pinkie. His thumb too."

"Perhaps. But it … "

Must he keep interrupting her when she was doing her level best here to get up from the pit, soar to the sky and secure the roof above her head? And the desperation he might refuse, lay like a lather on her bones? She glided forward then turned to face him.

"Doom Bar Hall is too precious to me. As you will see when I show you around, I am in every scrap of this place. In fact you might even say I am this place. That is why you should also know something."

"What?"

"I come with it."

Start as you mean to go on. Finish too. The blank cut-out she was inside meant it was nothing for her to stand here and offer herself like this. Once. Perhaps. But now? Given the alternative? Although equally, some might say, she had risen to this with a surprising fervor.

"I'm sorry?"

"Oh, I am too, Mr. Wryson, but I honestly have no choice."

He blinked, as if he hadn't known what was coming, or didn't want her, although he did have the good manners to smile. "Am I to understand? Are you … are you suggesting … "

Orwell's boots scraped on the scuffed floorboards.

"Dstny. Dsny, old girl, thart's what … you see … it's like this … I relemmber now …"

"Oh please, Orwell, do be quiet for once in your sorry life. Let's just agree I'll handle this, shall we? You can go to the devil for all I care. In fact, shall we say Truro marketplace if you don't button up?"

Yes. Gil Wryson wasn't the devil and he wasn't Divers O'Roarke--not that the devil troubled her, if she'd to narrow that list down. Divers O'Roarke now? Exactly how likely was he to be here in Cornwall?

Ignoring the wind banging the shutters, the batter of incessant rain cutting a silver stream down the moonlit glass, she continued,

"Now then, Mr. Wryson, these are the terms I place honorably on the table before you. They are very simple. Doom Bar Hall is my life. I will not be separated from it. So if you take Doom Bar Hall, you take me, to do what you will with. I'll be your queen, your housekeeper, I'll be your *whatever* you desire, because no-one knows this place like me. If you can't do that, if you have some other agenda, some other woman, for that matter, whatever you have, walk away now. I know I have not won Doom Bar Hall from you, that in a million years I may not have done that, but then again I never lost it in a devil's hand of cards, played against a man too drunk to know his own name, let alone the family one he's thrown away. These are my terms. I'm not leaving here, unless it is in a box. Do you understand?"

"Miss ... Lady ... ?"

Ignoring him, she lifted the glass to her lips. Courage flowed into her veins, all the way to her pounding temples. It always did when she made up her mind.

"In the circumstances, you may call me, Destiny."

Orwell tried again to struggle to his feet. "Dstiny. Don't. You ... you don't know ... "

"Orwell, I asked you to stay out of this. What you do is up to you just as this is up to me. I am doing this. I am keeping our home."

Her shell would anyway. What followed behind, a pallbearer at an unspeakable funeral might wince. She waited, a prisoner of the silence, the one existing in her soul, for Gil Wryson to speak. His lips cinched uncertainly, as if he didn't know how to approach this. Gentlemanly of him, but not the point.

"Destiny?"

"Yes."

"Well, I … I'm sure I can call you that, Miss … Miss Rhodes, if that's acceptable … "

"Why shouldn't it be? We're going to be things to each other, after all. Let's drink a toast to it."

"But what I was trying to explain, maybe not terribly well, that is true, and perhaps your brother—"

"Oh, him? He doesn't count for anything where this is concerned. Go on. Drink up. Plenty more where that's from."

"-- is too, is that I didn't actually win the game. So really … "

Her heart beat in such hope it almost felled her, although hope was something that had lived in the dark for the last two years. *Doom Bar Hall wasn't lost at all.*

Relief washed like an ocean, ambushing her as she stood there encased in tortuous, threadbare velvet. Her cheeks pulsed. To think she'd abased herself for nothing. But what did that matter? She downed the drink in one, wiped a mittened hand across her mouth.

"Then … if you didn't win …? What are you doin--?"

"No. I suppose that's what I meant when I said I wasn't a gentleman."

"I'm sorry, Mr. Wryson, you will think me thick as a sea mist—"

"Not at all."

"--but the truth is I really don't understand what you being, or not being a gentleman, has to do—"

"I'm acting on behalf of my employer."

"Your employer?"

So it was true? She'd lost Doom Bar Hall. Still, she'd made that decision before this man walked in here. How he looked, how old he was, who he was, had made no difference then. Why should it now?

"He thought there would be difficulties, you see."

"Apart from me brother lying drunk I can't imagine how."

"Well he did. And that was why he asked me to spy out the lie of the land, if you will. After all, this is quite a house to lose--"

"Do you think I don't know that? That is why my offer is the same because I don't intend to lose it--"

"*Especially when there's past associations.*"

"Past associations." She resisted the urge to finger her throat, which prickled as if a moth's wing was stuck in it somewhat of a sudden. "What do you mean?"

"I mean my employer once lived—not in the house itself—but on the estate, and is known to you."

"Known?"

She swallowed the astonishment sitting cold as marble in her mouth. There was only one man she could think of who'd done that but of that one man, she didn't want to think. Not when the blood drained from her face, the floor loomed so perilously close she struggled to stand in her black slippers and Orwell staggered to his feet.

"Dstny ... I triled to tell you. But you ... you ... Anyway, you're nlot seris ... "

"Unless the name Divers O'Roarke is unfamiliar to you, Miss Rhodes?" Gil Wryson's voice was oiled velvet.

"Divers O'Roarke?"

How did she say the name as if it was nothing to her, the name of the man who had cursed them, cursed her loudest of all?

Because she must.

"No. I believe I have some vague memories of him."

"Good, because he is waiting outside. I will be sure to pass the details of your offer to him if you still desire it."

Before she could think whether she did or not, whether some might say this was putting it rather strongly, or she should change her mind, a footfall sounded in the doorway behind her.

"Good evening, Destiny," clanged the sounding bell of hell and a voice she sort of recognized from there. "I see you haven't changed."

CHAPTER TWO

"Not changed? Oh, I think you're mistaken there, Divers, in ways you can't possibly begin to imagine."

Really? Well, just because she'd got in there faster than him didn't mean he'd no imagination.

If you let her speak to you, it is already too late.

"But let's not quibble when it's actually so very nice to see you back here in Doom Bar Hall again," she added, as if it wasn't already too late the first time she opened her mouth. She offered her pale, paper-thin hand for him to kiss too.

Destiny Rhodes? Or an abandoned place? A shadow that flickered on the wall while she'd burned away. Face whiter than blotting paper, eyes black as ink. Destiny Rhodes. Hadn't she always been glossed as lacquered furniture, eyes like gleaming black diamonds, lips lush as ripe peaches, fashioned in hell, every bit of her held lovingly in place by satirical design? But this?

Where the hell was the scent of ambergris and decadence, she'd breathed so freely, mainly over him? What the hell had she done to her flowing raven hair? Hacked it with garden shears, then hacked the comb? And what was this, 'nice to see you again' stuff, as if he wasn't enough of a plague about the place the first time round? A pox on it too.

If you let her speak to you, it is already too late. It always was.

Ignoring the hand she'd extended for him to kiss--that would be right--he set his hat down on a side table. Anything less would show it wasn't just too late, it was ten hours past midnight when it wasn't even a quarter to. The last thing he'd expected tonight? To bump into Orwell Rhodes in Daindridge's. Now he had though ..?

"Now then Destiny, there's no need to lie."

If his curses really were this effective though, maybe he should curse Lyon and be done with all this?

If you let her speak to you, it is already too late.

"Who says I'm—"

"I do. What's more I think I should tell you now, I overheard your little suggestion."

"Oh, it wasn't little, Divers. I think we can both agree on that. Given the things we once were to one another."

"Were we?" As for her being even remotely fazed that he'd heard her outrageous suggestion? Chance would be a fine thing. He shrugged off his coat, taking care not to breathe the subtle scent clinging to her like cobwebs—*lavender?* "You tell me. Well, little, or large, I daresay we can all make a mistake at times."

"Who says it's a mistake?"

"Well, the thing is, I do."

"I see."

"And, in case you haven't noticed, I now own this fine house." He slung the coat onto a chair. "So?"

"Well, so your friend there was say—"

He nodded to Gil to leave, thrust his thumbs in his waistcoat pockets. "That's why, for old time's sake, I'm going to suggest to you that you have till midnight to follow Gil there, out the door, also there."

"But …"

"Now."

"But that's only three hours away."

"It's four actually." He flicked his fob watch open. "One thing I have learned is how to tell the time. That's why I also know enough has been wasted. Midnight, Destiny. Before, is preferable. You know where the door is, I'm sure. You've lived here long enough."

A half full bottle of burgundy stood on the heavy oak sideboard, a set of hideous gold rimmed goblets by its side. It was time to snap his fob watch shut and taste what the house had to offer. He crossed the floor, stood with his back to her as the red liquid splashed like the unruly sea into the glass, the noise it made a sharp reminder of the sound that same sea made washing onto the sand at times. He held the glass under his nose, sniffed. A tang of blackberries. A definite winter bouquet. When it came to smuggling it was always the taste that counted though. Clearing his throat, he raised the glass to his lips.

"I'd offer you one but I don't want to take up your valuable time."

Yes. Physicality was everything in this job. And what exactly could undercut it in this instance? Certainly not her standing there with her dead eyes crouching in her skull.

"Oh, I'd hardly say it was—"

The French doors crashed open, the walls juddered, wind tearing around the room like a howling banshee. And with it …

Rose.

He coughed. Jesus. As if she was right here, the vapor of her dead breath, anyway, whispering on its dregs around the book lined walls. So he struggled to stand here.

Rose.

If you let *her* speak to you, it is already too late.

Rose.

Christ. How he wished they were all other things *now*. When not once in all the years since he'd lost her, had he felt her presence, not the times spent in bitter longing, the times he'd hung tales of his own deceit on the soundless stars. The only damn things to truly own the night sky.

Why the hell did he feel her here now, scuttling round the wainscoting of his life? Because she knew that what he should be here for, was the one thing he couldn't give her? Not if his limbs were pulled apart by the four horsemen of the apocalypse. If he was asked to dig his grave with her same breath.

Revenge.

He swallowed. If he did not speak, he was finished. In every way. "So?" If he did not sound as fine as a summer's day as he grasped the French doors and snapped them shut against the gale nearly taking them off their hinges, too. "The things we were, eh?"

"Yes, Divers."

"But maybe what you mean is the things we *did* to one another as children? Because it's so long ago, I honestly can't remember what we were. If you want to sit there like patience on a monument, pouring over the past and all the tiny and tedious things that happened there, wasting your valuable time that could be spent procuring lodgings—"

"But I am procuring lodgings."

"--that's fine. But I don't define myself by one moment. Despite how and why I left Cornwall, I'm not here for any kind of revenge if that's what you think."

"So you say, but some might say it's still revenge when I've nowhere else to go and not a farthing to me name, either. Surely even you can see that now and how sodding difficult it is for me to beg you, after all these years, to let me stay here? At least till I sort something out."

Damn it. *Let her speak*? So far he'd let her recite the bible, the alphabet backwards and three Shakespearean tragedies, all in that low, earthy voice of hers, which was why he wasn't letting her recite any more. At all costs he needed to shut the curtains as if it was no odds to him. He grasped the moth-eaten fabric—Jesus--tatters in his fingertips. What was going to fall on his head next? The ceiling? These were chimney pots lying in smithereens out there on the lawn. As for Rose? Her knowing Rose was here? Or not?

"I thought you were married?"

"Briefly. And I see I'm not exactly alone there either. Congratulations. I always knew, whatever some might say, some woman would be lucky to have you."

"Blind and old, was she?"

Still at least she'd noticed what glinted on his finger in the candlelight. His *perfect excuse to get rid of her* card. To think he'd argued about it. Now he could speak of his wife, his lovely wife, who he was head over heels over, with impunity.

"So?" He eased into the squeaking leather chair that had sat in this spot for so long, it was a miracle it hadn't sprung roots down through the floorboards. "What happened to your husband that he's not here to take care of you? Had enough of you, like all these other poor sods, did he?"

Her eyes darkened. "If you're meaning, am I cursed, are we cursed, well you of all people should know the answer to that. Still, if you must know ... about Ennis—"

"Not really." One question? If he could speak of his wife, his lovely wife, with impunity, *why the hell wasn't he doing it,* instead of mouthing off about Ennis? This was not about revenge, although in his defense he was back at work after being laid low. Another glass of that burgundy was probably in order, just to set things back on track--show her who was master here, underline to her about Lydia—although maybe it was that piss-poor it had caused him to hallucinate? Either that or it was that kicking he'd gotten months ago? Deliberately he stretched out his hand. "Why would I? But you're here, so where is he? Out in the storm with the rain crashing down? Hiding behind the books? Well?"

As if he didn't know. But her eyes had sunk to the back of her head. It was his duty to stop letting her speak to him—Rose too-- and finish the job.

"Fine." She exhaled sharply. "You know, some things just aren't worth this." Turning on her heel, she swept to the door.

Damn it but the hips were still more than half decent when she swished them like that. Cockiness came with the turf. But he was as drawn to them as he was to ram her eyes through her skull there— metaphorically. For the sheer hell of it. At least he hoped it was, that his tightening throat didn't say he was drawn to anything else. That he felt bad seeing her like this. That he felt ... quite a lot actually. Because this woman would cling and cling.

"Perhaps. But I'd like to hear it again."

She stopped dead in front of the open door. Apart from the rustle of the black velvet gown, like fallen leaves at her feet, the silence wasn't just as lengthy as the long boards of the room, it was as scarifying as salt in open wounds. It was also one he never should have broken. Hell's teeth, why had he done it? He *had* this. The past could not stand like an iron shadow between them, as if she still meant something to him.

"Hear what, Divers? That me Ennis is things you sodding well know alrea—"

He swallowed. Deliberately as he reckoned she just had. "No. Not Ennis." He'd started. Just like old man Rhodes always said. He might as well go on now he was drawn to the flame. "What you have to say about coming with the house."

CHAPTER THREE

"Are you ragingly insane, my friend?"

"Hmm? Sorry?" Divers O'Roarke let go of the door jamb and glanced round. Two glasses of brandy cast amber shadows on the wooden serpents. The ones that slithered along the sideboard, as opposed to the one that had slithered off up the stairs.

"Insane?" Gil set the decanter down. "After Eirwin, are you insane?"

"Why would you think so?" Divers cleared his throat, walked purposefully to the flickering fire. "This isn't what it looks like."

How could it be? Destiny Rhodes *had* been totally discomfited; her hands clinging like talons to her dress. His would have too if he wore a dress. Obviously he didn't. Not this far anyway.

'*I've said it, about coming with the house,*' she'd said. So of course, he'd also said he wanted her to say it once more.

Why not? He wasn't seventeen any more. The stupid boy she'd taken a wrecking ball to. Only *then* he'd lowered his gaze to her soft breasts, outlined in the clinging black velvet, the least he could do since he wasn't exactly going to get to touch them, what was more he hardly wanted to.

That wasn't so damned clever because *then* he'd seen that he wasn't seventeen sure enough. He was eight and perhaps he didn't just want to hear it all again because he'd simply wanted to make her squirm, either. What he wanted was something he couldn't believe. Even now.

If you let her speak to you ...

"Well, then." Gil picked up the two glasses. "Tell me what the hell it is, man, because from where I'm standing, and from where

Lyon is standing, I just know one thing. She can't stay here. You know that."

Divers eased down into the ancient chair, grasped the generous glass Gil offered. This was the way to end the day, especially now Orwell was sleeping it off upstairs. Of course Orwell shouldn't be sleeping it off anywhere on the premises. Divers was unsure how that had happened—oh, all right, he wasn't. Orwell was here because *she'd* said she'd leave if he stayed. So obviously Divers was letting *him* stay, at great cost to himself when Orwell Rhodes had made his life an even bigger misery than Destiny Rhodes, which was really saying something.

'*Midnight, you say?*' Destiny Rhodes had said and so had he. At least he'd said it earlier and he'd been going to say it again in this cavernous room lit by the mounting candles of memory and deceit, in the silence broken by the steady tick of the corner clock and the rain trickling down the window pane, leaving steamy patches in its wake.

But for some reason, when there were no gold medals for guessing which choice was the more odious to her. Him? The far distant relative? The family pauper? The man who had not got where he appeared to be by tilting headlong at a gate? Or the loss of this damned mausoleum? He'd then damn well said he was going to accept her offer. To make her squirm, of course. *Sort of anyway.*

And that was how Orwell had come up in the conversation. As far as Orwell was concerned, as far as Divers knew, he hadn't thrown himself in along with the house. Even if he had, he was hardly Divers' type.

And that was how Destiny Rhodes had said she'd stay and they would talk about it in the morning.

So now?

Now, apart from the fact she didn't know Orwell was still here? Well, he could see why Gil felt there was a problem. Divers eased further back in the chair and took a mouthful of brandy. Not the best. Tart with a trace of acid. In fact, probably like the stuff they cleaned their windows with in Kent, although that was down to the sheer volume flooding the place.

"Not that I see what it is, is your business, Gil, but I'm dealing with it. Obviously. I've not come here to waste the golden opportunity so kindly bestowed on me by Mr. Lyon. Miss Rhodes will be leaving in the morning. Her brother too."

Gil sat down in the chair opposite, the moldy one with the bottom sitting two inches from the floorboards. Christ but this flea-bitten dump had certainly seen better days. Imagine anyone being that desperate to hang onto it, they threw themselves in with it?

"Not my business? Maybe not. But, you saved my life, remember, when I was starving, when I'd nowhere else to go, when I couldn't remember who I was, didn't know where I was. I owe *you*. So you'll pardon me for talking out of turn. After Eirwin, she's trouble you don't need. *We* don't need."

"It just seems that way."

"Whatever it seems, man, do you need me saying what Lyon will do if you get involved with her? Unless that's what you want?"

He shrugged.

A possibility he'd not considered. Revenge in a very different form. Better than no revenge at all?

"You do know it was no odds to her who she offered herself to, just as long as she could stay here?" Gil sat forward. "Me. You. That spells danger in my book."

"I know what I'm doing. I always do. So can you please just drop it? Thank you."

Wasn't he the one who'd told Destiny Rhodes they'd talk about it *before* the morning? He could tell she couldn't contain herself. Yes. Her expression had been reminiscent of a dead viper's.

"I just remember her differently, that's all. Hell, the things she did in her time. But I've said it. Rest assured, tomorrow she goes. Do you think I can afford to let her stay here? Her drunken buffoon of a brother either? Well? I was just having myself a little fun, you know?"

He meant it. Let Destiny Rhodes stay and she'd soon discover things about him he couldn't allow to be discovered. Then what?

She'd slay him. So he steered clear of her tonight, finished the brandy, took the lantern lit walk onto the moor, signaled to Lyon things were on track. Vital when Lyon's nose was for a rat and Divers was that rat, back at work by a mere whisker.

As for talking before the morning? It was a dilemma because he'd sooner dig his grave with a twig than let her think he was eight again and too afraid of her to go near her. But what if he then couldn't leave it at that? He'd never known any man leave it at that around her. Look at Nick Trengouse, threatening to blow his head off with a pistol after she turned down his offer of marriage, look at Harold Penhaligan who'd gone to drink and the devil when she'd finished toying with him for giddy months on end. It didn't matter how changed she was.

Then there was Rose, here, waiting to ambush him. What would she think if he followed Destiny Rhodes upstairs, presuming the dead could think? So, over his dead body could he go up these stairs.

"Then tomorrow can't come fast enough, sir," Gil said. "Because if she ever finds out what your business really is she'll go to the law. Don't say I didn't warn you."

"I don't doubt it, but aren't you forgetting one thing?"

"What?"

"I am the law."

***

Hadn't changed? Her? As Destiny seized the tree branch, swaying about above her head, she acknowledged one thing. It wasn't that the branch was swaying so badly in the howling gale, it all but took her eye out. It was the cold cheek of those who hadn't the wit to look in a mirror at themselves and see they were as unlike the kind, malleable boy they'd once been, as she was from a talking horse. She'd only had to glance at herself in passing, in the bedroom mirror, the one she'd just sold herself to keep--to keep her pine cone garlands too—to see she was a pitiful, starving shadow of her former self. Her hair hacked because she was done with the world, her clothes as decorative as sackcloth and ashes.

Oh yes, gossip said that she was strong, stalwart, unfazed by any downturn in events, because gossip was vital in the circumstances when people laughed behind her back and thought she didn't know it.

But she must be fazed, fazed by *him*, to have prostrated herself at the toes of his polished boots. Surely not because she thought she could still dominate him and shocks one and two--knowing he owned Doom Bar Hall and finding him changed beyond recognition—had undercut her?

She had changed. *Beyond recognition*. The old Destiny would have secured him in seconds. As she'd almost secured that Wryson man, what with her warm smile and all. What a pity he'd been the wrong one.

Well …task one? It was Doom Bar Hall, or it was nothing. She was here, wasn't she? At least she was in the vicinity, the house walls rising up in their storm-riven shroud. Distant but visible.

What a foul night but, as if everything else wasn't damn well bad enough, there was the little matter of what was stashed in the summerhouse. If Divers O'Roarke got his hands on that, she'd hang. She'd need to stop him going in there till she sorted this with Tom Berryman—task two.

Hellish, wasn't it? And hellish too, that she'd had to brave coming out here first, with the threat of discovery hanging over her head, to do just that? Stand on tiptoes, hang that lantern, now swaying worse than the branch, on the branch, to let Tom Berryman know there was trouble. Some might say that was before she even got to Divers O'Roarke. Oh, and all the things she, Orwell and Chancery had done to him as children. Let her *not* sodding think of that when there were things she couldn't ever put right.

She inched a breath, let go of the lantern, stepped back. Thank whatever lord served her, it never pinged backwards, taking her right eye out, or causing her to win the set of grinning wooden teeth in the *I just had me head panned in by a lantern and now I need to belt back home to meet me lover, before he finds out I'm not there*, competition.

But at least now—*finally*--she could do that, despite the fact she was swaying worse than that tree, with hunger, what with all this shock and that, and her having left out breakfast and lunch as it was. As for the black ribbon the path was going to make if she left that lantern here? That was something she hadn't thought of. And sod all she could do about it either. Holding her hands out so as to keep her balance, she skirted the clumps of bracken.

Divers O'Roarke.

Expensive leather boots, grey greatcoat to match his eyes that put anything Orwell owned to shame, a silver fob watch on his waistcoat that would win him five minutes on the platform being ooh'd and ah'd at in the Penvellyn Fair *finest gentleman* competition. No small wonder. He won houses playing drunks at cards, cleaning out their wallets and throwing the family silver to the dogs.

How could he look so different though? Confident? Strong? Towering, despite the fact he wasn't hugely tall. His hair, tied at the nape of his neck with a black ribbon, darker and straighter. Nothing like that chestnut mop she remembered so well. Did he darken it? And why would he? Unless he was a peacock? As for him skulking into that tricorn hat in ways that would put the bogeyman to shame? Where had that and the sort of *not* so obviously Irish in terms of an accent, even come from?

How jealous was she, when she'd tried and outright failed all the years to get rid of her mother's northern accent, to sound more refined, in keeping with being Destiny Rhodes? Or, at least as if she belonged here where she'd been born? Oh, and what was that talk, or lack of it, about a wife? Had she died, run away? Been cursed too? A bit like herself, struggling along with the stony ground beneath her soles and the wind blowing her backwards, as she clung to her cloak ties, when by rights she should be in bed dreaming of Ennis.

Divers O'Roarke.

Who she better damn well hope was sitting in Doom Bar Hall counting the spoils right now, the risk she was taking coming out here. He might, for that matter, be knocking on her bedroom door. And here she was, torn between rushing--not because she was eager, that was for sure--and taking her time. She could be out for an evening constitutional after all, even if it was in the middle of a howling gale. Then again he might think she'd run away.

Still? Nearly there. *She was nearly there*. Almost at the garden wall, lying low beneath the scudding clouds. After that she just had to get through the garden, then in the back door which she'd left unlocked and up the stairs. Thank God.

Divers O'Roarke.

She clasped her cloak tighter. Very well, of course she, Chancery and Orwell had made things difficult for him and Rose. It was in that way children made things difficult for other children, especially poor, earnest children, with the sweetest smile. The kindest nature too. Why not stomp on his then chestnut curls? Grind his grey eyes and exotically-boned face into the gutter? It wasn't just what children did, some would say it was what she, Chancery and Orwell won first, second and third prize for doing.

Only now?

Oh God, only now, Jesus spare her, *what* the hell was that coming along the garden path towards her? A shining bright orb. *Shit.*

Forget *what?* How about *who?*

Not the Man in the Moon, or anyone going to win any prizes for trying to be him either, that was for sure, not with that purposeful stride and the tricorn jammed down over his eyes. A shiver crawled up her spine, followed by its sister in hob-nailed boots. Its aunts and cousins too.

And her torn between rushing home--not because she was eager, that was for sure--and taking her time too? No wonder her heartbeat nearly beat her ribcage to death and her feet slowed to a crawl. Her throat dried.

Tell him the truth? The real truth of Rose and Chancery that summer? Before he went a bit further and saw that lantern? The one she'd left for Berryman, dangling on a tree branch somewhere behind her head?

Out here? When he'd be as likely to accept it as he would a place on the roasting spit in hell? What kind of *local idiots'* competition was she trying to win? No. What she must do, was pray he didn't see that lantern. Or ask, as she slowed her steps to a snail's pace, why the hell she was out here. Pray her steps didn't falter any more than his did. That he was out here looking for her. Sodding unlikely though. Flash him her coolest stare. Especially now, now he drew level and her heart nearly leapt onto the path, under his fancy boots. Anyone could have left that lantern. *Anyone*. Including herself, to welcome Orwell home and just forgotten to take it down. But …? *But wanted to check in case it fell down and started a fire. Only to find it was stuck fast.* Well?

Besides? *His* head was down. Protection against the wind beating at his face.

"Divers." She nodded.

What kind of stare did he flash her in return? Only she couldn't see for the shadow cast by his tricorn hat. Maybe it was none at all?

"Destiny."

Oh God, just let her get past him. *It wasn't going to happen*. It wasn't … My God. It just had. He kept walking. So did she. Without falling down onto the ground, or looking behind her either. Just kept walking.

She snagged a breath. Then she snagged another. Maybe, for that matter he just liked moonlit walks too?

Did it mean he'd no intention of coming to her room?

She brought her gaze back to the path. Whatever he did tonight, tomorrow, whenever, there was another aspect of this. One she marvelled she'd forgotten, one that flowed like life back into her veins, breathed in her decayed pores.

Courtesy of him *everything she touched turned to dust.*

Why should *he* be any different?

CHAPTER FOUR

What should have been the last chime of midnight died silently in the clock case. Now he'd trodden the silver path onto the moor and left the lantern high in the huddle of rocks, he wanted his thoughts like a cold cloak about him. No chiming bells, or scents of lavender perfume rising in the iced moonlight as it had earlier when she'd sailed past him. No little frissons of excitement either.

He padded, a slow tread—no need to hurry--towards what stood before him--her door, the door to perdition. Reaching it, feeling, hearing, the hollow beat of his heart, he paused. A moment to turn the handle. A moment to unclick the door. A moment to slip inside. To look at her dark tresses of hair spilling on a damask pillowcase--*were moments that were never going to happen, moments he'd stopped the clock on.*

For a start her hair wasn't long enough to spill.

For a finish everything she touched, remember?

Once he'd have died to possess her.

That was then.

This was now.

Now *nothing* would stop him from walking on. Just as he had earlier.

As for what she'd been doing out there leaving lanterns tied to tree branches--at least someone had? In the middle of a howling gale at that? The morning would be the time to find out about that.

But he'd a fairly good idea. A fairly good idea what to do about it too.

The lights didn't just go down on this. They went out forever.

***

God, what was that scything her eyes? So mercilessly Destiny couldn't see a sodding thing? The sun? How could it possibly be the sun? She couldn't stand the sodding sun, and its hotly, pitiless, autumnal rays were beaming straight through the crack in the damask curtains.

As for what she hit her head off? Try the brass bedrail. It sounded about right. Ennis' face slipped, just as starlight had crept with silver fingers into her dreams too and he was going to kiss her. Now the sun shone, burning coals couldn't have fallen faster than Ennis's image from her clasp.

Smothering the groan, she flicked an eye open. Oh God, please don't tell her she'd done it again? Sat staring into the darkness and fallen asleep in her dress? She closed her eye again. Last night? *Last night* she'd had every reason to sit and stare into the darkness for hours, waiting, waiting, *waiting*. Not for Ennis to whisper her name in the darkness. God no. How the hell could she have possibly forgotten what she'd been waiting for?

Divers O'Roarke. Divers O'Sodding Roarke.

Flicking both eyes open, she sat up. Divers O'Roarke *who wasn't even here*. How sodding brilliant was that? Perhaps he intended to be faithful to this wife of his, whoever she was? And Destiny just imagined that little electric flicker that had passed between them on the path last night? Perhaps he remembered the exact wording of that curse?

The sweet, malleable boy he'd once been *would* certainly be faithful. This new, abrasive, cocksure, hardened man who'd looked her in the eye with shutters on his own and said they'd talk before morning now? Well he'd hardly be anything, least of all scared of a curse he'd uttered with good cause. *In his eyes.* At the very least she'd thought he'd want to know where she was last night. Had maybe even seen that lamp? So? Bravado, bluff call, or worse?

She glanced at the bedside table. *Great*. Was that why there was no such thing as her coffee? He'd told Lizzie *not* to spare her so much as a drip of water that was running down the window pane because he'd gone back on his word. So now it was going to be broadcast from the church pulpit, her husband had died rather than be married to her—*two years ago now*—and incidentally, just to shove the knife in, in case it wasn't far enough already, Divers O'Roarke didn't want her either. After she'd only gone and offered herself to him too.

The poor sods. What a shame if that was as much as would make their day sparkle. What would make hers was lying here till she died--quietly, without fuss. She lay back down and dragged the pillow against her cheek. That dream last night had been a torture too far to her. What else was left?

For that matter Ennis had probably seen how she'd considered affronting his memory. For the sake of a roof over her head. How could she? Even if it wasn't just any old roof?

No. It wasn't. And it wouldn't have been sodding necessary either if he'd left her properly provided for, before he only went for a trip over that cliff, now would it?

But he didn't know. How could she think these thoughts?

Still had only gone and sodding done it though, hadn't he?

Being said all over Cornwall, wasn't it?

Her throat dried. Forget the villagers. Did she sail from places with her head low? Shouldn't hell freeze first? Heaven have roasting spits?

So? Task one? At the very least seeing as Divers O'Roarke wasn't interested in her or her lamp? Rumple the bed, open the curtains, change her dress. If the villagers wanted something to choke over with their beer and bacon, they should have it. Especially if Lizzie was now in his pay. Then Destiny could go find somewhere else to lie down and die. She had to get up.

Dragging a breath, she stumbled across the floor and tugged the heavy damask curtains hard. Then she tugged them harder.

What the hell was wrong with the sodding things that they wouldn't open? Had Divers O'Roarke crept in here last night and sewn them shut? Tied the tops to the pole out of spite, so not only would she get no coffee this morning, she'd get no light either? Lizzie never had this trouble. She tugged harder. She could open a sodding curtain surely?

Not to save herself, the pole clattering off the floorboards, said. Not that it spoke exactly. That was something poles didn't do, largely because they were too busy panning in her head, on their way to panning in the floorboards.

"A-A-A-A-choo!"

The curtains, the lovely cerise and orange ones that had hung there since the days of Great Grandmother Endelienta--a long time ago to be sure but that wasn't the point—flumped onto the ledge like a broken-necked swan. That the place was plainly never dusted was the point.

"A-A-A-A-A-A-A-choo!"

And if it wasn't dusted, what the hell was she breaking her back, taking in smuggled bottles to pay that lazy trout, Lizzie and them other girls, for? Certainly not the good of her health. She'd probably caught all manner of awful diseases.

"A-A-A. A-A-A-A. *Choo!* A-A-A—"

Still so long as not a single, solitary person saw, or heard her trumpeting like a rabid elephant, she could still make A-A-A-A ...

"Good morning, Destiny."

Forget *show*. As in making one. How she never won the florin for *the best jump out of her skin, ever executed by woman, man, or beast*, was beyond her.

It was a close run thing what was worse. The thud as she stepped back and landed on her backside because her foot caught the curtain? That her spine jarred as she did? Or that the back of her head smacked off the floorboards?

Yes. Maybe it was a good morning, somewhere else in the world. Here in Doom Bar Hall it was the worst morning imaginable. Frankly, if her skull hadn't been panned in before it was probably fractured in three places now. Or that coronet of stars wouldn't be floating in the dust motes. But maybe that was heaven?

The floorboards creaked. Please don't tell her it was because *he* was crossing them. *In her direction.* Not only that he dropped to his haunches and extended his hand. Sort of. After a long moment's consideration when it was plain he must have died because this was over his dead body. "Allow me."

Was he mad? From Land's End to Launceston people avoided her like she had the plague. In fact it was probably from Land's End to John O'Groats. She couldn't get another husband even if she wanted to.

"Seriously, Destiny, before you go getting any ideas," she didn't move and he added, "I don't want my property damaged."

"Are you meaning me, by any chance, or the sodding curtain pole?"

"The curtains. Obviously I'm meaning the curtains."

Great. That he meant the curtains were his property was a plague cross chalked into the door of Doom Bar Hall. As expected as the sun rising. She needn't die in its rays today, when courtesy of this same man, she had it in her power to wither him to dust. She glanced at his hand.

What?

And have Ennis birling ten times in his box by affronting his memory with the man who was responsible for his death, even if it was purely to get revenge—and it would hardly be for anything else? She couldn't. What if he looked down from heaven and saw her?

Only think of the generations of Rhodes' who had stood here before her, before Ennis, before their baby, had all gone, though. So every day another drop of breath left her, because of this man, looking so prosperous in his nice charcoal waistcoat, a bunch of fancy lace at his throat, the smell of the ocean in his soft brown hair? But maybe she was afraid of that tiny flicker she'd felt on the path last night because he was a bit commanding? And he wasn't half bad looking either.

Think of the rhythm of her life, the things that anchored her now, the Christmas mornings, a gift for each of the servants gathered in their best around wreathed trestle tables, and punch, hot with cinnamon and pressed cider apples, served from the steaming wassail bowl that had been in the family for five generations. The little things she held onto in order to hold onto something bigger--the life, the one she'd carved from the ashes, she needed to know was still there for her when sod all else was and no-one would have her. If she'd had the courage to end that life perhaps, but she hadn't.

Think of how bloody entertaining it would be in the village, now she'd got her comeuppance. *Finally*. At the hands of a man who had cursed her *for nothing,* whether that curse had power or not? A man she'd greeted as warmly as a log fire last night. Telling him how good it was to see him when it was anything but, but how else could she have greeted him without being shown the door? A man who thought *she* hadn't changed, when she had, *beyond all recognition*. A man obviously determined to squash whatever iota of pity he'd *perhaps* had for her lying on the floor like a prostrate giraffe. Maybe for that matter he thought she was lying like a prostrate giraffe for that very purpose?

Now, maybe this curse was a load of old buckets of cod, but ask Ennis, Chancery, her father, her mother, and they'd all say differently, if they could.

So task one?

"Actually." Ignoring the proximity of his grey eyes, she grasped his hand. Yes. Task one had changed somewhat from a few moments ago, which was probably why her heart hammered. "I was expecting to see Lizzie."

"Lizzie? She's someone who hides in the curtains, is she?"

"Oh, you have no idea where Lizzie can hide on occasion. Curtains, wardrobes--"

"Lizzie? Are you meaning the servants?"

"Well, Divers, you might say I'm hardly meaning the stuffed parrots belonging to Grandfather Austell, even if they do have names. Glad you've cottoned on." She smiled. Keeping his hand of course. In fact, smiling gave her the chance to press it tighter.

"They're gone and--"

"*Gone?*"

Her heart stilled in its tracks. *Gone?* My God, was this what she got for touching him? And offering her most disingenuous stare men had threatened to shoot themselves over?

Grandfather Austell's stuffed parrots? The ones he'd brought all the way from Bristol? The ones that brightened the sitting room, even on a dull day? Even if one would win the prize in *the squint eyed stuffed parrot* competition and another for having no eyes at all?

"What do you mean gone?" she demanded.

"After some consideration."

"Why have they gone?"

"Because I told them."

"You *what?*" Oh God, don't let her thump her hands off his chest. Forget the disingenuous stare. She sprung to her feet. She believed she even let go of his hand, her throat was that thick she couldn't breathe.

"What I say, Destiny," he sighed. "Servants are servants, after all."

"Ser—"

"And you always pointed out I was vastly uneducated? Well, well."

The servants? She froze in her tracks. How could she be so sodding stupid? To let go of his hand and everything. Had it been the sodding parrots now? She hauled a breath.

"Oh … I think when it comes to education the record will show I never had—"

"*And* not that it's your business—"

"It's not, believe me."

"I gave them three months wages, so Penvellyn folks will think me more than generous."

"Right?" Well, lucky them.

"Before *you* start, that is."

"Well, I wasn't. Going to start, that is." She was, but then again there were times for not starting and times for not falling on the floor, times for yittering through her teeth too. "I mean Penvellyn folks and their thoughts are no odds to me. No, no, it's only the servants after all. And really, as you can see, they'd win the trout, in the *as lazy as one* competition, a share of it anyway. So three months wages shows no end of a generous spirit if you ask me."

Especially when he'd spent it for nothing if he was doing this to force her out. Maybe she should have been more of a threat to him, then it might have been four months wages? Five? Statues erected to her all along the road to Penvellyn for her services in getting sacked servants *six* months pay?

He rose to his feet. "Destiny ... Look ..."

What at? The door? No wonder her face froze and her eyes felt as if they stood out like flints. Why couldn't he have come in five minutes earlier? Before she'd decided to stand by the Rhodes' wassail bowl? When she'd still been more than happy to die in a ditch? Whereas now? More to the point, how could she have flared like that? When she had his hand and everything? She never flared like that these days. She ran her tongue over her lips.

"W-what at? You not coming in here last night like you said and now giving me more work—"

"You? Work? Well? Well?" He glanced round the room. "A new one on me."

"--to do than I had perhaps hoped, what with last night's storm damage to the estate—"

"Destiny, I really don't think that the storm damage to the estate is top of my list of prior—"

"But maybe you were afraid to come in here, what with that curse and that?" Oh God, please let her smile be the most hotly dripping and divine she could make it, despite the fact it was nothing short of shocking she was having to offer it. "But fear not, if you've come in here now, I must warn you, not only is it not convenient. I wouldn't want to be crossing that pretty wife of yours." Well, it was a thought now she considered it. "Especially as you're likely to be doing that when she arrives to find out you've only gone and gotten rid of all the servants."

"Nicely scored, Destiny." He shoved his thumbs into his waistcoat pockets. "But I think the servants would be the least of her complaints."

"Really?" And no prizes for guessing what would be the most. "Why's that? Because you're not rich at all? And here's me seeing straight through you the same as always? Well?" Not that she meant to or anything, when there was one thing he hated was to be reminded of that fact, but having nicely scored once, it was good to do it again. "After all, no servants? What lovely wife would be happy with that unless she was accustomed to it?"

Now he thought about it, it was probably why his face froze, and he flicked his gaze to the floor.

"Now then ..." Although her heart rose in her throat, she opened the wardrobe. Get out of here before he said *get out of here* and he might forget he was ever going to say it.

"Where are you going?"

"Oh, I'm not leaving if that's what you're thinking." Of course she could go out without her cloak, a late autumnal sun blazed from a cloudless sky. That was probably because the wind had tossed all the clouds to earth though. Why make this easy for him, by taking her place in the family crypt because she only went and caught pneumonia though? "Chance would be a fine thing. No. If there is one person who knows this estate, all the nooks, all the crannies, all the little fairy dells and places of legend that people claim—"

"Right. Legend, eh?" His enigmatic gaze flicked her as if he wasn't just bored out of his skull but bored out of his skull and about to put her out before he was bored further. "Now Destiny, I know you are desperate to keep a hold of all your tattered little—"

"Oh, not half as much as you will be when your lovely wife doesn't just arrive, she gets her head panned in by some of them tree branches I was out tying lanterns on last night to warn passsersby. They're rotten every one of them. The branches that is although some of the passersby haven't got much going for them either, what with some of the goings on here sometimes. And I know that. I know that because I know Doom Bar Hall. Haven't I only made it me business these last two years? Go on. Ask me anything you want and I will tell you."

"Destiny ..."

"Even, *when will I get out*? And I will tell you it will be after I sort them branches."

"Sooner rather than later then, seeing as there only appeared to be one. And Lydia is hardly likely to come that way."

"Lydia? So? She does exist then? I was starting to wonder." Why did his face freeze, for the second time, as if she was not alone in wondering? When really, if anyone's face should freeze over, giving herself away over that solitary tree branch, it should be hers? But maybe he froze at her ability to extend such a magnanimous hand of friendship, in very difficult conditions? In which case she was really getting somewhere. "She might come some other way and the end result could be the same. Go on, try me. And if you're not satisfied, I'll go now." Not going to resist that offer, was he?

"Try you?"

"Go on. I dares you. Bet you can't."

"Very well then, Destiny." He drew himself up. "Raven's Passage?"

"*Raven's Passage?*"

"Raven's Passage."

That crock of excrement everyone said led down from Doom Bar Hall to the cave at Ryland's Point and was stuffed with more treasure than the Orient? She hesitated as she fiddled with the hanger. Well, well? Please don't tell her he was another of these eyes-full-of-gold fools? And him rich as Croesus too? With how well that design business paid and everything?

"You did say," he added. "And yes, I believe that's what it's called."

She did too and if he was that fool, why not string the pony along, take him down to the kitchen and show him the entrance? The broom cupboard, for example? She edged her gaze sideways. It was an idea of course, but then again once he saw it was only a broom cupboard, maybe he wouldn't think it was a very good one?

"I'm ... I'm sure it is but ... well, what possible purpose would Raven's Passage serve except to make the walk to the shore dry on a wet day, for someone as rich as you? Herland's Dell now, which I do know, know well, and, if I may say--"

"But maybe I like being dry?"

How could he, when she didn't want him to?

"Here, and maybe you're just not as rich as all that?" Well? Despite what lay on her hands like a cold sweat, she set the hanger back on the rail. Rising to this really well, wasn't she? "Or you'd buy an umbrella, like an ordinary person."

Well? He would, wouldn't he? But maybe he wasn't as rich as all that? And that was the real reason he'd gotten rid of the servants?

He just didn't want her to know that when it would be good to know, what with her obvious talent in design and that, that, just maybe she could think about making some money, if need be, if the wife arrived, found out Destiny had flung herself in with the house and gave her her marching orders. Also, turning him to dust might avenge Ennis, how would it secure Doom Bar Hall, if the wife inherited what was Destiny's by right? It would mean she'd be shooting herself in the foot to touch him. But suppose she could string him some other way? With her stunning local knowledge and renovation skills? Yes. A girl needed to think ahead here.

"I mean ... I mean, let's face it, if you were rich why dismiss the servants when they're this close to the cliff face of local knowledge? Gossip too? I mean ... I mean, if anyone knows anything about a place and the nooks and crannies in it, believe me, it's them."

And when they didn't, it would be all their faults not hers too. How clever was that?

"But you said you did."

"I do. I was just expressing my surprise that you would be in any way interested in Ravem's Passage and all the gold it's said to contain, would get rid of the servants too when you're supposedly rich as Croesus, unless who you really want rid of here, despite what you said last night, is me?"

"You'd have to ask Gil."

"What about? Whether you want rid of me, or not? Or what you do exactly? I mean let's face it, from what I remember you barely knew the difference between a snowdrop and a pansy, a piece of satin and the thread to sew it into something. Here, from what I remember you couldn't win a game of snap either. Yet here you are only going and winning Doom Bar Hall in a card game *in Daindridge's* of all places, last night."

How the sodding hell was that in terms of co-incidences when for years there hadn't been a whisper--about him, about anything--too?

Had he fallen off the face of the earth or something? As for that look, that cool look, that cool, *unreadable* look he'd given her when he spoke there just now … That look would win every prize going in the *you've stumbled on something I don't want you stumbling on* competition. No wonder her heart skipped a beat. What was going on here?

How she faced him without a flicker of what she was thinking was down to one thing. He'd also been out there last night. *With a lantern too.*

As for how he faced her? He shrugged, his face expressionless as a piece of blank paper. But then he was hardly going to write *guilty as charged* on it. Let a single carefully combed hair stand up either. "About how it all pays. He's the curmudgeon about these things."

And yet, did it pay to face him without that flicker either? Especially if he was up to something he shouldn't be? *Like smuggling.* She wanted to stay here, didn't she?

"Right."

"But I suppose, while it might be nice for you to think I'm poor, I'll probably have to disappoint you. I just like to balance my books, not live above my means. Have you any idea of the trouble that—"

"Oh, plenty, the way my father ran this place into the ground loans, for this, loans for that and Orwell's doing his best to finish the job, so now a big, fat nothing is what there's loans for. That's why, putting everything aside, it would oblige me no end for you to let me check over the estate, see it's not going to cost you any more after last night's storm. I mean, if nothing else, we wouldn't like to be held accountable, because, I don't know about you, being rich and all that, but that is money I don't have. And while you might be good enough to overlook that fact--" he wouldn't but it did no harm to appeal to his vanity--"I wouldn't sleep easy. Given these past associations you spoke to that Gil about, it wouldn't be proper."

No, my God, not when some would say it was written in large letters, from one handsome cheekbone to the other, that she'd stumbled on something here.

As for asking Gil? Would she hell. Gil wouldn't answer her questions. But there was one man who might. Hadn't she left him a message last night with regard to what was in her summerhouse too? Maybe Divers O'Roarke didn't want rid of the servants to drive her out at all?

Yes. Talking crypts, pits, of fool's gold and tunnels, the time had come to do a little digging.

CHAPTER FIVE

This hadn't exactly gone as he'd intended. Some people might even add, as the door clicked shut that his attempts at *starting tomorrow to deal with Destiny Rhodes,* hadn't just failed, they'd failed so catastrophically, the success rates for landing a cat on the Moon by throwing it up in the sky, were probably greater. It was 'tomorrow,' wasn't it?

"Wait."

Ignoring the smell of moth balls, he tore a scarlet ball gown from its hanger. The scarlet dress, the emerald one, hell's teeth with bells on, the crimson one, danced from the hangers as if they were bloody alive. The burgundy one. Why the hell did she have to have a dress that shade? The shades he remembered her in. Of course pink, or pastel, or cream, were too boring for her.

Forget exotic siren written all over her, lips of beckoning sin, eyes like stars and all that stupid stuff. At sixteen, she'd been brash, beautiful and more knowing than King Solomon in a very different way from other girls. Earthy. Outspoken. Provocative. Dripping honey one minute and tight-faced sarcasm the next. And dangerous. Dangerous as a sea of sharks. She'd been casually, *not that different from what she was now in some ways.* Or she'd never have gotten one up on him.

"Destiny."

What was he doing even thinking about her at sixteen when she'd just turned tables on him? Firstly by sprawling on the floor like a helpless giraffe. So he'd touched her, for God's sake. Secondly with all that *other* stuff. He wasn't going to think about thirdly. But so long as he got her out of here before there was a fourthly, this was fine.

He bent down, gathered up the scarlet dress. Not the one to go after her carrying. Christ, weren't there any rags like that dress she was wearing? She was getting away from him, burning like Rome while he fiddled like some befuddled Irish ploughboy. He rummaged, yanked some silken effort from its hanger--black, beadless. She went. And she did it now.

Did he reach the door handle quicker because his boot caught in the skirt, or because he needed to catch her? Whichever it was, he whacked his nose off the panelling. He cursed, ran the back of his hand across his face. It wouldn't do to face her with blood dribbling down his chin. Physicality *was* everything in this job. Especially now he almost found her brass-neck entertaining, himself rising to it in ways it didn't pay him to. He tugged the door open.

"Miss Rhodes."

He straightened his shoulders, hurried past two moldering suits of armour and the grandfather clock, gained the wooden stairs. Gained the wooden stairs and clattered down three of them, before righting his fall.

"*Mr.* O'Roarke?" She paused halfway across the hall.

Rose.

Oh, Jesus Christ, rustling leaves on the staircase, when there was *nothing,* just his shadow on the bare boards. As if that wasn't bad enough, the dress sprung to life like a snake, the kind charmers coaxed from baskets.

"Something wrong, is there?" she asked.

"No." He shoved the dress, rolled up behind his back. "Not that I know of."

"So?"

But maybe she'd froze given the house ball *was* in his court? And it was. She hadn't stumbled on anything. "I was just ..." *Because if she had stumbled? And she compromised this? After that business with Eirwin? Or she thought she had a bargaining counter ...?* "...looking for Gil."

"I see."

So did he. That the door was there and he needed to put her out of it. Now he'd been stupid enough to dismiss the servants because to know him was death, he also knew Lyon *would* want her here for the time being, *if* she could shed a light on Raven's Passage, the thing that would give *him* the in. Lyon certainly wouldn't want her wandering the wilds of Cornwall, blabbing what she knew, until Divers had established whether that was all or nothing.

"I'll just be getting on my way then?" she added. "Check the estate for damage, that is? So your lovely wife—Lydia--doesn't come in to a mess. Because I wouldn't like to be the cause of any trouble between you."

So help him to whatever God there was, if she said that word *wife* again, she'd be wandering Cornwall a lot quicker than she thought.

"I hope you think you'd get to. Now, if you don't mind I've work to do."

He certainly did now.

And it didn't involve cooling his sweating brow, calming his pounding heartbeat either. Lyon would want her here, but not if Divers found that damned *in* for himself. He would now. If he'd to turn up every stone in this place, dismantle it piece by piece, he would.

She hadn't undermined him. He'd undermined himself. Now he knew this, he'd dig his grave with a thimble before it happened again.

***

Destiny leaned harder against her bedroom door, letting the beadless black silk fall from her grasp as the breath—rather a lot of it, in fact she probably sounded like a charging rhinoceros--rushed down her nose. After Tom Berryman had been as much help as a sodding Christmas pudding to an overweight donkey--who the hell was the Cleanser exactly?--and the smack in her soaring wings with the shovel, her attempts at digging had been, *Divers O'Roarke still meant to throw her out.*

Well, why the hell else would her gowns be in heaps on the floor, at the door, the black silk on the staircase? Unless Gil Wryson had come in here and sodding slavered all over them? About as imaginable as her waving a fairy wand and transporting Doom Bar Hall lock stock and barrel, *to the Moon*. Some might say he was the kind but she had her doubts.

That lying son of her aunt's husband was though. *A stepson*. For God's sake that was how tenuous the connection was. One even she struggled to remember. How could her aunt's husband do that to them all? Win the prize for *falling off his horse and getting his head stoved in by a boulder*? His first wife too, although she hadn't had her head stoved in exactly? But there was a connection with horses in that she'd had galloping consumption. As for *her* aunt marrying the grieving widower? Couldn't she have got someone else, who was footloose and fancy free for example? Who didn't ride horses either? Or at least took a bit more care when he did?

As for the world and its aunt for bringing Divers and Rose O'Roarke here? Talk about shutting the stable door after the horse had bolted. Why could she not have put them in a place for orphans like any decent, self-respecting aunt?

No wonder she'd sunk down against the door and slammed her heels off the floor. As for sounding like a screaming banshee? Well, the last thing she could afford to do was sink to the floor and lie here as useless as her gowns, a thread for the unpicking, could she? But she had sunk, so she might as well make a noise about it. Tom Berryman's point blank refusal to move that stash, and the fact that Divers O'Roarke saw her out there last night, were her undoing. To come back to find her dresses had all been hauled from their hangers, was the final straw. Why fight what she couldn't change?

If she had some dirt on Divers O'Roarke, perhaps, but there wasn't even half a trowel-load. As for the idea that her dresses were all over the floor because Divers O'Roarke meant to put *them* out only; had maybe even taken them out the wardrobe and put them on the floor because he wanted to see her in them? Well, pigs would fly through her window, without cutting their wings. Maybe if she'd stayed in her room, put on one of those dresses and been enticing instead of battling out in the storm to leave that lantern all for nothing? Maybe Divers O'Roarke had come here for that matter? Then what he'd come was out to see what she was up to?

She hugged her cloak tight, tighter than her stomach had drawn these last two hours as she'd battled along the headland and back. At least look on the bright side. The fact the dresses had been thoughtfully laid out saved her the trouble.

And truly? She was tired. More tired than if she was a hundred. Certainly too tired to go down these stairs and engage in another battle to no good end with Divers O'Sodding Roarke.

How much easier just to sit here and dream of Ennis. There was sod all point to anything else.

***

"Miss Rhodes."

"Well, it's certainly not them sodding parrots."

And no end of sodding wonder too. A fat lot of dreaming of Ennis she'd got done this afternoon with the sodding great racket that started up ten minutes after she sank down onto the floor. And went on. *And on.* Bang. Pause. Wallop. Pause. Bang. Pause. The thud of metal on stone *and* such an amount of plaster showering behind the walls--even if it was lucky there were any walls for it to shower behind--she'd thought she'd need to find that proverbial umbrella.

As for the inconsideration of those responsible for nearly taking the house off its foundations? Those responsible, for that matter, standing there in their shirt sleeves? Their breeches too, it was true. Sweating as they swung great pickaxes in clouds of dust. In what was the Doom Bar Hall library? When all she wanted was to lie there on the floor and dream of Ennis--what kind of widow was she for not doing it since this morning? Well, there would be no prizes at the local fair for guessing who they were.

"What do you want?" Divers O'Roarke added, landing another blow on the brickwork.

"Want? Well how about some peace and quiet for starters?"

Never let it be said she didn't know how to get it too. Not when, if there was one thing Divers O'Roarke hated more than her, it was being caught red-handed. Clasping the scarlet dress tighter, the one she'd scooped up off the floor, she swept forward.

"Gil, get her out of here, thank you."

When all she wanted was the peace to sleep?

"Gil, out now."

"Goodness." The sight of what was spread over the library table stopped her in her tracks. "You know, I haven't seen that—"

Well she hadn't. She hadn't seen this for ages. As for what it was? Grandfather Austell's map was what it was. His one of the house and grounds. Not that that should distract her or anything.

She held up a hand. Peace was a priority, but even if it killed her, surely the only way she should be leaving here was in a box? A pity she'd come in here raging when it was probably what he wanted and was probably taking that wall down to make sure he got what he wanted too. But she could sort that to her satisfaction surely, with what she'd come in here to sort it to her satisfaction with? That was the priority. She dragged her gaze from the map.

"When I have simply come to discuss the business of my things? Yes. And how worried I am that while I was out there today looking over the estate for you, there was an intruder in—"

"Things? What things?" Gil Wryson's black eyes gleamed with amusement. "You don't have any things."

"Really?" She cocked an eyebrow. "But I thought I did. Excuse me, but are you saying that—"

"Do you mind me asking what the hell you're talking about?" Divers O'Roarke wiped his hand across his nose. "Well?"

"My *clothes*, Divers."

"What clothes?"

"What ones do you think? The ones on me back. What else? And not just those. No. If it was those I wouldn't trouble you when you're obviously so very busy. My *other* ones."

"What other ones." He raised the pickaxe.

"This dress here for example. And the others up the stairs, lying on the floor of what *was* my room. I mean I accept now that technically speaking, what with you winning the place and all, that these dresses which someone plainly pulled from the hangers--"

"What about them?"

She fought not to drop her jaw. What did he think when he'd put them there? Didn't he give a proverbial that she knew it, that his friend here knew it?

"The fact that they were lying on the floor." Where she nearly lay herself, the shocking affront to Ennis's memory being offered largely by her heart giving that stupid bump at the sight of Divers O'Roarke's half naked chest as he landed the pickaxe in the wall. As for the lies he was telling? When she had him, by the balls at that? Hadn't he changed a great deal?

"The floor where, I can't swear to it but I am fairly certain, I never left them. And now, given that there's no servants to hold responsible for such adverse carelessness as not sweeping and dusting, and just maybe—maybe--"

The floorboard to her left creaked. "In *your* room was it, Miss Rhodes?"

She unpeeled the dress from her arm, shook it out. "Well, Mr. Wryson, I don't think this is yours, or his, now is it? But maybe you'll tell me it is?"

Gil Wryson wiped his hand across his nose. "I'm unsure how it might be legally."

"*What*? That you wear dresses?"

"That my employer here, Mr. O'Roarke—"

"Does? Well, I never did. Or that this is the kind of place you are planning on running here, Mr. Wryson. Goodness, I wonder what the locals will say to that? I know they like a bit of gossip. But men? Wearing—"

"*He* could argue—"

"That, that's all right?"

"--that when it comes to things being yours and things being his, absolutely *nothing* in this house is legally yours. And that goes for—"

"Really?"

Nothing? My God. They even meant to have the clothes off her back. And then what? Put her out naked? In the freezing cold? While they footered with maps in order to haul down walls? How awful was that? Why, oh why ahd she come in raging?

"You mean … you mean I don't even own me own petticoats? Me drawers neither? Is that what you're saying, why they've all been pulled from the hangers and dumped--"

"It's fine, Gil." Divers O'Roarke swung the pickaxe to the floor. "I'll deal with this."

"I know sir, I'm just doing what—"

"I know what you're doing, Gil, and I'm grateful but Destiny here looks as if she needs to sit down. Don't you, Destiny?"

"*Me?*"

Raven's Passage? Was that what Grandfather Austell's map was doing on the table? What he was doing standing here half naked taking down that wall? Divers O'Roarke that was. Grandfather Austell would hardly be standing here doing that and not a pretty sight it would be if he was. Heavens. Here was her thinking it was to drive her out? After all, why would you need a map for that? A pickaxe maybe? But a map? To take the wall down that was. Not drive her out. Raven's Passage, eh? Well, she never did.

As for her needing a seat? Not that she knew of. But then again, this Wryson man was quiet and earnest, two traits that went hand in hand with being fanatically, *righteously* driven, in her experience. When she'd been no end of amenable about that gaping, great hole in the wall too.

"Well, yes." She clasped her hand to her chest, seeing as Divers O'Roarke was asking and she wanted to diffuse the situation. "I--I suppose I do. Now you come to mention it. A little anywa—"

"Sir, I've told you what you must do about thi
s. About her. About this. About *everything*."

"I know you did."

"And I'm not saying—. It's just you *did* dismiss the servants."

"And?"

Was she mistaken? Was there the tiniest edge to the way Divers O'Roarke said that simple, little word. An edge that was still so dangerous, this was not the time to say,

"Goodness, you should be careful, Mr. Wryson, in case he dismisses you," as she dropped onto the chair, Divers O'Roarke very kindly set forward for her.

But maybe it was? So she did it anyway. She settled her skirts about her too.

"*Sir.*" Gil Wryson jabbed his finger at her. "*She needs to shut her---*"

Well, she did but it didn't mean she could do it. Not with all this going on. How could she?

"Take the afternoon off. As I'm going to do. *Uh.* I mean it." Divers O'Roarke stepped between them, resting a hand on Gil Wryson's shoulder. "Go acquaint yourself with the local hostelries, or whatever. That's a power of work we've done today. We can continue taking that wall down tomorrow."

She lowered her gaze. That would be in his dreams.

Of course it may all depend on what he said next. But, glancing at that map, she had a pretty good idea of what that was likely to be. She was more than dead certain about what she'd do about it too. Yes. Why look to Tom Berryman for answers when they were right here under her nose?

These dresses would be getting left on their hangers from now on and if they weren't she'd know what to do about it too.

"So?" He flicked his gaze over her. "What's so important you burst in here uninvited?"

Her dresses, hell's burning teeth and bells, was that what she was going to try breaking his balls about? Well, his work demanded his complete attention. The chair was as much as she was getting.

Not only was he going to deny going anywhere near her blasted clothes, let alone leaving them in a heap on the floor if she *dared* accuse him, with Gil gone, what the hell did it matter? Raven's Passage? Sure to be here somewhere. The house designing business was the best front going that way. As for her finding out he was a smuggler? Precisely what he wanted people to find out.

"Oh, I think it hardly matters now. Indeed I fear I've probably disturbed you and caused you to dismiss Mr. Wryson for absolutely nothing. So, please don't worry about it."

"Well then ...?" He lifted the pickaxe. "I won't."

Yes. Another ton of rubble showering onto the floorboards would do no harm at all.

"I'm glad you think so. But I'm really not interested in whether you do, or not—"

"I put your dresses on the floor, is that it?" The wall shook as he landed another blow against it. "What you've come in here to say? And berate me as you used to do all these years ago when I was ten and you were nine?"

"Maybe that was because I liked you."

"Just as well I never held my breath," he panted, tightening his grip on the shaft. All right, so that was unexpected. But if she thought he was stopping for that she'd another think coming.

"As for the dresses? If they were mine perhaps I would berate you. But from what your man has just pointed out to me--"

"It's what I use him for, pointing things out to people. He is very good that way. The best I've known in fact. It's why I employ him. To deal with things I can't be bothered dealing with."

And because he could be trusted. A hard thing to come by, not just in this world but the world *he* inhabited. That dancing, dark and shady place of gnarled shadows and twisted paths, haunted by the need to keep one step ahead where nothing could ever be as it seemed. Not even himself.

He dragged a breath. Christ, the real reason he'd sent the servants packing. Yes. He might involve himself with them. Their lives. Their struggles. *Their law breaking activities*. He lifted the axe.

"Look Divers, far be it for me to argue about these dresses."

"Trying to though, aren't you?"

"You want me to go, I understand. And I can't say as I blame you either. Not after the things Rose told you about me. And the things we did to you as children. You don't have to do things like taking the walls down in the hope of driving me out, you know."

Oh, here it was—nip, nip, nip--about the wall. Well he did have to and he was taking it down. She didn't know where Raven's Passage was? Fine. He'd find it for himself. And if she didn't like it—he raised the axe—well? The door was still there. For now. And welcome she was to walk through it too. In fact if he wasn't concentrating so hard he'd say so. As for her seeing that map? When it came to damns, he'd be lying to say he gave one. Enough was what he'd had of it all. Enough. Including the damned bickering with Gil.

"Now, Destiny, don't flatter yourself."

"I'm not. But seeing as these clothes aren't mine, perhaps you want me to remove them first?"

Right. Maybe his heart missed a beat but did she really think he was going to stutter, ogle, land the pickaxe on his toes instead of the wall?

Much as it might not pain him to tell her, women were things he sometimes had to involve himself with--a hazard of the job. In fact, sometimes he did more than involve himself with them, sometimes he watched them bleed over him to a death he neither wanted nor expected.

He tilted his jaw. "Now you're being tiresome, Destiny."

"Me? In what way?"

"What way do you think? But you go ahead." He tugged the axe free. "If you want to catch your death of cold, that's entirely up to you. I'm not lighting any fires to warm you."

"Well, it's not exactly up to me. I mean your man did say these clothes are not mine, so—"

All right? *Did she really think he was going to stutter, ogle, land the pickaxe on his toes instead of the wall?*

A button. It was only a button, for God's sake. Not terribly sensuously the way she undid it, at that. Not so his tongue hung out for something other than a jug of ale—this wall-breaking was tough work, after all and his ribs felt as if they'd been broken all over again. Obviously they hadn't healed yet. But he did land a blow. Why not? The hell with whatever else she wanted here. Doom Bar Hall. The dresses. A reaction from him.

"And I should add, you sitting here naked, is neither here nor there to me. If you think otherwise you'd have to do better."

She raised her chin. "I don't *think* that."

"So you say." He took careful aim.

"Fine then."

"Well then. Don't let me stop you."

"You're not."

Obviously. Or she wouldn't unfasten another button as he wiped his palm across his nose. It was still only another button. He tossed the hair out of his eyes. And that was another blow. A blow. A button. And another one. His throat dried but this was thirsty work and his ribs were murdering him. How many of the damn things were there? Buttons that was. He already knew about ribs. He hauled a breath. Blow. Button. Blow. Button. Blow. *Blow.* The judder went right through his body. Did her skeletal fingers tremble? He hoped so. Because where he was now he couldn't afford to let his kicked-to-bits ones ever make such a mistake. But that ivory sliver of skin sailing like a galleon across his senses ..?

He jerked up his head, sucked another breath. All right, just because someone did something as you didn't think they would, it didn't mean you couldn't see the smoulder at the back of their eyes though. A slow burn through frost. That it didn't touch you in places you didn't expect it to touch. He needed to think of Rose. Destiny Rhodes was hardly going to strip naked. And even if she did? It was hardly going to be anything more than water off his back, unless she pulled something spectacular out of the hat. And how likely was that? He yanked the pickaxe out the wall.

"Good," he muttered.

"Well, yes because I can't exactly leave here wearing them, now can I?"

He paused mid-wallop, flicked his gaze over the gaping hole *But what if she did*? Leave here stark naked, that was? Wouldn't he be as well digging his grave now--and not with a bent spoon either — as explain to Lyon what the hell he was doing letting a resident of

Doom Bar Hall leave that said hall without a stitch on her back? Suicide after Eirwin. He shouldered the axe.

"I am sure you can keep the clothes if that's your worry."

"*Sure*? Well, I don't know about you but my reckoning is I don't just speak for myself when I say we both know sure is seldom a certainty. Sure is a term that merely means you think so."

"I'm *sure* if Gil was here, he'd tell you we don't need a philosophical discussion. We just need you to keep your damn clothes on. If you don't mind? Thank you. Now."

"If you say so."

"I do say so." He stiffened his shoulders. Quite often in life the path you walked down was by another's design. Lyon. Destiny Rhodes. If it was *his* design now it would be straight cut to fit, an unrolled carpet he simply threw down before him to the place he wanted to be. No briars, no tangles, no rips to trip the unsuspecting. Destiny Rhodes and her brother, Chancery, had as good as killed Rose. The bastard had had his way with her. With Destiny's help. And then? *Then* was *now* in some ways. Him having to carry out Lyon's orders here, where Rose's ghost wandered every room and even these walls were bloody hard work. What the hell were they made of? Iron? He landed another blow.

"When it comes to that word *say*, let's also say no more about your damn clothes. All right? Believe me, they're hardly fit for more than rags. It's a mercy to let you keep them if you want to wear them so badly."

Because it was. This was a question of who was going to give in first. On this occasion, well? He'd had no choice. Next time now? There wasn't going to be a next time where she was concerned.

"Oh, I'm glad you're feeling so charitable when that is why I wear them because they *are* nothing frivolous, you understand? It's actually why I want to discuss the other gowns before I leave here, as I know you are almost certainly going to tell me to do. In fact you were probably going to tell me this morning. Last night even."

So she knew? Well, thank Christ. The trouble that saved him meant he could be even more magnanimous. Anything to get her out of here as promised *and* needed with the least amount of trouble. Finally the tide was turning. And he didn't see her making a nice speech about it like King Canute when it flattened her either.

"Gil spoke out of line and turn. If you want to know that you own these other dresses, then the answer is *yes*. Absolutely." He wiped the back of his wrist across his sweating brow. "So, the thing is—"

"You think I want to own *them*?" Why did she look as if cow pats were what he wanted her to own? "I don't want to own them. Goodness. I hope you think these dresses are something to me."

"Then if they're not why the bloody hell are you in here making a fuss about the fact that yes, I had my manky Irish paws on them?" He took aim at the wall. "Well?"

"I never said that. It's not something I would say. Think either."

"You didn't need to say. Because, let's face it, you never came in here to ask me about what you say you came in here for. So, talking clothes—"

"Yes? What about them?"

"Let's remove the kid gloves, shall we?"

"Well, I might if I was wearing some. But–"

"Take them, take the lot out of this house now and—"

"Thank you. Then I will. Now I have your blessing I was thinking of auctioning them, all proceeds to go to the servants you dismissed, if that is all right with you, that is?"

What? And have half the fecking county clambering over the estate? Lyon would love that. No wonder he took the pickaxe off the skirting board before he could stop himself. The man wouldn't just take the pickaxe off him, he'd be taking carpentry lessons to build the gibbet himself.

As for there being any prizes left for guessing how that would make him look locally? The poor-put-upon Destiny Rhodes, without a farthing to her name, nobly selling off her clothes to ensure those he'd shown the door to had coal and candles this winter, while she herself was starving on the highway. He'd never be accepted after that. *And he needed to be accepted*. The sooner, the better, the prize cock-up he was making of this.

He swallowed the burning knot in his throat. At all costs he needed to pull the axe out of the skirting board, carefully pull that brick there free. But more than that he needed to turn that tide back towards her, so she drowned in it, not him. Now. Before she somehow advanced further. Saw him for what he really was. He knew just how to do it too. He set the axe down against the wall, pushed his sweating hair back from his forehead.

"When I would like you to come to supper tonight?"

"*Me?*"

"Well, Destiny, I'm not meaning one of Grandfather Austell's parrots. Wearing one of these dresses as fine feathers at that either."

"*You* want *me* to wear one?"

"I wouldn't like you not to. That could be construed as indecent. The talk of Penvellyn, although from what I remember, being the talk was something you …" He flicked his gaze over her, that sliver of half naked breast in particular. "Well …"

"But I haven't worn any of them dresses since me Ennis died."

He cocked an eyebrow. *Them* not these. *Me* not my. Always a giveaway. Wearing one of these dresses would kill her. Did she think he hadn't worked out the reason she didn't? Well, however she'd come in here, whatever she said, this was one he was going to win, without straining himself too badly either, even if the last thing on the face of this earth he wanted was to sit down and eat supper with her.

"Then it's high time you did. Seven shall we say? In the dining room? The choice is yours. But let me tell you now, if you think I'm taking no for an answer, you can think again."

CHAPTER SIX

Seven? In the dining room? Right. And not taking no for an answer? Now some might say, standing against their room door yet again, as she was now, after she'd sort of peeled her clothes off--but not--that that hadn't gone so well. In fact some might say four words when it came to 'seven in the dining room.' *Over their dead body.*

Dress up? Look pretty? Eat food? Her? Not this side of hell. And they would be right.

How could she? Affront Ennis's memory further either if he was waiting for her on the other side and saw her doing this? Especially after earlier and Divers O'Roarke's shameless display of his chest. She couldn't. And they would pass their hand over their face and push their hair back from their forehead, when they'd give the clothes they'd never removed from their back to go lie down in that bed there.

But she wasn't one of them.

How could she be? No. That sodding bastard had flung down a gauntlet.

And if he thought, for one second, she was going to do anything other than pick it up, even if it killed her, he'd a big prize coming in the *another thought coming* competition.

***

There was—alas--only the solid tick of her heartbeat for Destiny to come downstairs to now Great Grandmother Endelienta's clock wasn't working for whatever reason—probably because Divers O'Roarke had taken the pickaxe to that too. Fortunately *her* heart was was already smashed so it was no real trouble to do this. Put on the awful Egyptian blue gown, aware that it hung on her like a shroud, run Aunt Kehelland's comb through her hair, pad, in her silver slippers, down a staircase which yesterday at this time had been hers. Orwell's anyway. The red gown? The other gowns? Not if you shoved three inch nails beneath fingernails. The one abiding light? She *wasn't* done.

How could she be? Ennis and Doom Bar Hall were at stake here.

All she'd done was dodge a little heavy musket fire in the matter of the dresses this afternoon.

Funny though that she hadn't wanted to think of how welcoming she'd once thought the family crypt was. As if this gown, much as she hated it, with its memories of that other world she'd once lived in, sucked strength into her veins. Yes. Or maybe it was the searing memory—the one she'd rather not think of--of how she'd only gone and unfastened her dress this afternoon? To ensure Divers O'Roarke never took her dresses out the wardrobe again, of course.

Whatever it was, when Tom Berryman next came begging for a place to hide his ill-gotten gains, the ones she'd deposit on the flowerbeds later, he could go to hell. Orwell could too if he didn't stop drinking like a whale. How happy she'd *finally* be walking amongst her beloved treasures. *And she would.* She bet Divers O'Roarke didn't think she could do this. When she could, despite the way her heart hammered in her throat, strangling her far worse than any satin choker and she'd far rather be mending that cushion cover she'd started on last week for the dining room, or dreaming of Ennis. Normally she'd time to do both but the inconsideration of some people knew no bounds.

"*For feck's ...* "

She paused. Had a plate just hit Great Aunt Modest's stone flagged dining room floor? *And* was even now lying there in smithereens? Her throat tightened. She hoped not. But so long as one of Great Aunt Modest's porcelain mazarine blue and gold patterned dinner plates hadn't breathed its last like Great Grandmother Endelienta's clock, it was … *nothing to get upset about*.

Even if on an early summer's day her life was so much better when she popped her head around the door to admire them in the light that peered through the heavy ivy fronds surrounding the window. The ones she'd strategically cut so the light poured, golden as honey onto that very spot.

The little things. The things some might say she held onto, to hold onto something bigger. The rhythm of the life with which she held herself together, knowing one break in the chain would bring her down. Because, let's face it, what the sodding else was there to hang to?

"I told you, this was sheer stupidity without any servants," Gil Wryson droned. "I've done my rock bottom best to serve you as usual but I warned you, just like I warned you that plate was hot, I was never engaged as a cook. You should have sent to the village, or better still shown her the door. Her and that brother of hers propping up the bar stool back at Daindridge's, hoping to win back a farthing or two."

"And I told you I will do just that when the time is right and not before," Divers O'Roarke's low voice—bossy, yet bored, sludgy as the river bottom, in fact--grated on her spine.

She tilted her jaw. Of course some might say that people who listened at doors never heard any good of themselves but she was so far down the lines in terms of ever hearing anything nice, did it matter? *Time being right* was a very odd thing to say, especially from a man who had probably broken her clock.

That thought that had been waiting in the wings came out and took first prize in the *standing center stage* competition. How right she was regarding the servants *not* being sent away to spite her after all. Her heart thudded harder. *He* was up to something good and proper.

Then there was the matter of him bashing that wall to bits. It could be his job. It might not be. Lastly there was the matter of him not wanting her to auction off these dresses.

This supper? My God, this supper, now she stepped back from it, wasn't an attempt to hit back at her. He *was* up to something here, something illegal. Something Customs and Excise would be very interested in knowing. Anonymously of course. When her own summerhouse was stuffed to the brim with what had partly helped fund the restoration of the house, it wouldn't do to be had up before the magistrate alongside him, bringing the Rhodes' family name into the mud trough. Unless she could strike a deal? To do that she'd need more information.

Let's face it, he hadn't asked her to supper because he liked her. Or intended on taking her up on her offer of herself. No. No matter how cucumber cool he'd been, terror that she was going to auction off these dresses must have gripped him. With hot pincers at that. This was surely her chance to find out why.

She glanced sideways, behind her, then sideways again. Sir Tredwynne's suit of armour shone in the flickering candlelight, *feet* from the dining room door. Get behind that and no-one would ever know she was there. Then she might hear what he really was up to good and proper.

Grasping her skirts she tiptoed a step then she tiptoed another. Thank God she'd had the foresight to order Chesten to dust behind the suit earlier this week. Destiny would be the first to deny it if she sneezed and was caught red handed, the first to say she was dusting, if Divers O'Roarke or his sidekick came out and caught her, though.

Thank God she hadn't got upset about the plate getting broken. It may have taken a while but finally the Fates were kissing her face. For that she could spare the odd plate. The odd wall too.

Taking a deep breath she wedged herself behind the suit. As she did, another clatter went right through her bones. It probably went through Sir Tredwynne's too, despite the fact he didn't have any. There were no prizes for guessing what it was, when what it was was as clear as the crystal jug on the side table inches from the edge of her skirt. *More* porcelain had just been murdered on the stone floor. It was enough to make her ... *stand here*. Take a breath. Walls and plates, remember? Walls and plates. Even if her eyes watered with the exertion of containing her fury. After all, it might be something else that had clattered off the floor.

"Well, the time better hurry up and be right before you break another plate, sir," Gil Wryson's laugh carried right across the stone flags. "Or there won't be anything to eat off, the rate you're going at."

My God. *Two* of her lovely plates--all right, they were his—*were broken*. Smashed beyond repair. She sipped another breath into her tortured lungs. Her lungs that were working like bellows in her chest. Two of the plates, the lovely plates, antiques ... *were not important*. Where was the cool, calm Destiny who never got het up about anything?

"They're damn hideous anyway, so they are. Only fit for the floor or the rubbish tip. You know, I'm probably doing the world a favor, breakin' the feckin' things, so I am. I mean *breaking* them."

"Aye, sir. You know? I couldn't agree more. Maybe we should smash some more?"

Not important? What? Stand here in the shadows when that sodding Irish as the sodding Droghedan pigs, bastard wasn't just wrecking the dining room, he was insulting her taste in plates *with his friend*?

Not this side of hell. She snatched her skirt. It was caught on the end of Sir Tredwynne's sword. Worse, Sir Tredwynne obviously either didn't like that, or wanted up it because he clattered down, one metal leg going one way, the other, the opposite. His helmet rolled in an arc around the floor. And not just his helmet, his sword, his axe, his breastplate, rolled and spun like knives in that game they'd played as children where you'd to sing if it ended up pointing at you. Except what she did was sneeze. Obviously Chesten never dusted a sodding thing, the lazy sodding heifer that she was, when here was Destiny taking in smuggled bottles and risking all sorts. to pay her too. Maybe Divers O'Roarke was right to have dismissed the lot of them after all?

"What the hell was that?"

As Destiny stood rooted to the hall floor, someone's boots echoed crisply across the flags. As for *what the hell it was*, wasn't that sodding obvious with Sir Tredwynne's gauntlet lying in the plant pot and his left arm trying to get up her skirt? And her sneezing like she'd shoved an elephant sized snuff box up her nose.

"A-a-a-a-a-choooooo!"

What was Divers O'Roarke trying to win? First prize in the *local idiot* competition?

"A-a-a-a-a-choooooo!"

My God. But if she didn't think of something when Divers O'Roarke stood there, large as life and twice as awful, his glittering eyes, stoic mouth and elegantly tied navy cravat, everything she didn't want to see in the candlelight, she was finished over two smashed plates. What did she want more? The plates, or the house, when she couldn't live in a plate? And he was up to all sorts?

Somehow, at an exorbitant cost to herself, she stiffened her spine, cleared her throat, set her jaw, fixed him with her calmest stare, much as her heart burned.

"What does it look like, Divers? Sir Tredwynne … fell. As I was crossing the hall he … he toppled down, nearly on me. Perhaps it was the vibration caused by whatever it was you broke beyond repair? How would I know?"

"Broke?"

All right *some might say* about the plates not being much good because she couldn't live in them, but she *wouldn't* and she *needed* to. In fact, given the way his grey eyes narrowed as they met hers, she needed to and more. To bite her tongue too. But it was all right—surely--so long as she didn't put any other feet stupendously wrong? And she wouldn't. Not if he broke every plate in the house. *My God, maybe the time was right to put her out now?* What it cost her to smile was probably as much as a mine-owner's fortune.

"But maybe I'm mistaken? Certainly, he has stood … *stood right here,* since I can remember."

He took a step towards her, flicked his gaze over Sir Tredwynne, then flicked it over her. Oh, he did believe her, didn't he? "That long ago, eh? Then you must be far older than I gave you credit for."

"Sir, I'd say that *if* that suit of armour fell …" Unfortunately, given how she needed to keep her mouth shut and forget about these plates, Gil Wryson wandered into the hall. "It was because *she* was--"

He spoke too. In a way that some might say wasn't exactly encouraging. But, on reflection and swallowing what leapt into her throat, at the thought of being marched out of here, they would be wrong. In all his life, one thing Divers O'Roarke had never liked was being caught red-handed having broken something.

"Me? What? Snooping? On you two? Are you serious?" She smothered a laugh. Who did Gil Wryson think Divers O'Roarke was going to side with here? "I mean, come on--behind some mouldering old suit of armour that means sod all to me and is now in bits, like whatever you broke, at that? Well I'm sure, if that's your worry, the suit can be put together again. Maybe even you'd be so kind, Mr. Wryson seeing as you're standing here, not doing anything else and Divers and I are going to supper? Well? At least I hope we are."

Silence fell like a cold blanket on the hall.

"Me? *Miss* Rhodes?"

"I am sure I did not mean to order you about, *Mr.* Wryson--"

"Good because it's not really in my line of duty, *Miss* Rhodes."

"—but Sir Tredwynne can hardly get up off that floor and put himself back together now, can he? And now there's no servants about the place, I suppose we must all muck in as best we can. And I mean, I would do it, but as you so kindly pointed out, it's hardly my property now, is it? What's more I wouldn't like to mess up the dress I put on especially for Divers after he asked me."

"Well, then." Gil smiled faintly. "I don't suppose it matters if the bits just lie there, now does it?"

Maybe it didn't, except to her. Letting the plates go wasn't she?

"But of course. You know, I never thought of that, not always being greatly known for my brains. But perhaps we should ask Mr. O'Roarke here, seeing as it's his floor? And he is a house designer and all? But maybe untidiness is the new fashion in London?"

She turned her gaze on Divers O'Roarke, staring at the floor in that way that measured a yard and knew to the nearest quarter inch whether it was short or not, even if he didn't know where. Probably in the fact *she'd* said *snooping* when Gil Wryson actually hadn't.

Oh God, it wasn't like her to pray but she did now. So hard she'd win the embroidered scripture verse in the specially made gold frame, in the local, *praying to live and fight another day* competition. But she wasn't just his enemy, the woman he'd cursed. Just maybe she was the woman who was on to him, enough to get behind that suit and break it? Who now asked him to prove he was a house designer? So, if he didn't ...?

"Well, Divers?"

He jerked up his chin, turning his ice-cool gaze on Gil.

"Let's do what the lady says, shall we? You go ahead and pick up Sir Tredwynne, while Miss Rhodes and I have the splendid supper you cooked. Not much, Destiny, I'm afraid, but better than nothing."

"Thank you, Divers. Your kindness is truly as exceptional as it is unexpected."

Was it hell? She was doing well here though, wasn't she? Getting him just where she wanted. Getting in between him and this Wryson man. Divide and rule. If she said so herself, she had concluded this part of the matter to her satisfaction and nothing he said would detract from it either.

"Don't thank me yet. When you're done picking up the bits, Gil, get rid of them will you? I really don't have any use for that old junk in here. It's not as if Sir-whoever-the-hell-he-was, is anything to do with me, now is it? Now then, Destiny, shall we have supper?"

The hell but this was the way to do it. Tonight was the night she got on board and gave him what he wanted to know. The name of her supplier. Then he got rid of her before she hid behind any more suits of armour. Fell? His backside. As for trying to play him over Gil? A few swipes at the junk in this dump and he'd see how canty she was then, thinking she was getting one up on him, indeed.

He shut the dining room door. Maybe shock tried to rake his scalp to see how her gown hung on her hips, when what he wanted was shock to rake her scalp at the thought of that suit of armour being binned. But anyone who knew her from before *would* look twice. The purpose in asking her here didn't include sleeping with her although he did admit, he preferred her in red. That blue was too close to damned crow's feathers. It hung like them too.

"Wait." He reached the dining chair before her. "You must pardon me. As you were always so fond of reminding me—"

"Me? Divers?"

"--manners were never my strong point."

Maybe he had broken these God awful plates that you couldn't see the food for the flowers on and consigned Sir-whatever-the-hell that mouldering heap's name was, to the rubbish dump? Maybe it made him feel all of eight again, standing in the darkness of that hallway with Rose, *he wasn't eight*. The last thing *she'd* be expecting was him to pull the chair out. He flashed his best smile as he grasped the carved orbs that topped the back posts while he was about it too, reeking the confidence he was master of.

"A great heavy thing like this isn't something you should attempt to move."

Bloody hell, he shouldn't either unless he expected a broken back for his trouble. He clasped the back posts tighter, so the veins on his knuckles stood out. How much did this thing weigh? A ton? Whatever it weighed while he could afford to look less than the suave person he purported to be, a man the world smiled upon, he wasn't going to, despite the fact that after earlier his ribs were bloody killing him.

"Then perhaps you should leave it? Personally it's something I never try to move. In fact I don't know the last time they were moved. It might even have been in Sir Tredwynne's time for that matter."

"Then how do you sit at them?"

"I don't as a rule. But you did insist. The trick was always just to squeeze into them. If you pull them too far you will only have to push them in again."

Now she told him?

"Not a trouble. Please allow me."

To do what? Snap his spine in two? He shifted his weight. They must have made men of the same oak in these days. She rested her timeless gaze on him.

"And if you push them too far in, you will only have to pull them out again."

Really? He straightened, trying to ignore the pain fisting his spine. Should he keel over now or what?

"There."

Hopefully he would have more success with the food even if Gil wasn't exactly a cook. Thank Christ the room was dark as the night sky so no-one would see if the food was any good or not. That geriatric yew tree just outside the row of windows and that bloody mess of ivy clambering all over them, no doubt wrecking every inch of the brickwork, meant there was hardly a scrap of light to be had in this dismal dump of a room.

Hadn't she ever thought about cutting the lot down, getting rid of these frowning portraits of her Elizabethan forebears, doing something about these dusty old flagstones, chopping up these chairs and replacing them with something more fashionable? It must be murder in here of a winter's night.

He could quite see himself as master of Doom Bar Hall. Without all this junk in it of course. But it wasn't going to happen. How desperate was Destiny Rhodes to have thrown herself in with it? Either that or she was blind as a bat, or off her pretty head? And she was still pretty, if you liked that kind of pretty, her troubled eyes glittering in the soft candlelight with a bandit's boldness, for some strange reason. Like? *All right, she wanted to eat him alive.*

But that was all right provided she was first on the menu. And after all, *he* hadn't knocked down that suit, had he?

Smothering his amusement, he crossed to the sideboard where a row of candles flickered in their tarnished sticks. The smell of beeswax was not a honeyed memory. It was like everything he remembered from his childhood here. Richly unwelcoming. "Some wine?"

"I don't mind if I do."

"Even if it's not the best?"

"What? When beggars can't be choosers? I mean, you will have seen the state of Orwell? You'd have to be blind not to and stupid not to know he has drunk most of this place dry. As for me? Well, I've barely touched the stuff since … since my Ennis died."

The lucky bastard. Still, who was he to judge? He tilted the bottle. It was time to begin the play. That bold, unholy look and the bold, unholy way she spoke said she was more than up for it. Well, certainly she was up to something. A little cocky riling wouldn't go amiss. Already he'd made some bad choices here, getting rid of the servants when isolation was *not* the name of this game *and* there had been nothing to say he'd have gotten involved with them had he kept them. Tonight he rectified that mistake by getting rid of her.

"That's not exactly what I remember of you."

"I'd like to say you remember wrongly and that's the whole trouble with you. But there. Tonight, since you've asked me to dine with you, Civility's my middle name."

Really? That would be a first. But all the better for his purpose. He knew what he remembered and what he remembered was right. Her sailing home from parties with claret stained lips. Sailing out to them too. An exciting, exotic ship. Unafraid of storms. At home in squalls. Wild as the wind on the sea.

There was no trouble with his memory. But then again the past was also a fabulously extinct land where memory bearing coffins had been nailed forever shut and sunk in crypts hundreds of feet beneath the ground. The past was what had got him into this mess. *Her. Eirwin.*

"Well?" He set the decanter back on the silver tray. "How about we have a toast then to the future and all the changes I intend making here? Here." He handed her a glass. "To the future of O'Roarke Hall."

"O'Roarke Hall?"

"Well, Divers O'Roarke Hall, then." He raised his glass. Yes, physicality was everything in this business which was also why he flashed another smile as he did it, rocked on his heels too. "No sense quibbling about it. I don't know about you but for me, Doom Bar sounds what it is. Now … " He lifted the lid off the nearest tureen. "Let's eat, shall we?"

Pea soup. Not his favourite but Gil had made no claims to be a cook and the smell could be worse. At least it smelled warm with a hint of mint even if it probably had no salt, stock and damn all peas, given the fact it looked like he'd dragged a bucket of water out the well and flung it in the tureen. Then there were the lamb cutlets he and Gil had slaved over. At least he supposed it was lamb. It had been hanging up on a hook in the cold press. It might be anything. The beauty of this? Beyond giving him something to extend the evening, what it was didn't matter.

"You have no problem with that, Destiny?"

"Me? Why should I?"

"Because you haven't drunk your wine."

"Oh? Well, then? I better rectify that." As she wound translucent fingers round the glass, her smile dripped more honey than a ten foot honeycomb. "Here was me thinking you meant the food because, let's face it, it doesn't smell the best does it?"

He shot her another glance. Clever, wasn't she, with all her amenability and pretence at being that teeny bit tipsy? But not as smart as him figuring out her stomach was probably empty as a drum and that wine would rocket straight to her head. And there was a cellar of it on the table. How did he know right now this was pretence? This was his world. As for that amenability, he was going to have to take a hammer to? His world too. By the time he'd finished with her she'd be singing like a canary. And the smuggling trails and spidery, shadowy web that operated here, the ways experience had taught him a local knew better than anyone, these would all be his.

He edged into the seat at her side, where he'd positioned his place. Preferable to sitting in what felt like another country. A sort of frozen wilderness for all it was a late autumn evening. Did people really need dining rooms that sat half a city? Even on a summer evening when the very bricks should swelter, the room probably needed heated. Things he would shortly use to his advantage here, although he wasn't fool enough to believe this was going to be plain sailing. Not given the hand he was going to have to prise loose from the tiller first.

"So?" She dabbed her mouth with the back of that hand, set the glass down. An *empty* glass though. "About your plans? What do you intend?"

"Lots. I mean the place needs a good shake up, brought into the present century, don't you think? We should drink a toast to that too." He stretched out his legs and reached for the bottle.

She shrugged, averting her gaze. "You know, you are probably right about that wine."

In fact he had the distinct impression she was about to put her hand over her glass. He waited, his own hand hovering. "I'm sorry?"

"Orwell buys it. Well … at least that's as much as I know. At least, I assume he buys it. One never knows round here, the amount of blind eyes that get turned to government business even by law abiding citizens. You have to be careful who you can trust when just recently the penalties have become so very severe. I don't know if you remember him, but last month they hung Griffin St. Gerren. Can you imagine? For smuggling that rubbish too."

So she did have fingers in smuggling pies? What else could she mean by blind eyes, law abiding citizens *and trust*? As for Griffin St. Gerren? He wasn't just a smuggler. Not the corpses he'd left on various beaches, damn the government for making it illegal to claim salvage from a wrecked ship if anyone was alive on it. Still, this wasn't taking long, was it? Three little words, Doom Bar Hall, plus one glass of piss poor wine she plainly knew he was trying to ply her with and she was ready to sing like a canary. *Unless she somehow thought he was plying her to get into her drawers?* A man of his sterling undercover qualities?

"Just the same, here." He reached forward.

The time had come to get gold out of this miser's tooth. Refuse another drink and--well? It would make it very plain to him she was onto him. And she wouldn't want to do that, now would she?

He smothered a chuckle. The first to want to burst from him in so long. "Unless you want to forget about the wine, if it's that--?"

"No. No. It's fine. Honestly. Just fill up me glass. There's nothing like breaking the habits of a lifetime."

"Just what I like to hear. Cheers." He nudged his glass against hers. "To the future. Divers O'Roarke Hall. I think I'm going to start--*properly* that is--with in here."

"Really?" She lifted her glass to her smiling lips. "But I thought you'd already started in—"

"Now then, Destiny, I said *properly*, didn't I? And properly it will be. No more, no less, the justice I intend doing this place, building on the work of generations."

"Oh. Well, cheers then."

"Yes." The mouthful he swallowed was long and satisfying. "These chairs, for example, the ones that came on the ark, I'm thinking '*bonfire*'. Along with the paintings. All these frowning ancestors. Getting rid of them will go a long way to taking the chill off the place. And I'm not even talking striking a flint. I mean it's not as if they're my ancestors after all."

"Bonfire?" One little word that was surely as good as the Doom Bar Hall three. A little word that would have her singing sooner when he put his proposition on the table because there would be nothing for her to do but sing. "Well, I suppose … now you come to mention it … it is quite cold in here."

"Then, have some more wine." He pushed the wine bottle towards her. "Yes. As for the colors, well, while I am a great fan of the French style, I don't know about you but I think this room would look best, painted plain, ordinary white."

Christ. Had he really said all that? As if he really knew what he was talking about. But then not many people around here would know whether he did, or not. Not even her. And that was the beauty of this.

Confidence, the first he'd felt since Eirwin, flooded. What kind of foolhardy way had he been carrying on lately? Certainly it was not in a way that reminded him of how good he was at his work, or that he was going to pull this job off. He had fallen low indeed. But this was an end of it.

"Amazing." It was such an end that, while the smile she offered was dripping with heat and honey, everything that was earthy about her, he saw beyond it to what wasn't. What wanted to take him by the throat and squeeze hard. "You don't think you would want to be in *Divers O'Roarke Hall* for a while first, though? Get the feel of the place before doing anything so major? I mean white walls and the French style, while all very nice ... "

"Just who is the designer here, Destiny? Hmm?"

"You tell me," she chuckled. "I thought it was you? But then again ..."

A nice try. But when he'd been beaten senseless, left for dead, had his ribs broken and his eye nearly kicked out, when he'd seen with his other one just how paltry bloody awful it was to be the law and the blood he'd failed to staunch seeping from Eirwin's shattered breast bone, did Destiny Rhodes really think it mattered whether she believed him or not?

Last night maybe? Yes, that was a mistake because he'd never expected to see what his curse had done, never expected to stand in this house again and face her, to find himself confronted by so many ghosts—and not just Rose. But tonight? It was time to land the fish. In many ways having this house from her was revenge for Rose.

He was here to work after all, even if *her* provocative essence was winding round his senses.

Maybe he was working though? Like old times? And that warmth and laughter oozing from her wasn't feigned? And all this wine on an empty stomach was making her more foxed than a pickled ferret? He just wasn't seeing it for the snake of that scent round his nose. But there was a good way to find out. Insult her further. He reached to refill both their glasses. It wasn't like he wasn't a master at keeping his own head clear.

"You know, it's too bad you don't like my ideas. God knows, but your family were never ones for design."

"Well, we can't all be good at everything."

"Or maybe at nothing at all?"

"If you say so. But then I never had the benefit of an education. I mean I'd have liked to ... *Hic*. But me father? Well, that daft old bugger thought I should get married. I mean? I mean, come on now, although of course, then I did. To the richest man in Devon at that. So just maybe he wasn't that daft and I didn't need an education, after all?"

Would she really find all this so damned funny, she nearly ended herself, if she wasn't soused? The woman was a grieving widow. One that same rich man's family had given a pittance to.

"Well, Destiny—"

"Oh, that's me all right. Destiny by name. Destiny by nature."

"The thing is—"

"Ooh."

"I will be away a lot in London, mainly using here for entertaining."

"Lucky you. *Hic*. Gosh, you can see what I mean about this wine. It's sodding rancid, so it is. In fact a definite bouquet of—" She sniffed the glass cautiously, then threw the contents down her throat. "Cat's pee."

"Now. I don't know about the state of your wine cellar—"

"Not very good. Certainly not worth getting hung over. Did you hear that? Hungover? That was a joke by the way."

"Indeed if you even have one, but it's important—"

"Oh, I couldn't agree more. Cheers."

"I leave the place in good hands when I'm gone. The hands of someone who knows how to cut certain corners. Someone who knows and understands they're being given a good deal, given they're no longer in control. Someone local who knows where to come by certain things at a good price for that entertaining, shall we say? The drink especially."

"Oh, the drink is all we need. Long live the drink. Here. Fill up me glass."

"What do you say, Destiny?"

She raised her chin, fixed her hot, glazed look on him as only she could in the darkening shadows. She even chuckled faintly right at the back of her throat. Trust him? Or not? Put the fishing net away or not? Even if she had every reason to tell him where to go, having that reason and acting on it, were two very different things. And did he really want so very much? How the hell else was she able to hang on here if she really was *that* impoverished? Besides, look at her. Did she even know what she was doing?

Any moment ... Any moment *now* ...

No wonder his mouth was dry with anticipation. She set her elbow on the table and in that instant her mouth hardened, her cheekbones sharpened and the light went out in her eyes.

"Tell me about your wife, Divers."

CHAPTER SEVEN

Bloody, damn bitch. Having filled the brass goblet with claret, Divers O'Roarke flung it against the fireplace. Not that it made a deal of difference. Brass goblets? Who the hell had brass goblets? They bounced all over the fecking rug, splattering everything with the contents. Dark red drops dribbled down the ancient stone. What satisfaction did that give him, standing here amongst the guttering candles and the remains of the dinner, in flickering shadow-light, that damnable smell of beeswax in his nostrils? He never lost his temper like this. Not so he wanted to rip the mantelshelf from the wall. He leaned his palms on the mantelpiece, raised his chin, growled through his clenched teeth.

"And don't say I told you so."

"I'm not," Gil said. "Just wondering what the hell you said."

"I told her Lydia was not for discussion. What the hell else could I say?"

"Look sir, if this is unraveling, you still have the Dymchurch consignment, the money—which *I* know you don't want but—"

"Well, if you know, why the hell are you—"

"I'm not. I'm just saying."

"Well, don't."

"So? A grieving widower? What's the problem?"

He made a fist. *The problem*? That even after all these years Destiny Rhodes' capacity to eat her way beneath his skin was undiminished. That she'd outsmarted him.

"Nothing. Nothing at all. I just ... " *Need to stop falling apart. Thinking Eirwin, seeing Rose.*

When having to have one of Lyon's spies come here was nothing out of the ordinary why fear that ordinary? Why not just agree to bringing in a Lydia? He had once before. On his first job.

"Well then … I take it that nothing is what she gave you?"

"She was always tighter than a spider's arse."

"Family loyalties, is it, sir? I suppose if they brought you up—"

"They didn't. That lot couldn't bring up a dead frog. My stepmother brought me up."

His stepmother who they'd despised and sent to live in that maudling farm cottage that was damp and stunk of pigs because she'd disgraced the family, running off with some Irishman whose tongue was the only silver thing about him.

Gil's footsteps echoed in the cavernous room as he strolled to the table to clear it.

"Well, then the point of having Destiny Rhodes here seems less than before, if you don't mind me saying, sir."

"You say what you want, man. You will anyway. you always do."

Actually he did mind. He minded terribly. Hell's teeth, why should he have Destiny Rhodes thinking she'd got one up on him when he was now standing in a ten foot hole? *And* to have the servants back would look like capitulation? When, it fact, it was her, or them now? Whoever would give him the *in*. And really, he didn't want any female spy of Lyon's here. The previous one had been old enough to be his mother, not his wife and still he'd had to fend her off.

He raised his chin, stared at himself in the shining glass.

"Children."

"Children, sir? What about them?"

The dark, liquid flicker in Gil's eyes said everything that was to be said about *his* brilliance.

"Yes. Talking want, that is what I want. I want you to go and get me some."

***

My God, what was that racket, that high pitched screeching racket? A dream? If so it was a sodding inconsiderate one, dragging her from the one place she could go and find solace, from the world, from her pain, the only place she could breathe. The satin winding sheet of sleep. Destiny hugged the pillow tighter. Hugged it over her ears. Oh God, let her get back to the dream of Ennis, alive, vital, a stray lock of hair falling over his eyes as he shielded them from the sun and told her, 'I love you, Destiny and I don't mind how much you drank at that table last night.' *Her* Ennis, surrounded by children.

Childen? She leapt up as if she'd stood on a fish hook. One for each toe as she sprung across the floor. What the hell was he doing surrounded by children? She didn't have any children. So what the hell were children doing here?

The scrunch as her nose smacked the pane sent shock waves spinning. She all but slithered to the floor.

Children? My God, was she seeing this right? Hearing it right was bad enough. But children *were* down in the grounds. Five? Maybe six. No, *seven*, there were seven, all different ages. The boy in the cloth cap and the coat not meeting in the middle, slouching on the edge of the grass looked about six. The two girls playing some kind of tag all over her herb garden looked *far too damned big to be playing anything* certainly in muddy clogs.

She blinked, rubbed her eyes. It wasn't a dream, or it would go away. The children were real. Had they heard she didn't live here and they thought because she'd gone they could run all over the place?

Well, they couldn't. Not over her dead body. Her feet, like hammers, struck the floor. Even before she reached the wardrobe she'd torn off her nightgown.

***

"**Y**ou." The screech, directed at the boy on the far side of the lawn, was out before she could stop it.

"Can I help you, Destiny?" Divers O'Roarke called from somewhere behind her.

"Presupposing I need any. Otherwise that will be the day."

After last night it would, which was why she tore across the gravel, her breath ripping holes in her chest, her jaw set, her boots scrunching on flying stone. No-one could help her, least of all Divers O'Roarke, who suddenly appeared at her side. Hadn't she broken her back tending that lavender border? Look at it. The stalks flattened, the tiny buds scattered everywhere. A herd of rampaging cows couldn't win first prize in any competition for doing any more damage.

Think of the evenings she strolled along this scented path, drawing the soothing fragrance into her lungs, the afternoons she instructed Lizzie how to make shortbread to put by for Christmas, of the mornings she sewed little sacks for all her drawers. The chest of wooden ones anyway. It couldn't all be gone. Not this border she'd nursed back to life after her father left it to die. Just like he'd left Doom Bar Hall. As much a ruinous drunk as Orwell. And she'd enough doing today what with that footstool needing mended and that cushion cover to be finished and the wassail bowl brought down from the attic seeing as Lizzie wasn't here to do it for her.

"These children ..."

The words tore from her, a sentence she couldn't finish. Even her black gown felt like a cage despite the fact it hung on her hips.

"What about them?"

"What about them? What do you think? I'm not for having children here. Look at the fine mess they're making of your lawn. Well?" She marched up to the crowd on the edge of the lawn. "What do you think you are doing here? All of you? Well? Leave here at once. This isn't your place. Go on. Be off with you, you beggarly brats. Now."

"Father?"

She swung her gaze around. Chestnut hair, grey eyes, perhaps three, or four *and* staring at Divers O'Roarke? Shock raked *her* scalp. It couldn't be. *He* couldn't be. And *she* couldn't have said what she just had either, could she? Doom Bar Hall, remember? She gulped

"It's all right, Molly." He placed his hand on the crop of curls as Molly's mouth wobbled. Oh God, she *had* said. "You have nothing to fear. We talked about this lady, remember? And we agreed, she's not as scary as she looks, as awful either."

Awful? She tightened her jaw. Molly O'Roarke? It was the kind of name he'd give a child, certainly. As for the look on his face? It wasn't just hangdog. It was hang the whole pack of dogs. My God. *It couldn't be.* Lydia was an invention. Surely? Anything less said *she* had it all wrong about Divers O'Roarke having things to hide. And she didn't. She couldn't. But what if she did?

"I'm sorry?" She was actually. "Are you saying *these* are your children?"

"Well … "

"All of them? Or just this one?"

Because this one was about the only one she could live with. At a push. Rather than live with the field mice and foxes in the hedgerows, that was. And yet, they couldn't *possibly* be his. Put aside the fact they were ragamuffins every one, except for *this* one, *that* boy, the one she'd first seen, was a Chaunchell if ever she saw one. The face long as four rainy days, the hair sandier looking than the stretch of beach between Ryland's Point and Penvellyn Cove. As for the two girls presently knocking the lavender for six? If these were Divers O'Roarke's, he must have been all of ten at the time.

Given that, given this wasn't just Doom Bar Hall *and* revenge for Ennis, this was a continuation of last night and that rubbish he'd spouted about *Lydia,* after she'd resisted his attempt to … *what exactly*? Chisel something from her she didn't want to give. That's what. Probably in advance of throwing her out of here. Task one? Task one was to swallow this sword.

Pulling that question about his wife from the air had been a stroke of genius. Something that just came from her inner core, regardless, as she'd sat there, listening to his talk to desecrate Doom Bar Hall, eating food she could barely swallow, *because she was the phoenix and talk was all it was,* when it left her reaching into the dark for something that was not there. Oh yes, dressing up had cost her dear.

It would be for nothing if she didn't breathe deeply of the lavender scented air, level her gaze fully on him, let him see this little game wouldn't dent her armour. Actually, as with last night, the situation wasn't without its entertainment. Him doing all this to get rid of her when she wasn't for going. *Or maybe because he thought she knew something she wasn't for telling?*

"Goodness. How amazing. You and Lydia must have known each other when you were children and you must have known Kenal Chaunchell's wife as well. You know, I didn't think you were so badly behaved, Divers."

"Would you have liked me better if I had been?" He took a swaggering step towards her. To intimidate her no doubt.

"Who says I didn't like you?"

"Do you want the list with your name at the top of it? Anyway, what makes you think they're mine?"

"The fact you claim to have had a wife. Lydia."

"I see. Well, indeed." He ruffled Molly's soft hair. "And that is why I feel for them."

"I'm not quite following."

"Lydie's greatest wish." His gaze swept the suddenly boundless garden, hovering here, waiting there as he dragged out every word. "What is more, I have you to thank for the idea, really."

"What idea is this?"

"Of opening Doom Bar Hall as a home for poor children."

She tilted her jaw. She didn't mean to but when the words she was going to say had been taken clean out of it, some might say, it was as hard not to, as it was to refrain from collapsing in a heap on the grass but that would give him the advantage. *A home for poor children?* Doom Bar Hall? The family seat of the Rhodes for generations? She was not going to be forced into a humiliating climbdown here, was she? He lifted his face to the sun, letting its warmth play.

"I see the idea surprises you?"

"Not really. No. What surprises me …" was that she never took her hand off his jaw, but then Doom Bar Hall was at stake, "is that you feel obliged to thank me for the idea. You don't have to do that, especially when it flies in the face of your plans for Divers O'Roarke Hall."

"In what way?"

"Well, last night I seem to remember you talked of many things. About entertaining, about wine cellars, about bringing people from London, to show off your extreme brilliance *at design*."

"Oh, I wouldn't call it that—"

"Oh, credit where it's due, Divers."

"If you say so. Thank you. Last night was my business side coming out. I like to dabble in many pies. It doesn't mean I'm going to eat them. Besides, a place this size?" He swept his gaze over the sandstone walls of what was actually her heart. Doom Bar Hall. Then he fished out his fob watch. "I don't see why—"

"Why don't you just put me out?"

Some might say the words dripped a dab more acid than she meant. What kind of way was this to speak when she wanted to show this was water off a duck's back? Certainly it wasn't in a way that said that water was trickling into the pond. Or made her believe it wasn't exactly what he wanted. But was it any wonder? *Why toy with her like this?*

He sighed. He sighed all the way to his boots and back again. He thrust his thumbs into his waistcoat pocket and contemplated the clump of horse parsley too. "Now then Destiny, why would I do that?"

"Because you're waiting for me to leave, that's why. And I can go, you know. I can go now. Just say the word. After all, the house isn't mine. But maybe you can't do that. Maybe you—"

Want something from me and it's not my body either, so why don't you just stop your silly games that I'm going to keep right on defeating, and your sighing and your languid pauses, were the words on the tip of her tongue. They were also the words that froze to her lips.

The rapid pounding of horse's hooves, on the path at the side of the house froze more than her tongue. It froze her scalp and it seemed to freeze Divers O'Roarke's too.

There was only one thing that noise could mean, unless he'd organized cartloads of children to be driven in from every corner of the southern counties. And it was
the one thing she'd dreaded most since Tom Berryman had refused to help her,

She jerked her gaze around. As she did the summerhouse jarred into her vision. Beyond it, the thought of the contents. Should she faint now and get it over with?

CHAPTER EIGHT

Hell's teeth, *Lyon*, right here in Doom Bar Hall, at the head of his not-so-merry band of men. Twelve of them at a quick count. Destiny Rhodes's face was white as the foam on the waves. It probably wasn't the only one. And yet, what did Divers have to fear? He hadn't done anything.

Lyon swung his booted leg down from the black stallion. Hopefully code for Divers to speak?

"I---uh—an explanation from your good self for this disturbance, sir, if you don't mind? There is some reason for the cavalry riding in here?"

After all, he and Lyon were meant to be strangers and Destiny Rhodes couldn't know they weren't.

"Orwell Rhodes?" Lyon's glinting blue eyes were at odds with his canny Scot's accent. His hardened, lined face, more pockmarked than the surface of the Moon, was too. He was not a man to cross. He was a man you prayed would never find out you'd crossed him. Even his coat and tricorn were stark as a hanging judge's and had a definite sniff of the gibbet about them.

"Not guilty." Divers shook his head. "And you still haven't explained what you're doing on my property."

Ignoring him, ignoring the men in navy coats whose horses had flown to a halt behind him, Lyon raised his chin. "Search the place."

"Now just a minute."

"Divers, I—" Destiny Rhodes' eyes flashed. It might have been to warn him to shut up. But maybe, after all, she was hiding something and it would put an end to all of this when she was marched off? An aviary of birds with one stone.

Lyon cast her an unimpressed glance. "Were you saying something?"

"I was wondering who you are and what it is you hope to find? We are simpl—"

"The King's man is who I am."

"But—"

"You're expecting Touse?"

"Touse? Why should I be expectin--"

"Well, a brief visit to the area, by my good self, ma-am, is all this is. I am what you might call his supervisor. I make it my duty to traverse the south coast, making my report to London. As for what I'm hoping to find?" His keen eyes swept the cloudless sky, like a hawk's, hovering, waiting. "Let's just wait and see, shall we?"

"Yes."

No, was what she meant. Her eyes burned even deeper holes in her head.

"But just so you know, I do not own this house," she added.

"So?" Lyon kept his gaze fixed on some finite point. "What are you doing here then?"

"What does it look like? Supervising these sodding children he only went and brought here."

Lyon's gaze wasn't the only one to flick her. Divers made a play of patting Molly's bony shoulder. Anything to hide what sparked at the unmitigated impertinence of her answer. If he didn't speak now, *if he let her speak instead* ... In this way she always did that could mean something, or nothing ... This way that even had Lyon struggling to impress her ...

"Someone has to before they wreck the place," she went on.

Speak? And say what? Anything would make it obvious to Lyon that for some reason he couldn't deal with this situation with his usual aplomb. Had gone and brought these children here. Perhaps because of her? Perhaps because of himself?

What earthly reason did Lyon have for being here unless he knew this? Knew about Rose? Divers' history here? Knew about *everything*? And the only way could have been through Gil.

"So?" Lyon returned his gaze to the horizon. "They're not this gentleman's then?"

"Hell, no," Divers asserted. "I only just won the place."

"Cheating at cards," she put in, her eyes spitting fury.

"Miss Rhodes, you know, and I know, that that game was—"

"*Sir!*"

Divers broke off mid-sentence. Nobly he had ignored the tramp of feet across the lawn, the buckets being let down into the well, the foray into the walled vegetable garden and the prodding of the ancient bushes, but now that the shout from the summerhouse was deafening? What had he to fear? As his line of work had always shown, half the southern counties would be in jail if the excisemen arrested people for *buying*. But harboring now? Providing a safe haven?

What a come down for the noble and ancient family and more importantly, her. What was he about to witness? The real reason she needed to stay in Doom Bar Hall?

So long as Lyon thought he'd done well and meant this to happen, wasn't this proof he was still the man for the job and not the one who was somehow struggling with it? In Lyon's eyes.

"Stay here," Lyon growled to the men closest. "Guard them. And let's see what this is about."

Divers endeavoured to look natural. No-one could exude Lyon's icy menace, except Lyon himself. The man wore his thoughts like a blank mask and was unstoppable as a winter freeze. If they weren't working together, Divers would tremble in his boots. Destiny Rhodes now? Even she must have wilted by now on the vine of her raging fury. He lowered his voice.

"Is there something you want to tell me? Something I should know? Because I don't think that man, whoever the hell he is, is for messing with."

She shrugged. "You tell me, Divers. And even if there was, why should I tell you? Well?"

"Something Orwell, by chance, knows about then? Because I have to tell you –"

"How would I know what it is, or whether he sodding does? Orwell is seldom sober enough to ask. But maybe you think I'm his keeper, although I'd say it is fairly obvious that if I was I'd have put him down by now?"

Divers cast his glance across the straggly lawn. "But that's your summerhouse from what I remember. And--" he broke off as a wooden keg was trundled across the stones. "Well … Unless I'm very much mistaken …"

Her face tightened, her wasted eyes didn't just darken, if they could have leapt from her face they would. A cornered viper couldn't look more terrified, or terrifying. Certainly there was life in her yet.

"But maybe that just walked in there?" he murmured. "Maybe someone broke in and left it? Or maybe you don't use the place any more?"

"And maybe you should just shut your sodding mouth unless you can say something constructive?"

Another keg and another was rolled onto the stone path. Christ how many were there? As for her not knowing? It was perfectly bloody obvious from her stare—also stony—she not only knew, she'd probably supervised putting them there. Surprising, she hadn't thought to move them? Or maybe that was why she'd hung that lantern the other night? She jerked up her chin, spoke through her clenched jaw.

"Is that man the Cleanser?"

"The *what*?"

Her eyes narrowed. "That man? Is he the Cleanser?"

Divers shrugged. How would he know who, what, the Cleanser was, that there was a Cleanser, after all? He was from London. Remember? It was why he feigned his most harried look.

"Now then Destiny, you'll pardon me appearing a trifle stupid—"

"Only a trifle? Why change the habits of a sodding lifetime?"

How fickle, how typical. Even with her back hard against a wall, so there wasn't so much as a twelfth of a quarter inch of space, there she went, snipe, snipe, snipe. But then maybe his most harried look was slipping? And he'd somehow given her his cocky, *physicality is everything* one instead because he was slipping too? Well, the main thing? As Lyon strode back across the lawn, finally Rose's name was a gentle breeze on *his* face. One he raised that same face to. Closed his eyes, breathed. Maybe he wasn't here for revenge but it certainly felt good, as women, as life--when life was good that was.

"Shit."

Hearing the mutter he flicked his eyes open. Not quite so canty now was she? In fact beaten to a pulp was what he'd say.

"You only just won this place?" Lyon levelled his gaze on Divers. "When?"

"Oh, let me think? Two nights ago."

"And you didn't know what was in the summerhouse?"

"I haven't exactly had time to look."

"Yes. Cheating at cards can be no end of time consuming, you know," Destiny Rhodes muttered.

He glanced at Lyon. "I haven't exactly had time to look at much more than the state of this dump. Maybe do a little work. I'm a house and garden designer, from London."

"With plans galore. Big ones. Big as his boots in fact, to take the family seat for generations apart—"

"Only because it needs it."

"--and throw everything in it to the dogs, when if you ask me, talking smugglers—"

"So whose house *was* it then?" Thank Christ for Lyon's timely intervention. "Who am I looking for here? Well?" He glanced from one to the other. "Or do I have to arrest you both?"

"Shall I tell him?" Divers kept his gaze trained on the spot somewhere behind Lyon's head, his thumbs in his waistcoat pockets. "Or will—"

"Me brother." The retort was fast as a bullet. But maybe she was about to throw herself in with Lyon? "Orwell Rhodes, seeing as you must know and *you're* going to tell."

"Who is where?"

"Probably Daindridge's or any of the other local hostelries within a three mile ride."

"I see." Lyon narrowed his eyes. "So? he's not here?"

"Not unless he's in sodding hiding in the bushes. Doing it well though, if he is."

"Well then, we'll just have to arrest you."

"Me? Are you serious? Me? Why would you go and--?"

"You're here, aren't you? So are these barrels."

"Yes. But—"

"But maybe you're going to tell me they walked into your summerhouse on legs?"

"Walk? What?" she scoffed. "These barrels? Now you're being no end of ridiculous. Trying to win first prize in the—"

"You can explain my stupidity to the magistrate. Take her."

Divers heard the ragged saw of her breath. It was not the way to speak to Lyon if only she did but know it. But this was Destiny Rhodes. A mouth at odds with the world. In a big way at that.

"Yes," Lyon continued. "There is nothing like a few hours in a cell to further the recovery of lost memory."

"Is this some kind of a joke?" As the two men grabbed hold of her, Divers forcibly restrained what surged through him like a high tide. The pleasure that rose in his gut as her throat tightened, her eyes lost the litle mark they had and the color drained from her cheeks, was the most he'd felt in weeks. Perhaps the most since he'd been beaten senseless and left for dead *by this crew*. "Because if it is ... Me brother, *my* brother---"

"You think Orwell did this?" Divers asked.

Drinking the barrels certainly but that was it. It *had* to be her. Nice to see the rat flushed out of hiding, even if that same rat had just ratted on its fellow rat. *The* salted mouth rat who'd helped drive ...

Rose ...

Christ. *Rose*, right there in his head, turning the bright day to ashes with *her* ghost's breath cold on the lawn. When here he was avenging her. Sort of anyway. *When she wasn't there at all.* Just the thought of her as she'd once stood on this lawn in a gown to match her name, her chestnut hair tumbling in the breeze. The day before she'd swallowed hemlock.

Destiny Rhodes gulped.

"He ... *He* ... "

Divers strove to fix on his most concerned expression. If Rose would get out of his head he'd do it with bells on. "I'll find him for you." Provided he looked. "Don't worry I'm sure you'll be out in a day or two."

"Not if it's down to him. I won't ever be free. How can I be? And, as for you looking? Do you think me head has buttons up the back and I'm going to win first prize in—"

"Enough!" Lyon snarled. "Now let's go."

"What? Are you meaning along the highway like a common thief?"

"Why not, when it's what you are?"

"Do you have any idea of the Rhodes' standing hereabouts?"

"Is that amongst smugglers and their ilk, wreckers, Miss Rhodes?"

"Oh, there's some here would know about –"

"I said, *enough*. Don't think to make things worse for yourself than they already are. Now ... *Bring her*."

Funny that. Destiny Rhodes didn't just like being the talk of the village, she dined on being the talk of Cornwall, so why baulk like a stallion at a gate it couldn't jump, *now*? Were some bridges just too far to cross?

Was the bit he saw here a kind of manufactured self that wanted the world to think she was worse than she was? And if that was so? When if it wasn't for Rose, *for what Rose said she'd done* ...? He swallowed. Believe that and he'd believe anything. Here? Now? Suicide.

Besides, there wasn't a heap of ashes Destiny Rhodes couldn't rise from.

He dragged his wandering gaze in about. What if Lyon really wanted a meeting with him though? And Rose, bless the patient, long suffering saint that she was, the one who knew in her heart and soul, his bitter loathing for the Rhodes family, wanted to remind him? This wasn't about Destiny Rhodes getting any kind of come-uppance. This was about riding alongside Lyon the same as always. Especially if Gil had gone to him. The children? After all, maybe, now he considered it, not the a best move on his part?

"*Wait.*"

Lyon jerked to a halt, his gaze sneaking sideways. Was it wrong to think he was waiting, like a cat for the mouse to lie down and die? "You said something, Mr.--? Mr.--?"

"O'Roarke." Divers stepped forward. "Yes. It happens I did."

"Something of interest, was it?"

"That depends."

"What on?"

"On the fact Miss Rhodes knows nothing. She is not who you want here."

"Think very carefully, Mr. O'Roarke. Who do I want here if not Miss Rhodes?"

Divers glanced at Destiny, her face whiter than snow, her mouth a pink slash. To land Orwell in it? Or not? That was the only question to answer here. Christ, he'd never played the role but he certainly felt like bloody Hamlet. Christ, if only he could walk away. For here, from this, from everything. He shrugged.

"I don't like to say."

Lyon turned fully. "And why is that? Didn't you say you just won--?"

"What I can tell you is Miss Rhodes is a visitor here. So whoever these barrels belong to it's not her. You're wasting your valuable smuggler-chasing time arresting her. I am willing to come along with you if that helps. Answer any questions you may have."

"Really?"

"Divers, you don't have to—"As expected her eyes nearly swallowed her face. But maybe he should face the fact she'd rather go with Lyon than be in any debt to *him*? "I mean it's ... "

"But I do. So?" He jumped in before she could add, *more than I can stand*. Ignoring the sweat coating his palms, he turned to Lyon. "I am happy to accompany you and answer any questions you may have. But I'd prefer it if we left this lady out of it."

Lyon cocked his head. "Fine. Leave her. Take Mr. O'Roarke instead."

"But—" Destiny Rhodes' throat fluttered. "Divers I really—"

Divers cinched his lips. "Don't want them to take me?"

"Oh, what do you think? Take the words out me mouth, why don't you? I just—"

He *tried* to cinch his lips, anyway. Well at least she didn't lie through her teeth about how good it was of him to take her place.

"I didn't know you thought I could take words out of your mouth."

All fine, when, *if* she did but know it, it wasn't--good of him to take her place that was. Only think of what she'd be giving him when he came back. And not her body either. In the meantime, the last laugh was about to be on her.

"Let me sort this out. No. I swear, I'll be back soon. In the meantime, why don't you see to the children?"

CHAPTER NINE

"So?" Lyon eased down into the wooden chair on the other side of the desk, his voice low as the bottom of the sea. "Would you like to tell me what the hell that was all about back there?"

Not particularly. Now Divers thought about it, he'd sooner dig his grave with a soggy piece of paper than admit he'd had Gil round up some children to get Destiny Rhodes to give him a name which he could have got from the servants he'd stupidly dismissed because he was failing at his job. Or just maybe he wasn't able to chuck Destiny Rhodes out? Because of Rose, or whatever. Complicated, wasn't it?

With Lyon, confessions weren't an option, neither was hanging by the neck until he was dead. He sat forward.

"Funny that. I was going to ask you the same thing. What the hell do you think you were doing arriving on my back lawn like that, unless you need to know something and this is how we are going to meet? I have this in hand."

"Not what Wryson says."

"Really? What about?"

"You tell me. Let us be clear, he's your man, not ours. And as your man, I felt obliged to listen to him on the subject of that woman."

"Woman? What woman?" Divers drew a breath of fetid, salty air. Penvellyn jail held the rancid odor of a salt flat at low tide, even if this was an office not a cell. It was damn chilly too. The walls were damp as if the sea had beaten on them so often, it now washed right though the crumbling, grey brick.

"He said there's unfinished business."

"And that's why you haled up on my back lawn because you believed him? When the man can't even remember his real name? Who he is? Where he's from? Anything?"

"He has always had your best interests to heart."

"Really? Well, he's all wrong about this one."

"Is he?"

The silence ticked by like a slow clock, carefully in time with the nerve ticking in Lyon's jaw. Imagine? Silence was Divers' favourite thing but if he didn't break it his gut said he was finished. He couldn't be finished. Over her? Gil doing this either. But fortunately he was master of this game.

"Destiny Rhodes and I go back a long way."

"So long you didn't seem to know what she'd stashed in your summerhouse."

"Any more than I know who put them there, that is true. Who she's hiding them for in other words."

"So you admit she is hiding them?"

"It's unlikely it's her brother. He's much more likely to drink them. Still, I'm glad you came round. I don't know what kind of results you are expecting after forty eight hours—"

"The usual ones. London is eager."

"Tell me something I don't know."

"They want names, Divers."

"And they *will* have them. Christ, when have I ever let them down? You either."

"What were the children doing there?"

"A front. Destiny Rhodes—. Well, she--"

"Won't leave? Is that it?" Lyon's gaze fastened on him, as if he knew about Eirwin, that Divers hadn't walked away from that as he should have. Now he struggled to stay off *that* path, *when he didn't*.

"Knows something. Obviously she does, or that stash wouldn't have been in the summerhouse. She also mentioned the Cleanser. But she's difficult. Always was. The whole family are."

"Then you should have brought in a wife for that."

"Obviously."

"The option was there. Is there some reason you didn't take it?"

"Destiny Rhodes would find out. She's the kind."

"All the more reason to get rid of her then, don't you think? Before she finds out you're neither successful designer, nor smuggler," Lyon continued. "That everything that's said about you is, in fact, a lie. And then, *then* you have no cover here."

"Fine." He shrugged. "I'll do it."

Because he would. Taken her place, hadn't he? So getting rid of her now would present no problem.

Lyon scraped his chair back. "Two days, which is very generous of me. Then I expect to find her gone. See to it. Results, Divers, are what I want to see. Results."

CHAPTER TEN

"So what do you want, Divers? About you being back here, that is? A medal?" She'd thought about it, winning first prize in the *most sociable girl in Cornwall* competition, that was, by greeting him with a glass of wine and the offer of whatever she could offer. But it was not quite how it came out now a ball flung by the Chaunchell boy nearly knocked her flat on her backside on the lawn. And then again, in her defence, her hopes that *he'd* be packed off to London for trial had just been dashed. And really, this was a very conflicted situation that way.

"Not exactly." Divers O'Roarke climbed down from the cart. "Think I'd wait forever for that."

He would too. But then again, her stash had been discovered and she'd nearly been arrested. What else could she do but demonstrate her eternal thanks to the man who had ensured she was standing here. Him not being up to his neck in smuggling and that. Hard to bear. But there it was.

"So?" She bent down, grasped the ball, heaved it back at Emory Chaunchell. "I entertained the children just as you requested."

"So I see." The grey eyes glittered like diamonds in frost. "An onerous task for you too, I can tell."

"Oh," she gasped."You have no idea."

Because he didn't. Or that she was so out of condition she could hardly tug a breath into her frozen lungs. Maybe it had been sunny earlier. Earlier wasn't now. Despite going in for her coat and scarf she was shivering. But, if she said so herself, even he could not fail to miss the way she'd got these children finally throwing the ball and not at her lavender bushes either. In her face maybe but not at those.

"We need to talk, Destiny."

"Talk?" Her throat dried. *That* was a pity. "Right."

"*Not* out here."

"I see. But what about the children?"

"The barrels are what we will be discussing. Now."

When she was doing her best here too, despite her shocking lack of breath and the fact she'd planned on sewing cushion covers this afternoon? Getting that wassail bowl out too. How could he? And so bossily.

"Right." She edged a breath. "Then, let's go indoors where it's private. I'd have said so a moment ago but that Chaunchell urchin has ears all over the place."

"Really? A lot of urchins do. It's something they share in common with the rest of the human race. Anyway, who says I'm the one with anything to hide?"

"Fine then. Then why don't we stay out here?"

His aura of command was undiminished by the casualness of the step he took towards her, just as she caught the ball too. "By all means, if you want the fact you're plainly a smuggler discussed out here in the open and being broadcast from the church tower in Penvellyn by nine o'clock tonight, let's do just that."

What kind way was this to carry on? Certainly not in a way that made her feel she would give her arms and teeth to call his bluff. Not when she couldn't shy away from the fact that her being put out of Doom Bar Hall might be being broadcast by ten minutes past nine because he thought that the barrels being discovered made her a very dangerous person to know. And maybe, what with his design business and that, he could do with *not* knowing her, either?

Her gaze clouded. Oh, she had fallen low indeed, down a cliff face at that, when all it took was a set of barrels being wheeled onto a path to hammer home the indisputable fact Ennis wasn't here to save her. So up had leapt sodding Divers O'Roarke instead. What was she trying to win? First place in the *pathetic widows* competition?

She was *never* going to get out of not giving a name, when she'd only gone and painted such a nice picture of domesticity too. Well, Tom Berryman, husband, father, grandfather, was someone she couldn't give up, not if she was thrown to ten packs of rabid hound dogs, each dog with ten inch fangs. She'd be lynched. Then? Well, then she'd be dead. Was it any wonder she hadn't really wanted Divers O'Roarke back there doing what he did? And despite him saving her and that, it would have been much easier if he'd been packed off for trial? But he hadn't. So what else could she do but jerk up her chin? Look innocent about it too?

"Fine."

Never mind Penvellyn Fair, never mind the county, or indeed the country, she'd need to win the world's *fastest thinker* award, by finding herself some other name. And she'd need to do it within the next five minutes too.

***

"Tom Berryman."

"Tom Berryman?"

Oh, all right the notion that she couldn't give the name up was vastly overrated. Did people really think she wouldn't and Divers O'Roarke would have to apply pliers to her teeth? When what she wanted was to get sewing her cushion covers and that?

Besides with a bit of luck, people round here might think he'd given Berryman's name? Get himself lynched and that would certainly put paid to his plans for Divers O'Roarke Hall. She nodded.

"Yes."

"I see. And he is …?"

"Griffin St. Gerren's uncle."

If he thought he was getting any more he wasn't. Not *right* now anyway. She'd thrown herself in with the house after all. It wasn't exactly edifying knowing all Divers O'Roarke wanted was the name of her supplier. When he was widowed, with no wife, who was not for discussion too? ? Nah. The thing was to dangle a certain amount of bait.

"Well, Destiny, I'm so glad you've finally decided to see sense."

"Oh, you'd be surprised at what I've finally decided to see, frankly."

She had. But maybe he was surprised and that was why the noise of the leaded decanter, the one that always caught the sunlight in its frosted clasp, slowly emptying, stopped? A pity. Much more of that *bounce, bounce,* sodding *bounce,* being all there was to listen to and she'd personally stuff that ball places where the sun didn't shine on that Chaunchell brat, given the flowerbeds she was having to sit gallantly *not* thinking about here. The lavender borders too.

Face it, the leaded decanter wouldn't be making any noise at all, would it though, unless her *overall* amenability deserved a celebration?

"I see." The smile carved generous grooves in his cheeks. He shrugged and resumed pouring. "Such is the thanks a man gets for saving a pretty pair of heels from dangling? Is that it?"

"Now Divers." She clasped the glass he offered. "Don't push your luck. Right *now* anyway."

"I'm glad you think I've any luck. Much less that I'd push it. But what you really mean is, even if you did know more, you wouldn't tell me."

"Says who?"

She did. But when he'd probably only gone and promised the Moon to that exciseman and was now going to have to come up with the goods, she was hardly going to say so, was she?

He could sink into Grandfather Austell's armchair and set his booted feet on the small table as much as he liked—she didn't like, but that wasn't the point—radiate as much confidence and command from the toes of these same boots to the dark lock of hair that lay across his brow, via everything in between, as he liked too. The point was keeping control of her finest cards, concerning Mr. Berryman and his barrels, till she could trust *him.*

And right now what with that *bounce, bounce, bounce* of the ball on the lawn outside proper doing her head in, now was the time to ignore the affront to her mother's table and keep offering her warmest, earthiest smile and most obliging manner. Because it stood to reason that if that *bounce, bounce, bounce,* reminded her of the countless times she, Chancery and Orwell would have swallowed swords rather than pass it to him and Rose, then it must remind him.   To think she'd planned on sewing her cushion covers this afternoon, instead of setting her face in gaping chasms. But that was all right. Guaranteeing the roof over their heads was far more important. She'd started well if she said so herself. At least she hoped so.

"Well, here's the thing." He sat back, tweaking his coattails so she was even more aware of everything in between. Or maybe he just liked to fidget? "I do."

"You do what?

"Say. Because I think you know more."

"Hmm." *Wasn't he the clever one*? Not a quarter much as her though, now she'd hit her stride. Trying to anyway. "Well, maybe I do? But, from where I'm sitting, I'm asking myself why you upped and galloped after that exciseman faster than if you'd wheels and rockets tied to your boots. I mean, let's face it, it's not as if you like me. Or wouldn't like me out of here, now is it?. And don't say, *says who*? Because I do."

Actually? A good point. Why had he done that? He blamed her for Rose.

"I mean, as you must surely see ..." She swallowed. Was referring to the *bounce, bounce* such a good idea? But he was staring at her intently as if she'd said something of great value. "What you said that ... that exciseman wants, is the name of the man who put the barrels in the summerhouse. Correct? Not the sodding path he wheeled them along from the beach. Because *that* wouldn't just make me even more complicit, more vulnerable, than I am already, it would land me in big trouble with more than that same exciseman, whatever his name is. In short, I'd be lynched."

"So? You're not going to tell me?"

"Hello? What did I just say?" Was he post deaf, or plank thick he hadn't heard it? But maybe it was the concept of her being vulnerable he was struggling to get his head around?"

Didn't he know what death it would be for her around here to say any more? Why the hell did he think she was playing on it? The truth about Rose and Chancery, wasn't a card she could play. "Anyone would think you were in that man's pay the way you're panning me head in about it. Because *frankly, truly*, what's a plain, ordinary house and garden designer needing names and all sorts for? Well? I've tried me best to be thankful. But if you thought I needed help out there, you were mistaken."

"Because that plain, ordinary house and garden designer needs something other than a name to give that exciseman."

"What? So I can hang?"

"I don't think it's unreasonable—"

"No. I'm sure you'd like that as revenge for your precious Rose, who, if you did but know—"

"I did see you out the other night is what I me—"

"And?" All right, so she'd lost her amenability somewhat but no sodding wonder. "Let's not sodding forget, I saw you. Far as I know it's not a crime. Last night? Last night you as good as offered me a position in exchange for something vital. Turning a blind eye."

Well, he had. She averted her gaze. My God. Was he after a name to divert suspicion from himself? Because he wasn't a house and garden anything? How shocking sodding was this? And how stupid was she to have as good as said so when he hated her guts? But then again he'd thrown her taking her place.

"Well then ..." The glass clinked as he set it down and rose crisply to his feet. "I daresay he will find out what he needs from getting that name."

Especially if *he* gave it? And actually if her head wasn't so sodding done in by this, surely even she could see that where this left her was quite nicely placed in just about every way it was possible to be nicely placed? If he was a smuggler? If he wasn't? Well? Forgetting everything else, including where the pieces anded?

"Just refresh my mind will you?" he added, placing his hands on the back of his neck so he could stretch his obviously cramped shoulders.

She raised her chin. "What about? Tom Berryman and how he gets the barrels up from the beach? And all these other things you think I know?" *And probably wanted for himself?*

"What you said the other evening."

"The other evening? What's the other evening got to do with Tom—"

"This house, Destiny."

And actually if her head wasn't so sodding done in by this, surely even she could see that where this left her was quite nicely placed in just about every way it was possible to be nicely placed?

When the words stopped ringing in her ears maybe? *Now* ... Now would be a good idea. Task one. Let a smile play even if her eyes felt as if they'd sunk to the back of her head. Trust him? As you would a poisonous snake. At least she hadn't waved her drawers about thinking he'd taken her place because he liked her. On both counts, that would be right. That she should hope for better things too.

"Oh, I'm quite sure you've not forgotten, Divers, so why don't you just drop everything about the children and renovations, Tom Berryman and all your other plans? Hmm? And get to what you've been dying, since you came here, to say? Trying too. I mean, muffed it a bit, I must say. But now you've done what you just did for me earlier there's no need to be shy." She drained her own glass.

"That's very good of you to say. I hope you think I am."

"What? Good, Divers? Well, *you* must be shy that is. I mean, do you seriously think that curse or not, I don't know you've never been able to resist me? Well? Because the thing is?" Although her legs shook, she rose to her feet. "I'm not good."

Did that take him off guard? The new commanding, sodding bastard that was Divers O'Roarke wouldn't want to look scared now, would he? Certainly not before little old her.

"Then I won't resist you. Be in my room at ten tonight. Is that acceptable to you, Destiny?"

Acceptable? Really funny this whole thing. Touse was the local exciseman here. Not this lot from where Divers O'Roarke had so recently hailed. London. What if they weren't excisemen at all? And *he'd* paid them to ...*what*? Only hail up here and threaten her, so he could then nip round the sodding corner with them for a bit, before popping back in a cart to get that name from her--that's what.

Having had a good laugh about threatening the widow. *Better still, maybe they were all in this together and who they really wanted to be in it with was Tom Berryman?* Best? These men had set about searching the place like hounds after a fox. As if they knew exactly what they were looking for, where to find it too. As if they'd been tipped off in fact. Tom Berryman would not have dug his own grave that way.

So if *he* expected her to baulk? About his room? About tonight? Giving her every reason now to walk out that door? Wouldn't he be waiting till kingdom come? When she *was* this nicely placed and the Fates were smiling. She gilded her lips in the brightest smile she could manage. She even fingered his shoulder, hard in its covering of soft wool. Leaned up on tiptoes to do it too. *Specially.*

"*I can't wait* are the words on my lips."

Even if she wished his breath wouldn't hang on her like that when it came to special things.

"Well, then?"

"Provided you do one thing."

"And what's that?"

"Get rid of these children. Who knows what I suddenly might find myself remembering then? Feel more disposed to talk about too."

Gathering herself, she glided from the room.

After all, he played with her. It did no harm to return the favor.

Carrots and donkeys. Play her cards right and this house would be hers sooner than she'd thought, without him, and the sodding children in it too. As for telling him about Rose and Chancery? Pigs would fly round the Moon first in pretty little silver bows.

CHAPTER ELEVEN

The sharp rap on the door, dragged Divers O'Roarke, from nursing the final dregs of the warm amber liquid in the crystal goblet. His gaze shot to Gil, sitting in the battered leather armchair opposite, before he could stop it.

"Christ." The word spilled from Gil's mouth. "Not—"

Divers held up a warning finger, kept his voice to a low rumble. "It won't be her but I swear to God if it is and you snitch a syllable of it to Lyon—"

"Me?"

"Like you did earlier--"

"Divers, I was just worried about you, man. Look ... after Eirwin, do you blame me? I know her death cut you deep, I know you felt to blame, that you were involved because that's what the job demands. You can say what you like about that. It's obvious—"

"What is?" He wasn't about to hear another word on the subject of Destiny Rhodes. Especially when this might not *even* be Destiny Rhodes, although equally, he'd sent the servants packing, who the hell else could it be? He set his jaw. A little menace did no harm sometimes. "Well?"

"Nothing." Gil ran his fingers through his lank dark hair. "You know you can trust me. I thought--I thought that--"

"Then I'll trust you to get the hell out and let me deal with this. My way. *Now*."

Lowering his voice, he flicked his gaze and his thumb to the adjoining door. Gil could find his way out from there. Divers had had it out with him and had known him too long to believe he had anything less than Divers' best interests to heart. Besides, snitch to Lyon about certain things and he'd be dangling alongside Divers. The court didn't exist that would spare either of them. And however much Divers appeared to be messing this up, it *was* a surface apparition. *He had this.* He had to.

"And don't say, I told you so, either." Divers set the empty glass down on the side table.

"I won't." Gil rose. "But if there's *anything—*"

"Saddle a horse for her. She's *not* staying. And find where her brother is—"

"Penvellyn."

"Good. I want him out of this house tonight too. Throw a bag for him onto the lawn and lock the main door."

Another rap. Of course there were those who might say he shouldn't have come upstairs but why should he skulk downstairs, giving her the advantage? No. *If* Destiny Rhodes was at the door, he'd open that door, looking as if this was what he expected, even if it wasn't just the last thing he expected, it was the last thing he wanted.

Fortunately she was hardly going to get into bed with him. Even if she was, he wasn't going to let her. He'd sooner dig his grave with a tea leaf. Besides, not only did he remember that curse, he intended on living to a ripe old age, although sometimes he wondered. If it was worth it too.

He waited till Gil had gone before opening the door. Take her? With her hatchet-jaw, dead eyes and that *dowd's, plain as crow's feathers and looking like them too*, dress? The world would grind to a halt and die on its axis, if women presented themselves to their potential lovers like this. He wrinkled his nose. Or would it?

"Destiny."

"Well, Divers, as you can well see, it's hardly Grandfather Austell's stuffed parrots."

"*And* charming as always. Or is that something that doesn't come with the house?"

"I didn't put it on the table. I didn't know it was required." And yet she spoke in that earthy way that meant it really didn't matter whether it was or not. As for the lavender scent? Please don't let his nose follow it. "You did say you wanted me here at ten. You did not say I had to be civil about it."

"Well, that's where I'm sorry to disappoint you but—"

"What? You want me to be civil?"

"Why change the habits of a lifetime?"

"So what's the disappointment?"

He stared at the passageway as she swept past him through the door.

"The children. Yes. You specified my sending them away. I didn't. Well … I mean, I said they can come back again tomorrow morning. If you think I am going back on that, you can think again. So really Destiny, given your terms and what you must understand, I want for Lydie, I don't see …"

"Oh, that?" His heart sank to match the armchair the squeak said she'd doubtlessly sat on. He just didn't want to drag his gaze around to check. But when he'd decided he didn't want, or need, to hear what she had to spill either, '*oh that*?' was neither expected or nearly good enough. *Obviously* she was disappointed. She just wasn't going to say so.

"Yes. That. So?"

"Well, I don't know about you but that was just something I said. On reflection, I quite like children. They are actually very nice. Well, some of them anyway. Yes. Ennis and I had very much hoped for some. But that never happened this side of hell. *God help them if it had*, I hear you thinking. And you'd be right. But God would have been helping you too. I wouldn't have had to come back here if it had happened."

He turned to face her, ignoring the fact she sat there like a black shroud. A sad day when Destiny Rhodes didn't know she should dress for a lover, though. Should sit there, her eyes like desolate stars in the candlelight, bleating her and Ennis's great love of children too, like a plaintive sheep with its backside stuck on a wire, except she wasn't a sheep and her backside was stuck here.

"Anyway?" She cleared her throat, thin in its mourning brooch. "You did say to be here at ten and it's ten. So?"

"I'm glad you can tell the time. I wouldn't have liked to go to sleep not knowing." Fortunately it wasn't Divers' place to let pity trickle into a single ventricle of his heart. These chambers were already dead as the dead they housed. "I wouldn't like you to go to sleep not knowing either that--"

"What? That I'm so very unappetizing you want me to go?" She flicked a stray strand of hair behind her ear, bit that suddenly succulent looking lower lip. When she'd as good as killed Rose too. "Well?"

"Frankly, do you want me to answer?"

"If you feel you must."

Truly? It would be nice to leave her with something, despite everything she'd done, everything she'd said, the fact Rose would find even more corners to ambush him from, she wasn't unattractive. But how could he? Lyon had spoken and he would speak some more too if he got wind of some of the contents of that conversation earlier. In fact he'd do more than speak. Divers had a name. While it would be nice to have some more—and Lyon would want more--he hadn't thrown down this gauntlet for that. Maybe he was simply seeing spectres that weren't there? Destiny Rhodes had always been a great player of men, their hopes, their fears. Despite the dull eyes, the fact she seemed, on the surface to be sleepwalking through life after the great blow it had dealt her, last night had proved she was also fighting for her life here when she had turned tables on him. So chances about what she knew about this operation, were things he wasn't prepared to take. Not after Eirwin. Not when Lyon could be on to him.

"The question is this. I cursed you. I cursed you and your brothers –"

"One of whom—"

"Blew his brains out at midnight. Do you seriously think I didn't trouble myself to find out?"

"Oh, I'm sure—"

"May everything you touch, turn to dust."

"Sorry? These words are not ones I remem—"

"But I do. So, on reflection, given how many people have done just that around you, how even this place has pretty much done the same, and there's your other brother, a sad drunk—"

"I am sure there is no need to talk about Orwell that way, even if it sadly is the truth, because of--"

"Do you really think I'm going to let you touch me with so much as a twenty foot pole? Now, you have half an hour. Gather your things, take whatever little tarnished trays, or cross-eyed parrots—"

"Cross-eyed parrots?"

"--you want. And go. Leave. Hell if it's money you want, I'll even give you some."

He dug in his breeches' pocket.

"I hope you think I want your money."

Just as well when he'd have to write her an 'I owe you'. But maybe it just eased the amusement flickering in his veins, to be magnanimous when he'd scored one about these bloody awful parrots, belonging to her equally awful, bloody chiselling, peg-legged, frog of a grandfather, who, to even have one parrot, never mind five of the fecking damn things, must have been a pirate.

Divers could quite picture the old skunk with them sitting on his shoulder. No wonder his stepmother had run away. Hell, the pity was she'd ever run back. A nice woman from all he remembered. As good to him as his own might have been had she lived. In a way thank God she'd died before he'd uttered that curse or he'd feel responsible.

"No." He eyed her squarely, spoke in his deepest, most impressive voice. "What you want, is me here tonight. But as I said-_"

"Oh, you always were the cocky one."

"It's not cocky, it's not self flattery. Me here tonight, falling into your trap. A woman whose heart is blacker now than it was then, which is really saying something, who thinks she can waltz in here and lead me like a siren onto the rocks. Please don't look as if you're astonished. I know the pretence that is. Just think of the fact you gave that name."

"Because *you* sodding asked me to. Do you really think I'd have done—"

"A first for you to do anything someone asks you."

"As for *that* night, *that* one you seem incapable of forgetting—"

"Can we just leave that night out of this? You see, I think what you did earlier shows the kind of woman you are and what you're prepared to sacrifice in order to stay here. Perhaps have *your* revenge, in some way? Correct? For Ennis?"

"Me? Oh, chance would be a fine thing, especially what I'm starting to thin—"

"And if you were prepared, why would that be?" That she should sit there and say what she had, shouldn't just cause alarm to creep like a vine from his fingertips to his face, it should send it snaking back down again, squeezing the breath from his body. When the most she could resort to, without any kind of proof *and* Lyon at his back and her mixing with smugglers, was cheap trickery though? No. The thing was to face her down with his usual cool. After all, what rabbit could she pull from the hat that would change that? What hat did she even have, let alone rabbit? "You tell me when if anyone deserved to be where they are now, I'm looking at that person, " he added, "So that sacrifice won't include me. Now … " In case she was in any doubt, he stood to the side of the door. He held it open too. "This isn't about revenge but I want you out of here within the hour."

"Really?" He'd the satisfaction of seeing her throat tighten. Unfortunately his groin did too. "Oh, I think it's about revenge all right."

"Now Destiny, nothing is further from the case."

"When you won't even hear me out about all the things I have to say?"

"I don't need to."

"The things I know."

"You told me earlier."

"No. I never did. Not the things, the real things, the things I know that—"

"Destiny, there is nothing. *Nothing* you can say to me here tonight that will make me change my mind about letting you stay here in this house that you don't own because your brother threw it away in a game of cards. A game that was not rigged, contrary to what you may think."

Because there wasn't. So if she got a little fraught, that bright, glazed manner crumbling like a sea wall that had stood so long it didn't know how to fall down? Well? It was hardly his concern.

It was on her to stop being wilder than that same sea that hit it. And on him to end it now. The most she could do was take her fists off his chest before leaving. So long as it wasn't his broken ribs it wasn't exactly anything to fear.

"Whatever you may think or say about that," he added. "If it's now little smuggling paths you want to tittle-tattle about, and how these barrels--"

"Things you don't know."

"--got into your summerhouse."

"The things about Chancery and Rose."

"Chancery and Rose?" He cocked his eyebrow, glanced at the floor. "Chancery? Not a name you should speak in connection with her. Not and expect to keep—"

"Well, I will mention it."

He tightened his grip on the handle. Better that than on her neck what shot through him in that second. What was this but a cheap attempt to stay here? An attempt he could not afford to let undermine him. "The door, Destiny."

"They were in love, Divers. Something you never knew."

In love? Chancery and Rose? With difficulty he swallowed what knotted his throat. Staunched the breath that bled from him in that second.

How low could she stoop? *How far could he let her?* The wonder was he didn't annihilate the floorboards, with the intensity of his gaze in that second. But at all costs he needed to keep this casual, use every ounce of his training.

"And that was why he raped her, was it, and, talking children—"

"Well, of course she was always a saint. She had to make up something when my father forbade the match, rather than face you with the truth that she was pregnant; me aunt had just died after all. She had to implicate me too, that I didn't just put Chancery up to it. I egged him on, when Chancery loved her. He wanted to marry her."

That he managed to keep standing upright at the door was a miracle on a par with Christ rising again after he'd had nails driven into his hands and feet.

A miracle such as he had never witnessed.

All this was about, was her staying here. To that end she wouldn't just cling to the coal dust, she'd cling to the air. At all costs, this was a moment where he needed to bring everything he'd ever learned in his line of work to bear. About staying calm, about being measured. About not thinking of these times when he was eighteen that he'd hungered, thirsted for this. Destiny Rhodes at his mercy.

Lyon *had* to be appeased. One thing Divers wasn't ever going to be was dust. As for listening to a single word that dripped from her serpent's tongue?

He'd sooner slice off his ears with a blunt knife. Because what it meant was he'd cursed her for nothing. Fallen into Lyon's clutches for the same reason. And he hadn't. He couldn't have. For Christ's sake why would Rose be here for any other reason but to warn him to stay away from Destiny Rhodes? To demand the revenge he hadn't come here to take from the woman he couldn't seem to take it from?

"Well, she was certainly a saint compared to you. Not that that was much manner of hard. As for revenge? If this was about revenge, it would be revenge to take you into my bed and give you exactly what you deserve. But I'm not going to. Now, in case you haven't seen it, the door is here."

She gathered her skirts. Relief pounded through his narrowing throat. She rose, walked towards him, not as quickly as he'd have liked. So it strained every fibre and sinew in his being, not to grab her elbow and shove her out of the door, the way his mind reeled. But what she'd said was a taunt he *wouldn't* rise to, whatever else she said.

Her gaze, dangerous as that same serpent's tongue, scorched him.

"Such a pity Divers, when you never know. I might actually have got to like it. But maybe you're just too scared of that curse ... "

CHAPTER TWELVE

"So ... Dstiny? Whoring yourself s'now?"

Get back to her room. Shut the door. Sleep. Eat. Face the day ahead. With Orwell's voice roiling over her? His hand descending on her bedroom door, the one she'd just opened? And the smell, the one that was worse than the inside a keg of ten year old brandy—off ten year old brandy—making her gag? Or it might if she could rise to it.

So he'd been standing in the darkened corridor listening? To what? Hardly her moans of ecstasy. The ones that only the other night she'd thought she could rise to in order to convince her new lord and master how delighted she was with the present arrangement.

"*S'now*? I'm not doing anything *s'now*. Nothing I know of anyway. But if you're meaning *now*, well, Orwell, it is certainly better than drinking oneself now, isn't it? Especially to death. Now, if you will kindly excuse me--"

"Do you think slo? Wilth him? D'stiny, you ... look, old girl, you're a Rhodes."

Tug her wrist free. Get inside her room—task one. Shut the door. Sleep. Eat. Face the day ahead. The one that wouldn't be spent here. Not now. Not ever.

"And a fat lot of good that's ever done me. Now, if you're done, clutching me wrist and breathing your stinking brandy fumes all over me ..."

He swayed. "Look, you *shid* trouble yourself about that, about ev'rything, given what's been said round Pnvllyn about *him*. All tht's being ... whativir."

"Really? So then? Go ahead. Tell me."

"Ahhh, so you're interested now are you, little sistre?"

"If it will get rid of you quicker."

"Such a pity that's for me to know and you to fin—"

"In other words? Nothing. Nothing's being said. Nothing you remember anyway."

Accept the fact it was—task twenty. Feel her eyes burn in her head. Duck inside her room, as she did now. Shove the door shut. Stand against it. Feel the smooth wood press against her spine. Accept there was no day, no day ahead. Nowhere to go. Nothing.

She'd failed. How the sodding hell had she failed? She stared across the room at her reflection in the mirror. Obvious, wasn't it? Because she looked like some sodding old crow who'd win first prize in the *sodding old crow* competition, that was why. Even if she wasn't cursed, she'd win sod all prizes in the local fair competition for inveigling a man into her drawers. For making them run a mile, jumping every stile, in the opposite direction perhaps, but that was about it.

As for spilling beans about Rose and Chancery? Trying to win something in the *I'm an idiot, humor me* competition, maybe even the *see how nice I am really*, or the *I have nowhere else to go* ones, having come last in the other two? Her face crumpled. No really, had she, or had she not, gone to that room tonight, with the express intention of securing the roof over her head with all that she knew? Getting into bed with *him* if need be? The man had cursed Ennis, *who had only gone and left her flat*. And it *was* revenge if she turned Divers O'Roarke to dust. Sometimes, in life, you had to put out to get back in.

Just because he'd stood there more commanding than Genghis Khan, it was no reason to come back here with her tail between her legs. Get the bejesus knocked out of her spine by a door handle either.

"Sod off, will yeh?" She fumbled for the key. It clunked off the floorboards as the door battered against her elbow. "Because I'm telling you now, you can do this all night if you want to but over me dead body are you--"

"Destiny—"

"—coming in this ro--"

"Destiny, open the door."

My God. *Divers O'Roarke*. Let her faint on the floor now before she lived to be a second older, except she couldn't faint on the floor. She'd be trampled on. As for what he wanted, nearly taking her off her feet like this? Well, if it wasn't to make sure she didn't leave here with a stuffed parrot up her skirt, or down her bodice, it must be that his beauty sleep had been a bit disturbed, what with the noise she and Orwell had been putting up and he was here to put her out a bit faster?

"What do you want?" Fail to face him up as he burst into the room though and she was finished. "Am I just not moving me backside fast enough for you? Or is it, that when it comes to gathering my things, despite what you said, I have none? And you want to be sure I don't leave here with something that's yours, like my petticoats, for example? Or something else that's already on me back? Like this dress?"

"Not especially if you want the truth? In fact I can't think of anyone who would like it. It's that hideous."

"Where's Orwell?"

"Lying on the floor, I expect. Along with Grandmother Tintagel's table." The floorboards creaked as he strode to the wardrobe, yanked it open. "But to answer your question, you have things all right."

"Grandmother Tintagel's table. You broke me Grandmother's Tintagel's table?"

"I never said I broke it. I said it was lying on the floor where it best belongs, damned old bat that she was."

Dear God, it was too much to bear. No wonder she sprung across the floor.

"You want *me* to take that?" The red dress he tore from its hanger, despite the blows she rained on his shoulder and arm, was one she wouldn't wear if she was stripped naked and thrown out into an Arctic storm.

"Oh, Destiny, Destiny, if you did but know what I want."

"Oh, I know." She thudded her fists off his chest, the sting of fury so hot, she could barely get a word out that wasn't mangled by her failure to breath properly. "It's not good enough that you're throwing me out, you want to select what you throw me out in. Show those, who may not know already, what me true colors are?"

"Then show them, Destiny." She gasped as the dress hit her chest. "Show *me*. Now. Because coming to my room dressed as you are right now wouldn't invite a man to open a chest containing fifty thousand pounds in gold, if you must know, let alone invite one to the dark and dusty death that *supposedly* waits from touching you."

"Seeing as you did the cursing you should know whether it's *supposed* or not."

"I'm not afraid of you. That's just something you've always liked to think."

"Oh, I don't like to think. I know."

"Whether I'm attracted to you is another matter."

Attracted? She clutched the folds of the scarlet dress tighter against her breast.

Task one--*Get back to her room. Shut the door. Sleep. Eat. Face the day ahead.* Remember? She *was* back in her room. She *had* shut the door but now, *now he'd opened it*, was it possible that facing the day ahead could be *exactly* as she'd prayed coming along the corridor?

For one thing too? Well? And was that why he stood there cool as a cucumber? Sort of anyway. Cooler than her anyway which some might say was hardly difficult.

Everything she touched, remember? All she needed to do was put on this dress which she hadn't worn since Ennis died, his face bloody as its color. She could, couldn't she?

"Well then? I've news for you." Her throat tightened as if there was an iron bar across it. Tightened so she could not speak. But she would. She would speak. She would do this. "I'm not doing this."

He stepped closer, his iced gaze skimming her face. "Not even to see me in hell? Well. Well. Oh, I should think it's what you want. Let me remind you if you can't remind yourself."

"No." She shook her head. "Let me remind meself. The reasons I don't wear this dress. This color."

"*Look* in the glass there." The way he grasped her and swung her towards the glass gave her no choice but to stare, as icicle cold as she could now, at what met her. At eyes that belonged to an alien constellation. At a starved crow failing to put on its finest feathers. His breath, warm male, brushed her cheek so she could taste it, taste him. "And tell me that woman is you, that you don't see what I mean?"

Somehow she jerked her gaze away, her mind from the images she wasn't going to let fill it here. Images of him. Of her. Images that would win her first prize in the *needing to contain herself* competition. Did he think she didn't see he wasn't serious?

"And that is somehow something to you? After all, unless I'm very much mistaken, not ten minutes ago you told me to go."

"Well, maybe that was because I don't want *that* woman." He leaned his chin on her shoulder, so all she could see was his eyes, liquid silver in the candlelight. "But this one, the one *I* know you are inside, let me see that one. Show me. The real woman. The one that could light a man to his doom and lead him dancing down *these* paths."

"Divers, I am."

Because she was. There was no 'real' woman. *This* was what she was. It was also as much as she was showing him, the way her heart hammered. Anything else was a betrayal of Ennis. Already he'd be affronted seeing she'd stooped low enough to be a foot below ground level.

So, if Divers O'Roarke thought he could beat her down lower still about this dress, he'd a big thought coming.

He gestured at her reflection. "*That* dress, Destiny."

"Divers ... I've not said, no--"

"Where are the clouds of ambergris?" He strode back to the wardrobe. "The trailing wake of debris?"

"You will find debris if you don't let go of this. And that debris will be you. And I ... I will have some say in—*Put me blue dress back.*"

"Says who? You? When I'm the person who's about to turn to dust? Now choose, Destiny. *Choose.* Blue? Or red? What do you think? What is more, I don't believe that curse."

"Well, more fool you because I'm telling you now--"

"No. Fool *you*, Destiny. For ever listening to a load of old balderdash. Spoken by my good self—"

"So you say but you're not the one living with it."

"--it's true but balderdash nonetheless."

"No. No, it's not. It's—"

He stepped towards her and bent his head. My God, what was this? Something she'd not experienced in years? Something that could not be calling her bluff? Something that took away any thoughts of thrusting her feet down through the floor to the deepest regions of hell, where they would be immediately impaled on twelve inch honeyed pikes and have wasps set on them? When she was lichened stone? And she could not afford to do this for any other reason than to turn him to dust?

However much she might sometimes have cursed the fact no-one was leaping up and down to come near her--certainly not anyone in their right mind—it was two years since Ennis. Two years, to come to this realization. Divers O'Roarke actually kissed not too badly for Divers O'Roarke. He actually kissed in ways that sent every bit of her spinning to places she belonged in. Hot. Wild. Dark. Places where her mind emptied and there was only this to hold, to cling to, to want, *to need.* A hunger that shrunk her mind, melted her bones.

"So? The dress?"

Did she speak? *No.* He did. Definitely. What was more his forehead was pressed against hers, his grey eyes inches from hers, his warm scent, soft breath, catching hers when she couldn't let it.

"Let's put it on, shall we?"

"Divers, I really ... I truly ... *beg you* ... to let this ..."

"No. Don't speak. Not tonight. I let you speak to me the night I arrived and I shouldn't have. I've already let you speak to me tonight about Rose, about Chancery. Tonight, I'm doing the speaking. Now ... "

Speaking wasn't all he was doing. Just as she told herself--tried to anyway--that him here was the answer to all her prayers, why did his fingers have to find the ribbon lacing the bodice of her gown. Tease it through the eyelets too? So they brushed her breasts? His fingers that was. Why did his scent, subtle oakmoss invade her senses?

When it was what she needed—them to do this anyway--why protest though? Just because her breath was somewhere down in the pit of her stomach? And she somehow feared to go on? Her? When all she had to do was touch him. The body was a treacherous thing but nothing she could not overcome.

"It was the truth what I said about Rose, about Chancery. Anyway, that wasn't what I was going to say, if you would just listen, not take my dress off me. I mean it--"

"Oh, I'm taking it off all right."

"No. No, you're not."

She froze. The dress had pooled at her feet. It was as much as was going to.

"So, what are you going to say? Hmmm? That I've no right touching you, kissing you, making you wear this particular dress? Well?"

The scarlet blur in the mirror crystallized into flesh, into blood, into lips red as rowan berries, into eyes black as the night sky and softly swelling breasts. Crystallized into him, pressing his mouth to her neck to the place where he must feel that even her pulse was flickering, to his arm tightening about her waist. *In this dress.* This awful dress, he'd somehow slipped over her head. How was that?

"But I do Destiny. Tonight I have every right. All I want is you in that dress."

If he'd lavished these caresses on her years ago would she have sneered at him? Or was that why she had? Because what rose in her might have got her into trouble then, just as what rose in him now was something he probably couldn't fight?

Well, she could. She could still. In fact some might say she would. She knew exactly how to too. She could not feel these things. She dragged a breath.

"Divers … Divers, I know that. I know all you want is me but … there is one thing you should know."

"Not tonight."

"One thing I am trying so very hard and even more patiently to tell you."

He raised his head. "What is it?"

"You see …"

Not Rose. Not Chancery. There was probably not a thing he wanted to hear now his fingers cupped what was probably heaven to him--her left breast, so her breath caught and her heart missed beats. Still he murmured,

"What is it you want to say?"

"This dress isn't the one I was going to pick."

Really? Well, what one was it then? One of her *made to make a man celibate for life,* specials? When she wasn't made to live in the dark. Or he wouldn't be here. Not when the bluff she thought she was calling, with her talk about dresses, might not be bluff at all. When underneath all that, underneath *everything,* did she really think he couldn't find the woman she was, if he had to? He had to now. Because the dark was his place of safety and he wasn't in it right now. Not since he'd left that room needing to know more and somehow walked into this. He met her gaze in the glass opposite.

"Well then, how about we remedy that?"

"Because I—"

"Don't really come with Doom Bar Hall, is that it?" He pressed his mouth to her ear. "Think very carefully before you reply. You angered me, yes, with your talk of Rose and Chancery *and* everything you said about them. About me."

"Everything I said was the—"

"Because these things would make anyone angry. But if you seriously think I'm going to insult either of us, by saying, *because you are so grief stricken for Ennis, you've given up on life,* when seriously I have to ask myself if I cursed you for nothing, you can think again, as I know some part of you would prefer. Just as I also know you are grief-stricken but the real you wouldn't want me to know, because the real you would rather die than admit to such things." Now, that ignited some small spark in her taut body. "So, how about you lower your tightening shoulders and answer straight? As for you touching me?" He lifted his head. "In many ways I am dead already I have been for months. So there's nothing you can do to me that hasn't already been done. And don't tell me a woman like you hasn't thought about it."

Her eyes glazed. "Oh, please don't flatter yourself I'm *quite* that bad that I would wish you de—"

"Thought about *this*? You, me, now, tonight."

"I—"

The tremble was something else, which was good when the last thing he wanted was her knowing he was doing his damned best not to quake in his own boots now he'd gone and landed himself in a situation he'd never intended being in. No wonder his heart hammered and he felt he'd immersed himself in iced water.

"I mean, you're cursed. And yes, I'm to blame. Even if you hadn't felt anything for Ennis, don't tell me loneliness would be your master. That you wouldn't desire someone to break that curse. Because, let's face it, who's going to?"

Her throat tightened beneath his fingertips.

Doom Bar Hall. Doom Bar Hall. He felt it in the faint tremble that lay on her skin like shimmering water, the sole reason she did this. But really so long as by morning he could kick whatever sandcastles he built here down, what the hell did it matter? And he would. There would be no repeat of the Eirwin situation.

Or were, *it would be nice to break that curse,* the words that didn't escape her. Was Doom Bar Hall what she reminded herself of here because of the things she couldn't let go of.

She shrugged. "Very well. If you say so."

How gracious. And yet? The winged brows, her eyes, dangerously smouldering as pointed stars? Set so far back in her head, how did he rescue them? No wonder Nick Trengouse had nearly killed himself over her. She was totally unfathomable, *and*, despite *everything*, no longer what she was then but so much more. Delicious in fact.

Hell's teeth. Kicking his sandcastles down, remember?

Him, losing his mind wasn't on the table here. She could even put the blue dress on. A woman battling herself like this deserved to.

He knew that as he cupped her chin, bent his head, pressed his mouth to hers, felt her lips open slowly beneath his. And then, get hotter, darker, deeper. *Not Eirwin, not Eirwin, not Eirwin*. But then, *he wasn't Ennis*. He knew that too as he pulled her soft body against his.

What waited in the dark when the only escape now was to look a complete damned fool by walking out?

He'd cursed her.

For nothing if what she said was true.

He was as damned to walking out as he was to staying.

But staying was all he could do now.

CHAPTER THIRTEEN

"Now, despite the fact that last night you were that far towards drowning in your cups, you refused, I want you to tell me something."

Despite the fact she never ate breakfast, Destiny set two cups of sweet, hot, chocolate coffee and herself down at the table. Where else but in the trembling cold of the dining room? Some might say they were without servants, it was doubtful Orwell had noticed the fact, although he did raise his head and stare at her, as best he could anyway given that staring and staring straight were two different things where he was concerned.

"Know? Old girl?"

"Yes."

"What about?"

"What do you think?"

Of course the chances were Orwell had probably forgotten he'd been in the corridor last night, let alone that he'd accosted her, probably forgotten who she was for that matter. She tucked a loose strand of hair behind her ear.

"Well?"

The slurp set her teeth on edge. Even if she had served his coffee in an old stone cup she'd found in the kitchen as opposed to the mazarine blue, the least Orwell could do was swallow the contents without sounding like a hippo had its snout in the cup. And was drinking through it too. Why had their father wasted good money on an education for him when the only thing he'd ever learned was how to drink? Not exactly winning any prizes for doing it quietly at that. Having satisfied himself he'd slurped enough for one morning, he set the cup down carefully on the saucer.

"I'm sorry old girl, the fact is I can't."

"You mean the fact is you can't remember."

"It's not that. It's that you are assuming … You are assuming I heard any—"

The door swung open. Late autumnal sunlight shafted across the table bathing the cup in gold. There was only one of two people it could be since the only other occupants of Doom Bar Hall were seated at the table. Although she struggled to do it, she lifted her gaze. Naturally the Fates, desiring to continue their campaign of spitting in her face—did they think it needed washing or something--and then demanding she rise again, decreed that of these two, it should be the one she least wanted to face after last night—this morning rather when he'd taken his clothes and left as if she didn't exist.

Her shoulders stiffened, the breath tightening in the pit of her ribcage. And yet she *must* face him. Wiping spittle from her chin was nothing she wasn't accustomed to, after all.

Her heart skipping the tiniest beat in her shrinking ribcage though? A certain part of her tightening too? Well, last night had been interesting. But when she was still Ennis's? Task one was to forget last night. Yes. Seriously. Her body's response too.

What was it she'd thought the night she decided on this, after all? *She could surely manage a few ecstatic moans where required.* And she had.

That was all there was to it.

The things he'd said before a curtain came down on what happened next? About her being lonely? The kind of woman who was obviously desperate for certain things? Well, people could all make mistakes at times. She intended mopping up this one.

She raised her chin. "Divers … I thought you'd gone out."

"Destiny, Orwell." He headed straight to the table. A spoon and a bowl of something he'd obviously made for himself, clinked and clunked as he set both down, eased into the chair opposite. "Is there something you want to ask me this fine morning?"

"Me?" Destiny's scalp shrunk. Task one? She willed her heart back down her ribcage. Even if he had overheard her, he was hardly going to give her anything, now was he? "Well, I don't exactly presume to speak for Orwell here, of course. Despite everything he *can* string sufficient words together to form a sentence but I, personally, can't even begin to imagine why you'd ask."

"Because I overheard you."

"Really? Well, in this instance I fear you are hard of hearing. In this instance Orwell and I—"

"Oh, my ears are in good order. At least last night they were."

Or he wouldn't lift his spoon to his mouth like that, his eyes cutting like a comet in her path and then, with casual deliberation and the merest flicker of amusement, swallow whatever was in that bowl.

"So? What do you want to know?"

"Know?" Apart from the fact she wasn't going to rise to this? "Apart from the fact it's plain as the nose on your face that not only--"

"My nose isn't plain."

"Well, that's debatable. But, in this instance, I'm sorry to disillusion you, I am afraid—"

"You? That's a first."

"--not only did you—"

"I'm a smuggler." The silver spoon clinked as Divers O'Roarke skirted it around the gold-rimmed circumference of the bowl. "Is that what you're trying so hard to find out you're asking Orwell there?"

There was no denying the quiet blanket that fell on the room, on her veins and heartbeat, the fact her coffee cup would have clattered into her saucer, were her head not so panned in already.

And yet, why would he tell her that? Because it was another bluff? What she'd been trying to find out yesterday?

"Wouldn't that be interesting? You know, I should never have guessed. And a wrecker too, no doubt?"

"Yes, actually. As Orwell will tell you. Or he would if he remembered, except he was probably so drunk when he heard it, he's clean forgotten, that he heard it and also that it's what's being said in Penvellyn about me."

"As it is being said about half the county, old chap." Orwell shrugged. "I wouldn't pay it any heed."

"You can believe what you choose. Why do you think I wanted that name?"

She cleared her throat. "What name?"

"Now then Destiny, while there's some things you may forget, that name's not one of them. Tom Berryman."

Her scalp shrunk further. Shrunk so it clung to her skull, in fact. That he was telling the truth about being a smuggler was wishful thinking. She certainly wasn't going to win first place in the *right load of old cobblers* competition by running to that exciseman about it, although some might say, it was very tempting. Not when that man might not even be an exciseman.

"Because you needed something to give that man. Surely?"

The chair couldn't be scraped back—obviously--so he rose to his feet without scraping it. He threw the spoon down on the table where it shone in the sliver of golden light, fixed her with his calmest stare as he pushed his thumb into his waistcoat pocket.

"No. Because I want to speak to Berryman, that's why. So I lied to you. And you fell straight into the trap. So, let me tell you that and spare you the business of going sneaking behind my back to Orwell there, or anyone else. Everything I appear to do is a front. A front for what I really do. Do you honestly think that designing houses and gardens pays that well?"

"Well, now you come to mention it, if I thought it did--"

"Well, it doesn't. What you choose to do with the knowledge is of course up to you given you want Doom Bar Hall. Now, if you will excuse me, I do have matters to attend to."

***

"**D**estiny, old girl. I say, old girl, come back. Stop it! Where the blazes do you think you're going?"

"Where do you think?" She tightened her flapping cloak about her, feeling the crashing waves surging hundreds of feet beneath her, the wind tearing the breath from her body and the hair up from her head, as she battled on. *Excuse Divers O'Roarke*? Over her dead body now.

"But Tom Berryman's cottage isn't this way."

"That old fool's cottage? I hope you think I'd go there."

"Then—"

"Where? Well, if you were sober you might know what happened yesterday, apart from you soaking up more gin and brandy than a wad of blotting paper and berating me for being in his bed."

"Tom Berryman? You were in Tom Berryman's—"

"Oh don't be ridiculous. The sky would fall first and topple all the rainbows." She only wished it had. And knocked her out. Then last night wouldn't have happened. "Credit me with some taste. And don't pretend you don't know whose bed I'm talking about."

"But I don't. I only thought … "

"You? Think?" She smothered the tears of laughter scalding her throat. "That's a first, I must say. Plainly you *don't* think or you wouldn't think I'd be in that old grandfather's bed. No. A man came to the hall yesterday. I think he is the Cleanser."

"The *who*?"

"The Cleanser. Someone Tom Berryman seemed terrified of. Too terrified to move that stash."

"Stash?"

"Yes. Stash. I didn't tell you because you'd have drunk it. So anyway, this man arrived and he arrested me. *Yes.* But Divers O'Roarke? Well, he took my place. Why do you think he did that? So he could have Tom Berryman's name from me and not content with that—no, when has he ever been content with anything—he came to my room, after trying to throw me out the house, along with Grandfather Austell's parrots."

"Steady on, Destiny." Orwell adjusted his hat—the solitary sign he was sober--in the tearing gale. "Are you saying that he brought Grandfather Austell's … "

"No. He didn't bring anything. Are you just not listening to a single word I'm saying?"

She swallowed the gust of wind tearing down her throat. What was she saying exactly? That, after she'd said her piece about the dress, the man had as good as begged her to take him to hell, that this wine-dark, consuming passion had so gripped her senses and his, even now the thought of it, was enough for her to feel his hands, his mouth, on her body, underneath that dress? That she'd struggled for a few minutes when she opened her eyes this morning, to remember Ennis's? His scent. His touch. *And she needed to remember.* He was her life. Even if he was dead.

But it wasn't just that. If it was just that, the ground wouldn't be crumbling beneath her black boots, trickling to its death in the crashing waves. It was the tiny pinprick of light at the end of the tunnel she'd seen in that second. A light that said she was living again. She'd felt alive. When she couldn't.

She wasn't living again. She'd never be living again. Never. Not given what living did to you. So why not blab what she now knew? *To Touse.* Before Divers O'Roarke wanted more, before he looked at her as if he knew her pain? When he damn well didn't. Said things about being dead. Even if he had let her keep the dress on in that second she'd felt like a scarecrow without it, which was really saying something when she hadn't wanted to wear it at all? Could he read minds, this man who was certainly *very good* at certain things, whose body—God, how had he come by that? And how could she have let it do what it had to her?

No. Her ability to turn people into dust had vanished. *She* was the one who was crumbling. So really, she couldn't rely on that and she couldn't get back into bed with him either. Not even to avenge Ennis, or get back Doom Bar Hall. Why should she? She intended mopping up this one, remember? Not thinking terrible thoughts. Like it was Ennis' fault she was in this mess. Like she was living.

Although the wind gusted Orwell's words across the waving bracken, she heard them clearly enough.

"I say, old girl, do you want me to call him out?"

"And shoot what? The sky? A tree trunk? Your foot? No, what I want you to do is go back to Doom Bar Hall. Keep him occupied till I go and see Touse about this man, this Cleanser, or whoever he is, because one thing I do know is a set up when I see one. And I'm seeing one now, between him and Divers O'Roarke. Oh yes, I've joined the dots all right."

"But what if Divers O'Roarke finds you've turned him in? What the blazes am I meant to say if he asks where you are? For God's sake, you can't do this."

"I think you'll find I can do this and more. And so long as he is taken away you need say nothing. Just tell him what you have to, offer him a drink, do *whatever* if he asks for me. Just don't spoil this for me. *For us.* This is our chance, perhaps our only one to take back Doom Bar Hall. Whatever he says he won't give it back. Don't you see?"

"But what if he will? Hang it all, *I* lost Doom Bar Hall."

"Goodness, finally you noticed. Still, if we take it back I just might be able to forgive you, so long as you don't lose it again."

"But look here, have you thought—"

She drew an ocean sprayed breath, eyed him squarely. "More than you have lately, I do assure you. Now go back. Go on."

"But Destiny, you mean that you're willing to betray a man you— well—you—"

"*Slept* with? Oh, say the words and be done. Like everyone else has probably said around here--s*lept with to avenge that poor sod of a husband.* Let me say it first and save you the trouble. Slept with and--"

"*Did* that, knowing you could just turn him to dust? Hang it all, it's anything you touch. Isn't it, old girl? And it seems the best way with a beggar like him, is to do just that. Touch him and--"

"If it were that easy, you, like Chancery, would have blown your brains out, long ago. Go back now, Orwell. Last night is not for discussion. Certainly not with you. In fact I can't think of anyone it is suitable for discussion with."

Well, she could, but it was too late now.

"For God's sake, what if this is a trap? Do you hear me? I mean, ask yourself why the hell he'd tell you he was a smuggler, unless … *unless he wants you to go to Touse?"*

"Why would he do that? And even if he did, it's a chance I'm happy to take to be rid of him. Do you understand? He told me to do what I wanted with the knowledge, in order to get back Doom Bar Hall. *This* is what I'm doing."

"*Destiny.*"

She hurried on. Yes she had offered herself with the house. But she couldn't, which was really saying something. Tom Berryman *had* quaked in his boots at the thought of the Cleanser. It would be nothing to how Divers O'Roarke would follow once that same Cleanser found out he'd been betrayed.

And she was just the one to do it. A problem shared was a problem halved, after all. Surely? And, if ever one needed halved it was this one.

***

"**S**o? She took *this* bait then?"

Once he'd have died to possess *her*, now he just might if the snap of Lyon's telescope, the brass one, that was Lyon's pride and joy, was anything to go by. When *he* shouldn't have possessed her too.

Had Lyon hit him over the head with the telescope he couldn't have felt more stunned--by his ability to keep his expression bland and utter that immortal word, *bait.*

What else was *he* meant to do though after last night? Destiny Rhodes, but not Destiny Rhodes? A woman he'd once thought so exotic, he'd even believed the stuffed tigers prowling the sitting room in frozen poses moved whenever she walked amongst them. Had he always been besotted, or what?

"Looks like it," he muttered, staring across the windswept moor. "It's where that path leads, after all."

He edged back in the damp bracken, biding his time until the shadow of a boulder fell across his hands, then he slipped round it and eased to his feet. If nothing else the fact that Lyon wasn't long about joining him said the bastard was as satisfied as it was possible for the bastard ever to be satisfied. Generally that was not at all but what else could Divers do but have his favourite visitor? Hope.

If Lyon now headed for the horse that was tethered to the blasted tree trunk, that hope would be rewarded. There was no doubt who Destiny Rhodes was on a royal progress along the perilous cliff path to see. That minion wasn't Divers O'Roarke. Something he should have known when he'd overheard her and Orwell this morning. Tigers were always striped.

Maybe if he hadn't tiptoed into the dawn?

He'd had to. Any longer and he was risking himself in a situation he'd never meant to be in. Where was Rose's whisper when he'd needed it most? Certainly not when Destiny Rhodes had said she and Chancery had been in love and the thought had led him along that corridor. Because Rose had been different that summer. So now? He swallowed, relief flooding as Lyon's hawk-eyed gaze sat on his horse's back.

"Well then, I best be getting back into Penvellyn. It would be wrong to disappoint a lady. I wouldn't want a capricious creature like her changing her mind about giving you up."

"Look, I know you think I shouldn't have told her anything but how the hell else was I going to keep Berryman in play? You'd have to arrest him otherwise and then I can't get a foothold on the ring. Getting a foothold on the ring is all that counts."

Ignoring his sweating palms, he set his tricorn back on his head.

Lyon thrust his booted foot into the stirrup, squinted at the dwindling sun as he pulled on the bridle to yank himself up. At last the bastard was going and Divers could relax for the first time since he'd woken up this morning trapped in the tangled folds of a dress he should never have asked Destiny Rhodes to wear and never would again. Not when he'd dreamt of the moment Eirwin had been shot. And that dress was her blood on him.

Lyon clicked his tongue raised his face to the sea-sprayed breeze cutting across the rough moor.

"What I think is you should have put her out as you were under express orders to do, and then let me deal with Berryman still being in play, *provided* she stayed in the area."

"She might have gone to him."

"As you say, but it's not like you to disobey. Don't do it again."

Fair enough but plainly Lyon had never tried putting Destiny Rhodes out of anything. Still, from now on, Divers wouldn't stray from the path. Lyon couldn't ever know how he'd done this so often, he'd strayed into becoming one with these people. Felt the thrill of taking gold. The agony of having to betray them. Lost something he'd cared about.

Not this time.

Now he'd clawed this back and was going to play a new game here, he'd sooner dig his grave with a bent twig, a dead bumblebee.

However he'd cursed her, rightly, wrongly, or indifferently, over his dead body and tattered soul would there be any repeat of last night.

CHAPTER FOURTEEN

"So Miss Rhodes, what can I do for you?"

Should she just say, *jump off the cliff* and be done with it? As the craggy faced worm who'd tried to arrest her yesterday, eased down into the wooden chair on the other side of the desk, Destiny did her best to do the same.

Before anyone even asked her where Touse was, *Touse* had shown her *in here*. But she bit her tongue and fixed on her tranquillest stare. A problem halved, remember?

"Oh, it is more what I can do for you."

Because it was.

"Really? And what's that precisely?"

At least give this man his due, there wasn't so much as a flicker in his eyes as he apprised her, it made it easier to face him coolly when yesterday's humiliation still scorched her hair roots, given she hadn't expected to be facing him at all.

"The Cleanser." She swallowed her rising gorge, the alarm that would have taken her by the throat otherwise. "What, if anything, do you know of him?"

"The Cleanser?" Lyon sat forward as if she'd taken him entirely by surprise. But maybe she was mistaken? Maybe Tom Berryman had been in his cups? Or trying to win first prize in *the mule stubborn* competition when he'd refused to move that stash--despite braying as loudly as that same mule, about this mythological creature? Maybe she'd had to do a quick turnabout on this man *not* being an exciseman, it didn't mean he wasn't the Cleanser. She sat forward.

"Oh, please don't look as if you have no idea who I am speaking of. When I think we both know who it is? Hmmm?"

"Do we?"

Of course, the blank look was expected. *But what if she truly was mistaken?* And here she was, Destiny Rhodes, of the house of Rhodes, committing a folly on a par with walking barefoot on hot coals, with her toenails covered in paraffin. Accusing this man because Tom Berryman had behaved as if the devil had crossed his path and this one looked to have horns?

"I see." No wonder the fine hair on the back of her neck stood up. "Well, maybe I'm wasting your time then and there's no such person?"

"Oh, there is a Cleanser, all right."

"Right."

"And we should most definitely like to put our hands on him."

"Really? And that is why you look as if you'd like to snap that quill pen, is it? Because you can't?"

"I'm just surprised you have heard the name when I was assured yesterday that you knew nothing of any smuggling rings hereabouts."

How sodding rich when that same smuggler had as good as sold her over a barrel and only said it to save his skin? "Well, I don't. That is no lie. The Rhodes never associated themselves with smugglers. Wreckers either. The Rhodes have never been less than decent, honorable, law abiding people."

"And yet, yesterday, unless I am very much mistaken, we removed several barrels from your summerhouse, the kind that law abiding, decent—"

"Because I didn't put them there."

"I see."

So did she, that the words had tumbled out before she could stop them. But really this was not going as she'd hoped. And it wasn't just that there was something deadly in the silence that sat on this man shoulders like a cobra, about the blackness of the velvet ribbon that tied his lank brown hair, even the crisply pressed bunch of lace at his throat either.

"Well then?" He tapped the feathered end of the quill against the desk. "Who did? This Cleanser you came in here claiming you know so much about?"

How sodding rich was that?

Not rich at all when just maybe, when it came to skin, it was time to save hers?

Besides, she'd given Tom Berryman's name to another smuggler to keep Doom Bar Hall. Of course she hadn't known at the time it was to a smuggler. Now she did though, why not do this? Ignore the ice-cold shiver that inched up her spine? Halve her problem?

"The man you brought here yesterday. Me house guest. Divers O'Roarke." She cleared her throat. "So yes, to answer your question, I do think I know who the Cleanser is."

"Go on."

What? No exclamation? No demand to know how she knew this? Just his eyes sitting on her like festering maggots in the sea-washed darkness. Except the room wasn't dark, there was no sea washing against the walls in the darkness. No sea, period. Just the smell of it, wafting in the window. She lifted her chin higher. To do less would say Divers O'Roarke's behaviour last night undermined her. She straightened her shoulders.

"I think I said. Didn't *he* tell me himself?"

"What? That *he* is the Cleanser? When was this exactly? In your dreams?"

"I beg your pardon?"

"I asked you to go on."

Intensely aware of Lyon's gaze boring holes in her, she lowered her own. Very well, to agree here would be to see Divers O'Roarke hang. This man, this creature, this part of her past, her childhood, her adulthood. And not just that? If it was just that … well?

And she should care when she couldn't rely on herself any more? And he'd broken bits of herself last night then discarded them like old shoes this morning. Just because she'd already fallen that far, was it any reason to let herself fall further?

A problem shared *was* a problem halved. Surely? Some would say hers would certainly be when she got him out from under her feet. In fact, when he was hung her problem wouldn't just be halved. It would be gone completely. So could she start thinking of the reward for turning him in. Doom Bar Hall, which he'd only gone and nicked from Orwell in a card game. Well? Not what had happened last night. And how he'd kissed like nothing on earth and seemed strangely vulnerable.

What if he used the honourable seat of the Rhodes for generations as a place to hide his ill-gotten gains? All right, she accepted she'd done that. But that was to fund the restoration, keep the place on its feet and the servants in jobs. She hadn't stolen these kegs.

What if he got arrested? She'd be strung up with him. Anyway, she'd come here, hadn't she, to land them both in it, *him* and *this man*?

So? That may have changed a bit in the interim, the principle was the same. Why start and not finish? She passed her tongue over her lips.

"He didn't in so many words. No."

"Actions speak louder did they?"

Damn him. "I *mean* he never said he was the Cleanser but he *did* tell me he is a smuggler, a wrecker too, and I'll thank you not to imply otherwise as to how I know but to keep a civil tongue in your head. He said that he uses his business of designing houses and gardens as a front. You'd have to question why he ever came back here, what he was doing in Daindridge's the other night. I know I have been. So why shouldn't he be the Cleanser? Well?"

"Because some say the Cleanser is an exciseman, gone to the bad."

"*Really*? Tom Berryman certainly seemed—" She bit her tongue. He was not the person to mention here. "I mean, Divers O'Roarke has always been as dishonest as the day he was born."

"That's as maybe. Being dishonest does not a smuggler make. It is not an offence in law. Consider the jails if I was to arrest every dishonest man, woman, or child. For that matter the jails don't exist that could hold them. Have you never done anything dishonest? Is sitting here like this *not* what you might consider dishonest?"

Destiny fought the images of barrels that bobbed into her head, fought not to finger the back of her neck too. Her? Dishonest? Had she ever heard the likes? Hadn't she come in all honesty to get Doom Bar Hall back? It was scant protection for what this was really about. But how could she face what this was really about? What? Right now? Her throat tightened.

"Well, if you're not going to listen, I should at least like it noted that I came here in good faith, should you discover that, at the end of the day, he—"

"I would need proof, Miss Rhodes."

What was he saying? That Rome was not built in a day? By God it would have had she been a builder. She sat forward.

"*Proof?* Isn't the fact these barrels were found in my summerhouse proof enough that you can hang him at the Penvellyn crossroads, a warning to any who cross the law here?"

"And let the crows peck his bones, eh?" Lyon chuckled. Despite the fact the sound was not unlike these same rattling bones, she nodded.

"Yes. Why not, if he broke the law and put these barrels there?"

"Oh, I'd like to hang the perpetrator, believe me."

"Then why don't you?"

"Well here's the thing, Miss Rhodes. He said it was you."

***

*H*er? Opening the door to her room, *obviously* Divers Roarke's rather, which was probably why he was facing what was also technically *his* looking glass above *his* mantelpiece now too, Destiny did not feel quite the same as the woman who had left it earlier.

Still--let her heart sing joyful songs of elation--she *had* been to Lyon. She *had* allied herself with him. In a way. Not the way she'd hoped. True. But so long as she could put aside the rankling words, *'You say one word of what I am about to reveal, to anyone and I will personally see you hang at the nearest crossroads for smuggling. Do you understand?'* was it so bad, really?

She did understand. *Lots.*

That Orwell lay sprawled in some or other state of inebriation, snoring in a chair and Divers O'Roarke stood here with his back to her, wearing a coat, meaning he'd gone out, was not ideal but it was to be expected. She was Destiny Rhodes, after all. Able to first guess everything and anything. Even if her latest second guess had sort of backfired in a way that had scorched her eyebrows.

Doom Bar Hall was still at stake. *Doom Bar Hall*. What Lyon had said meant that Doom Bar Hall was still on the table. She'd keep quiet all right *at a price*. Of course, while she'd wanted to say as much to Lyon, somehow it had seemed safer being a serious contender for winning the golden apple in the *keeping her mouth shut*, competition

In truth? At *that* point she'd struggled to say anything at all. Any reaction had been tempered by Divers O'Roarke's treachery *towards her*. The payback for everything she, Orwell and Chancery had ever done to him. The payback she must now overcome in order to face him down coolly as if it was no trouble to her and last night was nothing. That his treachery, after she had extended the hand of friendship towards him, was pitiable really.

Imagine *not* being able to move on in *your* life, even after having heard the truth about Rose and that particularly stupid time in Chancery's life, certifiable on a scale of idiocy—*Chancery would marry her, indeed*. No wonder their father had had an apoplectic fit and told him where to go.

Now, some might say she could not move on either. But the fact was that curse uttered for nothing had killed Ennis, as surely as if Divers O'Roarke had pushed his carriage down that ravine that night.

So, mustering her cold calm—what else could she do?--she stepped inside the room and closed the door.

"Divers. And Orwell too? Amn't I the honoured one?"

"Where were you?"

"I'm sorry?"

Her throat tightened so the breath stuck in the back of it. What if Lyon did indeed agree to let her have Doom Bar Hall when this was over but then Divers O'Roarke didn't because she'd gone to Lyon?

Despite the deep breath she dragged, her mind emptied except for one thought. She should never have done it.

So long as she didn't say she had--and why should she?—and Lyon could be persuaded to say it was about something else, this would be fine.

"Divers, exactly why would you think I would go anywhere? Well? Apart from round the garden?"

"Because I know you."

"Really?" Ignoring Orwell snoring like a pig in her best armchair, squashing the antique shawls belonging to Grandmother Tintagel, she edged into the other chair. "How glad I am that you clarified that. Well, then, let's drop all the pretence about where I went when you know perfectly well, it was hardly along the cliffs to the bay, round the garden either. And you told me you were a smuggler in the express hope that I wouldn't. Came to this room last night too. Indeed have done everything to cloak your questionable deeds when I'd say you've used me and this situation all along. You even had Tom Berryman's name from me by false means. Please don't look shame-faced about it. Well? Let's drop all the pretence, not just about where I went and why, but what I heard there too."

"Heard there?"

"And talk, talk frankly, shall we? About exactly who you are, why you are here and what I would like from the situation."

She peeled off her gloves. Yes. She had meant to say nothing. Why should she when he had done her the very great courtesy of insulting her? It meant she could be more measured than an inch tape despite the desire that had risen in her hot and dark, to take a mallet off his treacherous head. Lyon was *his* boss. Not the other way about. Why shouldn't *he* pay for her silence? Why shouldn't she be exactly as Divers O'Roarke thought? He'd probably planned Lyon telling her the truth in advance, *with Lyon*. And she'd only gone and moaned shamefully in *his* arms.

"Now, why would I do that?"

"Because I know you of old, Divers, I also know you lied. So please, don't insult what intelligence you believe I have by continuing to do so."

"Are you sure you're not speaking of yourself and the little web you always liked to spin, to sit in like a spider too."

"Goodness, the name's Destiny, not Arachne." Anyone would think he didn't know that Lyon had told her *everything*. Why should she be played with like this? "No, Divers, you have me fair and square. Do you really think I'd choose risking being put out of here, over choosing Doom Bar Hall? That is why, having been to Lyon and told him everything, I am allying myself fully with you and will say nothing to anyone about the dirty little game *both* of you are playing here."

CHAPTER FIFTEEN

If she'd flung a bucket of snakes in his face Divers O'Roarke couldn't have felt a sharper sting of surprise. *Him? And Lyon?* Not in his book as such. "I'm sorry?"

"No, you're not. That would be a first. And *much* as I played games in the past, I admit it, I don't now."

Much was the word on the tip of his tongue about the games she played all the damned time. She was playing one now. But the knowledge spider crawled with inch long spikes attached to each leg, across his scalp. That the thought she might not be playing didn't just make him catch his breath. It made him feel that what breath he did catch might conceivably be his last. But how could he very well let it be?

He dealt in wrecks, smuggling and dead men. It was only possible because he always stayed one step ahead. It was unthinkable to fall behind now. At all costs he needed to cling to the belief that as long as Lyon hadn't told her everything, he would survive to the next step. She jerked up her chin.

"And really you should learn to do the same about leaving games in the past because it frankly seems to me games are all you've played since you came here. So firstly, I don't want any more talk about children coming here. This is Doom Bar Hall, not a halfway house for waifs and strays because let's face it, Lydia never even existed, did she?"

"What?"

"What I say. And since she plainly didn't and that wedding ring is false as you are, neither do her dearest wishes. So please don't give me any more of your sodding fairy tales, any more of what my father would have called *bull*, about her, that either, or indeed, that Molly is anything more than some local child you've dredged up from somewhere. Secondly, the same goes for Doom Bar Hall itself. Since you're hardly a designer—"

"Says who?"

"Lyon does, Divers. Since you're hardly a designer and that is a complete fabrication, if you think you can change so much as a cushion cover here, I will go to Tom Berryman and Steben Padstow and all the other smugglers whose names I know—"

"So you were damned well lying?"

"Through every tooth in me head. I will tell them everything. And you can hang me and these same teeth from the gibbet at Penvellyn crossroads because there is nothing else in my life that truly matters, not since the night you cursed me for something I never did, that Chancery never did. *Because Divers, you cannot kill a corpse.* Now? Yes, or no, do we have an understanding? That's all I need to know."

Oh, how well he knew the killing of the corpse bit. Wasn't he the walking evidence? Christ, was it possible that curse *had* worked, that he was turning to dust? Why else would Lyon do this? Unless it was because Divers hadn't put her out? He dragged a breath, set his face in its blandest lines. Vital when he'd sooner dig his grave with a broken shoelace than show her he was in any way troubled.

"Well, if you and Chancery never did it, if you were so damned innocent and Rose and Chancery were in love—"

"Which you do not for a second of a second believe. No. As I've just said, *secondly*, you will leave Doom Bar Hall as it is—"

"As it is? I'd be doing it a favor, any poor, slavering, brainless idiot would if they, or I, set a match to this dump and its contents. These damned moth-eaten parrots for a start."

"Corpses, Divers, corpses, that is largely what the contents have been since you cursed us, for nothing, a thought you will have to live with, but perhaps that was what you thought you were doing last night? Or did it just make it all right for you to come to my room as you've been wanting to do all the years? And it was your chance, finally to let go of something you hadn't been able to because you were holding it in your heart against me. Anyway, thirdly, you will leave Grandfather Austell's parrots out of this, when it comes to talking ill of things. When this is over, as I know it will be, in return for my silence and blind eyes, I want Doom Bar Hall, which you plainly won under false, possibly rigged, pretences, because let's face it, you couldn't win a game of snap as a child--"

"Because you and your unholy damned brothers wouldn't let me, talking rigged--"

"But we're not talking them, are we?"

As he swallowed the ire that scalded like acid in his gullet he didn't even have the satisfaction of seeing her flinch.

"The past is the past, remember?" she added, her face stonier than anything the Medusa had laid waste to. "You don't live in it according to you, although you have bitten my hand of friendship to the bone--"

"Is that what you call it? Well, maybe that's because, when it comes to hands of friendship I'd sooner shake hands with a viper."

Amusement lit her eyes. "Not the impression you gave me last night. Well, however you choose to spend your time, I know what you expect me to say here." She pressed one slender hand to her breast. "'Why would I do that? Go to Lyon? When you'd throw me out? Dear me, no, I went for a walk on the shore. I do that sometimes when I want to clear my poor, dear little head that's being bamboozled by more lies than Herodotus told the rest of time.' But it's not what I'm going to say because it's not what I did. I did go to Lyon and I told him everything. And *that*, plus the fact you gave *my* name to him yesterday, is what he told me."

"What?"

"Oh, I'm not the one lying. Calling your bluff either."

Maybe the past was the past in her book? The one he was reading from plainly needed binding with metal chains and locking with bolts and bars, that he even uttered so stupid a goddamn word. But Lyon *had* obviously laid his cards on the table and Divers was struggling to take refuge in the fact Lyon wasn't playing with a full deck, unless he'd somehow pulled the joker from the pack, about Eirwin, about the stashed gold, about how involved Divers had got on the last few jobs. *About how he could leave all this if need be.* All he had to do was lift that stash.

His throat dried, his palms too, dried so it felt as if the skin fell off them in crumbs.

Christ, she'd undercut him in *every way*. At all costs he needed to pull the ace from the flames, speak as if this was no odds to him, as opposed to odds that were fully stacked against him. Odds that could see him dangling by daybreak if the real truth came out.

He offered his blandest stare, the one you could take a chisel and a blacksmith's hammer to and not make an eighth of an inch dent in.

"I don't doubt it. But the fact is, if that is what he said, then as ever, he's a lying son of a whore."

He was not the only one.

"So you say."

"It's what he does for a living."

"I didn't know there was such an occupation. Whoring perhaps. But being a son of one?"

"You're angry about some of this and rightly so."

"Me? Do you see me angry?" She gave a faint, low throated chuckle. "Think I'm in any way put out?"

"Says the woman who went to him in the first place, because you damn well did. Well, here's the thing Destiny, whatever you think, I never gave him your name yesterday. *You* just want to think so."

"Oh, here we go. At least I do think. Unlike some."

"Because you just can't help yourself, can you? Why do you think I told you what I did? Because I knew you'd go scuttling along that road like a spider. And you did. So now you're caught in the web."

"I think when it comes to webs, I'm hardly the one trapped. But, it's all right. I won't breathe a word. Why would I when you're the law, the one commendable thing about you, even if the rest is lies and obfuscation, including how well you're doing in London?"

"And that bothers you does it? How well I was said to be doing while you—"

"But I no longer come with this house and you will no longer try and put me out of it. You can say what you like so long as you give me your word."

"My word?" With pleasure, given what that was worth. "Or should I say 'me' word as you sometimes do? Well here's the thing. You could have had everything else but that word isn't worth the syllables that form it. Lyon's the law, Destiny. And you cross him at your peril. Me too. You think you're a corpse? You don't know the meaning of the word."

"And you do?"

The pity wasn't the hit she scored. The pity wasn't the way he stepped closer, clasped the chair arms to lean closer still. The pity wasn't the way he breathed the subtle lavender wash of her scent, stared at the lush dark fringe of her eyelashes, her lips so close, like the rest of the mysterious lines of her dress, her hem resting against his boots. The pity was she'd no damned idea *what* she was dealing with and despite everything he felt obliged to warn her. As if somewhere in his heart, she had a place.

"I know you'll find out if you blab a single word of any of this to anyone, just what it is to be a corpse. No terns, no conditions, no firsts, or seconds, or even fives or sixes, because you'll be dead, dead in ways you cannot begin to imagine. It might be you are anyway when I let him know you come with more price tags than a diamond ring. Do you understand? So let's see how willing you are to pay that price. Seven o'clock. My room. For supper. I want your answer. And dress appropriately. The last thing I want is to see you in crow feathers, is that understood?"

"Over me dead body. The clock's tongue can chime seven, eight, nine, ten. It can strike twenty four, twenty five, a hundred. And it will be over yours *if* you try making me. Make me leave here either."

***

"**D**estiny? You came?"

"Well, it's not me garnet necklace walking in on its two feet."

No. She hadn't died. No. It wasn't the sole reason she was here. Although it would have been the sole reason if she wasn't. As the clock struck five she'd understood, one thing. That was the team of excisemen, disguised as painters--London painters no less--who'd arrived, and, by the time the clock struck six, deposited their scaffolding all over the dining room floor and table. After, some might say, she'd given specific orders about that too. Did he think she didn't know what he was about here?

Having come back down off that particular ceiling though, wasn't she about to win first prize in the *having the ace up her sleeve* competition?

And while she understood he was meant to be playing the part of new master and house designer, she'd be playing that ace too, if he didn't get that scaffolding out of here again by the time the clock struck ten.

'I would need proof, Miss Rhodes,' Lyon had said.

And so, her gown, her necklace, indeed the imaginary cloak she'd stitched herself into, with all the exquisite brilliance of needlework she could muster, while not empty seas, were seas of absolute tranquillity, even if the problem shared hadn't just grown. It had sprouted such gargantuan feet and legs it was now a problem, quadrupled.

She raised her chin high above the garnet pendant she'd fastened around her neck, the one she might have worn at Christmases here with Ennis except they'd never spent Christmases here as a couple. He had been such a great one for Pangbury House that way. *And* his family who had never been especially great ones for her.

"As for making any remarks about that curse—probably on the tip of your tongue—please allow me to forestall you, although the choice is yours as to whether or not, I come in. That is, if you've forgiven me for going to Lyon. But please, don't pretend that you told me you were a smuggler for any other reason."

His gaze flickered in that way that said he'd had enough of her. He wasn't the only one. But it was too late now to take any of this back and really, given he'd handed over *her* name then had her in his bed, why should she? Torture herself about it either? Was he torturing himself?

"Look Destiny, as I said earlier, all I want is your—"

"In a minute. I mean, you are very, very clever, Divers. If I had only known from the start, for example, that *you* were the Cleanser …"

"*Me?*"

She squared her shoulders tight in the crimson gown she'd chosen, despite the fact it well nigh blinded her. Of course Divers O'Roarke wasn't going to win any prizes for looking anything other than surprised. As if a goose hadn't just walked over his grave. It had dug it first.

"Yes. It's very clever of you to express your surprise. But yes. *You.*"

He let go of the jamb, stepped back, walked to the side table before the fireplace--the chipped old wooden one, she'd almost forgotten was in this room. Clearly it was all the invitation she needed to sweep forward in a rustle of crimson silk. An invitation she accepted.

"So?" Amber liquid splashed into two small brandy glasses. "Who told you I was the Cleanser? Lyon?"

"Lyon?"

He handed her a glass. "Because as I said earlier, Lyon talks a lot of rubbish."

"Oh. Well … A bit like you then?" She sank into an upholstered seat.

His eyes narrowed as he toyed with his drink. "If he told you that, he's lying. So? Answer the question. How do you know I'm the Cleanser?"

Was she right to think he sweated a little? "Simple."

"Go on."

"Oh, I put two and two together. He did say the thinking is the Cleanser is an exciseman and you are an exciseman."

Another toy with the crystal glass, shining against his waistcoat.

"And that's your reasoning, is it? Nothing Lyon said?"

"What's wrong with my reasoning?"

"We can all add two and two together. The trouble is whether we're any good at simple arithmetic."

"God, this is tedious. Brain hurting in fact."

"Well, it's good to know you have one. Although if you did, you wouldn't have made five on this occasion."

If that was so why was the smile less assured than usual? He strolled to the window and glanced through the darkened glass. "Maybe even six for that matter."

"Really?"

Of course *he* was going to deny who he was. But he'd hardly be looking out the window, now would he, unless he expected immediate arrest? Or her to have gone to Tom Berryman and told him who the Cleanser really was? And for there to be a mob on the doorstep?

Not that she hadn't considered it. For old times' sake she wanted to give him a fighting chance. And besides, she didn't want some mob rampaging through the garden, generally wrecking her plants.

"Expecting visitors, are you?"

He shrugged. "Not that I know of."

"Well, it's just you told me to come here for supper which--"

She attempted not to glance sideways but was it any wonder when it was nowhere to be seen?

He cleared his throat. "Right. So I did."

"So?" My goodness. What a chance to discomfit him further when he wouldn't want that discomfort reaching Lyon's ears. Won this, hadn't she? Without giving a thing away either when he'd only gone and thought he was in the running in the *biggest bossy boots in Cornwall, she came with more price tags than a diamond ring* competition. She smiled—wildly--rose to her feet. She wasn't going to have to get back in his bed either. And nothing he said would change that fact. "Where is it then? In hiding?"

"Not exactly, just down in the kitchen where you're going to make it for me."

"Me? Divers?"

Even though he'd just pulled the whole idea from the air, he nodded. "Why not? As you'd say yourself, the sodding parrots are hardly going to fly down there on their little stuffed parrot wings and things and make it now, are they? That's because they'll probably be too busy laughing their little parrot beaks off imagining Destiny Rhodes in the kitchen, when she probably can't fry a bit of butter. But here she is attempting to cook for the Cleanser. At least she thinks she is. Cooking. And doing it for the Cleanser at that. *And she's going to go running to Lyon to tell him she is too. So? Let's get this over with. Supper made by you.*"

"Really?" she said after a long pause. A moment when the sweat droplets, the ones that had come out when she mentioned the word, *Cleanser,* as in *maybe he should just dig his grave with the spade helpfully provided by Lyon,* stopped dancing slippery jigs across his brow. "I thought we could just dispense with supper."

"Dispense?" He didn't just step closer--enough for the toes of his boots to brush the hem of her gown—he traced his knuckle over her cheekbone. "When just maybe you could get that proof you want? Why would you want to do that? Because you're probably not going to eat it? Being as that might insult Ennis's memory further than you have already?"

"No." To her credit she didn't pull away. Not fully anyway. But the glazed smile that wasn't a smile at all, told him how much she wanted to. How much she wanted to take her hand off his jaw too. "Being as you never meant to make supper, because you thought this afternoon was the very last you'd see of me. And then, when I saw these painters arriving—"

"They were arriving anyway. I have to look the part."

"So you say, but--"

"I do say." Did she like when he was commanding? Because he sensed it was something she loathed even as she was drawn to it. So he liked it as much as he liked the thought of living to his next birthday, which in some ways was not at all. "Because you've never had to live in my world. See the things I have had to see. Last night was very nice. I can understand you *not* wanting to repeat it, empty, grieving widow that you are. I understand how difficult it must have been for you," before she could move he slipped his thumb beneath her chin, "which was probably why you ran to Lyon this morning. You think I don't know that? That I'm the only one with ghosts around here?"

"Oh, I think you don't know anything. You may think you do—"

"Oh, I do. I know enough to know you think the dead watch us and you wonder what they make of the things we do. And in that panic this morning—"

"No. I think the dead have better things to do."

"Really? When you can touch me and turn me to dust? And still you did that? Went running to Lyon. Funny that."

"Glad you're laughing." There it was again, that smile that was anything but. That smile that yet was so damned delicious, it made his heart pound. Just as her lost, wasted eyes, the evidence of that curse, filled him with longing to bring them back to life. A longing he needed to squash. What kind of way was he in that being undercover now meant he could accept *anything*? Babies with their brains bashed out? Women with their throats cut? Eirwin blasted to bits all over him? This kind of betrayal? The fact he couldn't have made this about revenge? *That he now needed to take hold of this*? Well? He smoothed a stray tendril of hair back from her forehead.

"But maybe you were right to go to him if you're somehow gettting involved with me."

"I hope you think—"

"I don't think. I know. The funny thing is I also know what was in my head that night I cursed you. It was everything you *cared* about."

"That's not what I remem--"

"So I think that makes me safe enough, don't you? Ennis too, if he's looking down from whichever little cloud it is he occupies. Sitting there all day with nothing better to do. Playing his little harp, singing his hosannas, the endless Hallejulah Choruses and ditties. Unless of course, he's not in heaven?"

"Why wouldn't he be?"

"Because he outraged St. Peter when he married you."

"No. He never did." She dropped her gaze but not before he saw what burned in her eyes. Ah, the hits he scored here. "He loved me."

"Well, more fool him."

"Ennis wasn't a fool."

"Oh, we were all fools then."

"How dare you."

"I could have loved you. Any of the men round here could have loved you. But that wasn't good enough."

"What? You somehow think I wanted any of you? With your country clodhopper boots? And your smell of pig farms clinging to your hair?" Obviously she hadn't or her voice wouldn't tear, her eyes wouldn't glaze, her hair ping loose and he wouldn't be standing up bravely—given his earlier broken ribs--beneath the sudden rain of blows on his chest. "And your *mired in the fields of Kinsale* accent?"

"That was then, this is now. Cheer up. If he's in hell the chances are you will meet again. Now. *When* you're ready, you come and join me downstairs. No bluff. That choice is yours. But I will have your answer. And if you think you can turn tables on me, in any way, go running back to Lyon with tales of things I'm not—yes, I do know you well--you can't. The kitchen, Destiny. Or the door. Just don't think it will be neither, do you understand?"

She did, she must. Why else had she stopped trying to beat him half to death, her eyes glitteringly hot but cold in her head? Wild? Uncontrolled? Dangerous? Hot tears glazing her lips?

Her earlier running Lyon *was* in vain. She couldn't wither *him* to anything. But her thinking she could run back there again with the fact he was the Cleanser? Not in a month of Sundays. Maybe he cared for very little? *That* much he did care for.

She exhaled sharply. "I know … I know you somehow think that. That you think you know this. Know me. But you don't … the truth is you don't know, anything."

"You let me be the judge of that."

"No," she breathed. "Because you're wrong. About why ... About why I am driven to do what I did today. Why I couldn't stop meself, if you must
know the truth, even knowing it was something I shouldn't have done."

"Oh, I understand all right. I also understand there's nothing you can say to me, about me being the Cleanser, or this supper you don't want to make, or eat, or the pack of lions you'd like to see me thrown to, the sole reason you couldn't stop yourself."

"If only. If only that were true." She passed her hand across her nose.

"And are putting on such a good show. But *nothing* you say to me will change what I know. It comes with the turf in this game. And believe you me, it's a game I'm going to win. Because I'll tell you something else, remind you of it rather, about Lyon and why I need that answer--"

Her throat tightened, the words dripping from her. "The night. The night I lost Ennis, I lost more. Far more than you can ever know about."

"Well, we all lose Destiny, I think that much we can guarantee about life. So, if you don't mind, I'd appreciate if you'd stop giving me what your very own father used to call—"

"When they brought him in. When they brought him in, cold and dead and in bits on that board and they asked me ... they asked me, was this him, I lost our baby."

Christ Almighty.

"And just in case you're wondering ... "

"I'm not." How he found his voice? Kept it measured? He *had* this. And nothing she said would change that, remember? Not her forehead suddenly pressing against his, because he bent it, her breath, sticky as honey, on his lips. *Even if it already had,* what *lurched inside him.* "Believe me. I'm not letting you speak to me. It's the kitchen, remember? So if this is a ploy, a ploy because you won't go there and cook--"

"I don't know. I don't know if I can have any more."

"And last night, I never thought about that and you did? Is that it? What you now want to beat me up about, tell me that's why you went to Lyon and why you now want to go to him with the fact I'm the Cleanser? Compromising this whole operation here which he will not let you do?"

"No. Last night I never. I never anything. Because last night I were living."

Her breath caught. Her hands did too, against his face. He should take control. He had control. But everything, from her skin, beneath his fingertips, to the knowledge that she might be telling the truth about Rose and Chancery, crashed like waves into the empty places in himself. He couldn't move. He couldn't do anything for the feel of her mouth on his--hot, hungry demanding—except kiss her back, in the same way. *When it could be anything to get out of cooking that meal.*

Forget being in command, he just wanted her, the same way as this kiss. Her body, warm, wanton, earthy, demanding, was against his, her heartbeat hammering beneath his fingertips, her mouth, full of every secret she'd ever kept. Every tiny bodice button, one, two, three, tore from his clasp, though. The smell of the exposed silk of her skin, her scent, was nothing to the ragged saw of breath, to her gaze meeting his, hotly dark, wild, inviting. Things he'd struggled to say about her since walking into the library. Things he'd known damn fine could not be wasted by grief, so their breaths, wild, jagged, strangled the air.

"Come on then, what are you waiting for then?" The pant, the glazed look in her eyes? Did she tug her skirts up, or did he? Did the mattress creak beneath his knee? Had he ever had a woman want him in this basic, animalistic way? "Now, Divers. Now." Wrap her arms around him? Straddle him? Hold him? Kiss him? Her fingertips cupping his face? Skimming beneath his shirt to the bare skin of his back? So everything was an all consuming flame?

Tomorrow she'd regret giving him this inch. So long as he didn't regret taking it, it would be fine. It was only sex. What he'd had with Eirwin, after all.

At least he hoped that was all it was.

CHAPTER SIXTEEN

Touch him. Turn him to dust. Get back to her room. Shut the door. Sleep. Eat. Face the day ahead. Touch him. Turn him to dust. As she ran her tongue over what appeared to be glass paper stuck to her lips—enough to make her gag--Destiny fought to focus on the words hammering at her eyelids, along with the cold grey shaft of light demanding immediate entry.

Morning. It was morning. How could it be morning? Anything approaching it either when she was lying here fit to win *the sleep for Cornwall* competition? She forced her eyes open. Then she snapped them shut again.

God Almighty. Divers O'Roarke standing at the lovely cream, inlaid with the nicest, most delicate green and red fretwork, washstand, half naked was as much as she needed to know. Alas—because now she did know, her gaze stuck to the sight. The waist was especially spectacular. Narrower than Ennis's. And would you just look at the corded strength in these shoulders, the muscles that rippled beneath the tan as he poured a ewer of water over his soft dark hair? She'd sooner not although some might say she opened her eyes again to do it specially.

Not that she meant to, or anything, but sometimes people didn't do what they meant. As for her still being here? She removed her gaze from the tight outline of his buttocks in his corduroy breeches, gathered the sheet around her and pushed a foot out of bed. What?

Stay here? Having won the feather headdress in the how to make a sodding *great tit of yourself* competition. Hardly.

"Christ."

The jug smacked against the top of the stand. Just as she was thinking that lugging barrels ashore really agreed with him too. He inhaled sharply and bent forward over the stand. She hesitated.

"Divers ... Are you--are you all right?"

He exhaled sharply but didn't turn round. Goodness. Was that curse working after all? That wasn't so good, given what he'd said last night. "Never better."

"It's just I can't say as you look it."

Another grunt. "Before you go thinking this curse is working, neither would you be if you'd had your ribs broken."

He dragged his head up as if he felt her cool lingering gaze on the base of his spine. To have asked if he was all right might seem crass when what she should really want to know was that he wasn't. His ribs were, after all, nothing to what Ennis had had broken. His back. His legs. Blood on the board. Blood everywhere. Thick, dark, sickly sweet in her nostrils. Ennis was who should be here. *But he wasn't, was he?*

And last night?

Divers O'Roarke straightened his back, glanced over his shoulder, his mouth cinching. "Yes. I'm sorry to disappoint you. A hazard of the trade is all this is."

"Well, if you will play with fire."

He rubbed the towel over his hair. "Yes, well, I've done that all right."

What was that supposed to mean? The way his gaze rested on her with that gemstone glint of hardness too? That she'd betrayed him to Lyon? And still he'd let this happen? When a fat lot of good *that* was *if* touching him did no good unless she cared for him? She should stop it especially now he stood there displaying every inch of his more or less perfect torso.

"I see. Found out were you? Well, I'm sure you don't need me to tell you you'd be safer crossing the devil than smugglers and wreckers, seeing as you already know it all."

"Well then, seeing as you've outstayed your usefulness, the door's there." He let go of the washstand and strolled to the scuffed chest of drawers.

She blew out a long breath. *Last night she was living*? *She just wanted him to know why she was driven*? To do what? Forget she came in here with the ace in the pack? Even if the past never stood like an iron man between them, fall again and have no-one to break that fall? Fall again and be smashed in the process? No.

"I do know that. I have lived here for most of me life in case you hadn't noticed."

"Funny that. You never sound like it."

"Says the man who speaks with a false tongue because he's meant to be a successful businessman and he's quite wiped the mud of the past off his fine leather boots. Looks as if he colors his hair and everything. I'll come back for my things after, seeing as there's no-one to bring them and I'm so obviously not welcome being as I speak funny."

"I *never* said that."

She hugged the sheet against herself. "You didn't have to. Now, if you don't mind I've a room to go to."

"Fine. Just don't use it as an excuse to snoop because you won't find anything."

"Really? Who says I either want to or that you're worth snooping on? Chance would be a fine thing you know."

The door handle was in front of her. Now she'd had the final word, he'd be hard pushed to top it and there was nothing to stay for. She grasped blackened brass. That was when he spoke.

"By the way you're wrong, Destiny. Firstly, my ribs weren't broken by smugglers. They were broken by excisemen. When they kicked the bejesus out of me and killed a woman I was involved with."

***

Right. Well, that hadn't gone quite as she'd hoped but at least she was back in her room, with her dressing gown about her, sitting at her dressing table, even if his bed sheet was on the floor.

"Destiny."

Or should she change that *at least* to, she *was* back in her room, with her dressing gown about her, sitting at her dressing table, *his* bed sheet on the floor, till the door creaked open and face as long as a six fiddle cases, and twenty four rainy days, Orwell walked in. The last person in the world she wanted to see right now, when whatever he'd blundered in here with, was something she couldn't listen to.

Not a lot of peace in the world, was there? She'd really planned on mending that tapestried footstool. The one by the side of the dressing table. But plainly that would have to wait till another day. At least she'd done something with it today. That was refrain from booting it across the hearth given what Divers O'Roarke's words had raised in her—the excisemen had attacked him bit anyway. Why? Because the rest was just him being vile about her. Not worth kicking anything anywhere over.

The attack bit now? Why was that? Because they'd also put two and two together and made the four that said he was the Cleanser? Three and a half anyway. If it was four they'd have arrested him. It wasn't like she didn't have a million and one other things to do--that didn't sodding involve her involving herself more with Divers O'Roarke either. Unless he'd made it up?

"Now Orwell, unless you're coming in here to tell me something new of interest, why don't you go somewhere else? Daindridge's. The Hollow Tree. Wherever. Because really, while it might not look it, I'm rather busy right now." Hoping he'd take the hint she reached for the tiny bottle of lavender scent that stood like a sentinel before the glass. He clicked the door shut. Sadly on her side of it.

"Well, old girl, while it pains me to say so, perhaps *if* you weren't in his room last night—"

"Listening at doors, were we?" So long as it wasn't to her assaulting a Crown officer. "A change from drinking at them, I must say."

"You should be glad I do, glad I've come here, to be a brother to you as I have not always been in the past."

"Door's there, Orwell."

The floorboards creaked beneath his leather-soled boots. "I have come here sober, which again, I will confess, has not always been the case—"

"You can say that again but don't get too excited. It is only nine in the morning. And Lyon did take away that stash which you were probably helping yourself to, despite what you said to the contrary."

"For which I do humbly apologise."

"What? For being drunk half the time? Or helping yourself to that stash?"

"Destiny ..."

"As for being humble? What's that? The first time for everything?"

His brown woollen waistcoat swum into view in the mirror. "I have stopped drinking since you went with him, Destiny."

"Let's not hold our breaths." She set the perfume bottle down, reached for the comb. "That was just two nights ago. But maybe I should have gone with him sooner, then you'd be sober as a—"

"I don't like it."

"What? Being sober? Well, I suppose you'd find that hard."

"You being with him."

"Says the man who lost Doom Bar Hall so far as I can see, to a man who didn't use to be able to play snap too."

"They say he's the Cleanser, Destiny."

"Really? And I'm the man in the moon. I go out at night and I fly up into the sky in a pair of silver breeches and shine me light on the world."

Well, she was, *if* Orwell had heard it from some of *his* cronies. When the walls had ears and these ears were called Divers O'Roarke, *that* was worth risking Doom Bar Hall for?

No. Look where scuttling along the cliff path had gotten her yesterday, because of what he'd done to her nice, safe world. She'd need better than that to scuttle again. She'd need to do it in this *couldn't give a proverbial* fashion for a start and if she couldn't give a proverbial, why do it, when Divers O'Roarke thought she couldn't help herself and she could? Or she could until a few days ago anyway. God, she did feel like something when she was with him, didn't she? But it was a something she couldn't allow. In that respect it was better to sit with her head panned in.

Orwell grasped her shoulder, his spittle peppering her skin, when she'd just gone to a lot of trouble to dab perfume on it too, so it would need done again. "Will you listen to me? Believe you me, I went to a hell of a lot of trouble to get that information."

She breathed out long and hard, fixed her gaze on her sewing box. Hadn't she planned on doing some sewing after all? Why not just go ahead? "Drinking, was it?" She unclasped the box. "Next you'll be telling me you're not what you seem either. That you're secretly really working for the smugglers and all this drunkenness is an act. A man comes into an area--from London no less, or should I say he returns--and he wins from its errant master, a house that has been in the family for generations. But goodness, the errant master wasn't errant at all, despite being years in training, he was only *pretending* to be a drunk because he was meaning to lose the house. All in order to catch a mythical figure called the Cleanser. Oh, really Orwell, if you weren't needing help before, you most certainly are now. Now, if you don't mind—"

"The Cleanser *is* no mythical figure. Will *you* listen to me?"

"I'm trying Orwell, but so are you."

"He's an exciseman gone to the bad."

She swallowed. *Exactly what Lyon had said.* What if Orwell *had* gone to trouble? Real trouble? What if Lyon did have some inkling and that was why he ordered that woman killed and Divers O'Roarke left for dead? He just didn't have the full proof?

Funny that he'd said—no, *she* had--something similar, about people not quite being what they seemed, in certain pays and all that, that had then come to be so.

Chance? Or something that would win her a golden booth in the Penvellyn Fair *best fortune teller* competition. She slipped her gaze to the door. Could she afford to be caught listening though, any more than she could afford not to listen? Probably neither. And if she signalled to Orwell, or if she put a finger to her lips, he'd probably ask her why she wanted him to shut up. She'd just have to pretend. She cleared her throat.

"The Cleanser? Excuse me while I smother a yawn. It's really very tiring listening to a load of old cobblers. *The bad* indeed? Well, maybe he is bad. Maybe he's very bad and that's why I like—"

"Well, if you're going to be as big a damned fool about it as you've been all your life--"

"*My* life? Oh, hark at the prize carrot winner in the *loudest braying donkey* competition. Let's talk about your life for a moment—"

"*Your* life. At least I've tried to do something. I've tried to warn you. Just remember *that* when you end up dying on the end of some bullet meant for him. Because if *I* know, then it stands to reason I'm not alone. But maybe because you've slept with him, you don't want to hear this now?"

Dying? The words swung around her head. like the beating of an albatross's wings. *Killed a woman I was involved with.*

My God. Obviously all so his cover wouldn't go sky high. Was that it?

Right now, that cover was someone else.

Her.

***

"**W**ould you mind telling me why the hell you told Destiny Rhodes I was an exciseman?"

As Divers O'Roarke scanned the leaden sky that stretched like eternity above the rugged moorland, felt the stir of the chill breeze on his forehead, he went places deserted by angels but the alternative was worse. Besides, despite the agony in his ribs and the knowledge he'd let Destiny Rhodes past every defence going last night—worse, he was in danger of getting beneath hers, when a tombstone probably still waited--he'd met with Tom Berryman.

Not particularly successfully. A meeting was still a meeting though. Berryman was in no doubt Divers meant business and would and could undercut him, had his ear to the ground, could hire the men to help with a little light unloading of a ship already under sail from Calais. At least Divers had said it was Calais. Lyon narrowed his hawk's eye on a piece of browning bracken, gathered the reins of his stallion so he could sit it better.

"Why do you think?"

"No. you tell me. Because Destiny Rhodes isn't just the last person in the world you should trust, *if* she was the last, the very last she'd still sell—"

"Because, unlike you, I don't have time for games."

Lyon's gaze was enigmatic. Frost iced the back of Divers' neck.

"What games?"

"Any you might be playing. Principally with her."

The thing about Lyon? You knew everything but nothing of what he was really thinking. Hand him a farthing out the goodness of your heart and he'd still need to know where both came from. The farthing and the goodness. Probably your heart too.

To lose *his* cool, no matter how close to the raging seas he stood, was to lose this. The thing was to smile, calmly, shrug dismissively. Show, for once and for all he had nothing to hide. Because this job right now? He didn't. And he wouldn't.

"*Might* be playing? Oh I think you should assume that I am. We need her to play nicely. It's something she was never exactly good at."

The wind whipped at Lyon's hat and his stallion's mane so he took a second to steady it, although his gaze remained set elsewhere. "Really?"

"Yes. Believe you me, if anyone knows that, I do. You telling her could make it difficult, her, a potential threat. But I think you can take it as read that these games I seem to be playing are because she needs to understand there's nowhere she can go here. She's against the wall. And that's the place to keep her."

"I see."

"Good."

"It will be when you explain to me if she's so hard against the wall, with nowhere to go here, what's she's doing over there on the sea path? Unless I'm very much mistaken, that *is* her there, isn't it?"

***

Well, she never. Lyon himself, cantering towards her on horseback across the rough moorland. Just who Destiny was on her way to see. She smoothed the skirt and bodice of her coat, waiting as the stallion splashed through the glistening puddle a few feet from where she stood, without splattering her with mud too. And while there was a faint taste of frost in the air, it wasn't too cold. Things *were* looking up.

"Miss Rhodes." He tugged the reins.

"Obviously."

It was perhaps not the most civil way to greet him but what was there to be civil about? He'd threatened her. Still she was prepared to overlook that in favor of the fact that when he heard what she had come to say, he would, if not kiss her feet exactly, at least afford her Doom Bar Hall and take her out of this sod awful situation with that sod awful man who kept getting in the way of her life. Probably sod awful too but there it was. She straightened her shoulders, vital when her heart wasn't just battering the bloody Jesus out of her ribcage--her ears too--it rivalled the waves crashing on the rocks beneath her. Then she levelled her most penetrating stare on him. After all, it was hard to sleep with a man and then betray him. But it was nothing she couldn't do *now*. Besides he was nowhere about.

"I mean, I do take it that it is all right for me to leave Doom Bar Hall?" Task one? Sound civil.

"That depends on exactly what you're leaving it for."

While some might say it killed her not to take issue with his unprecedented cheek and arrogance, she allowed herself to be buried. After all, when this was done she'd be in charge. "Well, actually—"

"Go on."

At least she hoped she'd be the one in charge. *Actually* though, how was she meant to be the one in charge now another figure strode towards her through the bracken, his face grimmer than a storm-lashed sea. A figure she really should have known would be about somewhere. Divers O'Roarke, resplendent in his grey greatcoat and black tricorn, his knee length boots flecked with mud. Her heart clenched. Her stomach too. As for her lungs? They suffocated. Was he following her? Meeting with Lyon? To do what? Compare notes on her *obedience*?

Thank God she'd not said anything. *Yet.*

"Good morning, Destiny, we meet again." Divers O'Roarke scrunched to a halt. A not very pleased one at that. As if he knew what she'd come here to say and that something was not that he was going to win first prize in the *nice, wonderful in bed and that she liked him* competition.

How could it be? Lyon must be as keen to catch the Cleanser as half the smugglers between here and Dover. Divers O'Roarke's face was guiltier than every sinner in the Bible's all rolled into one. Truth should be spoken. Shame the devil her father had always said. And by God, no bigger one existed than the one standing there in the steel grey of a leaden sky, the wind teasing the loose strands of his dark hair, his eyes like polar caps. Handsome. There was no denying he was handsome.

She moistened her lips, offered him her coolest stare. "Indeed we do."

As her mother had always said, handsome was as handsome did. And now? *Now she was part of it.* A very dangerous part. A part that might see her end like that woman. If that meant betrayal, so damn well be it. Her Christmas garlands would look lovely in the library, after all.

Funny how she'd forgotten about them of late, when they were amongst the most important things in her life.

"You were going somewhere?" he said in that voice that smoked holes in her spine. Still she faced him. Cool. Blank.

"You might say. Then again you might not. But if you must know, although how you can't know, given this is me standing here. Well? But, yes, happens I am here and happens it's something I have to tell this man here, I'm sure he will be most interested in."

CHAPTER SEVENTEEN

As Divers O'Roarke set his hat on the library table, the one that now might not see the wonderful brass goblets gleaming by the firelight's flame at Christmas, something that would only bring a tear to her eye to consider, *if she'd any left to cry,* Destiny knew one thing. Task one was not Doom Bar Hall. Task one was getting her hair—what there was of it anyway—to stop standing on end.

"So?" His hat was followed by his coat which flumped into the sunken armchair by the empty fireplace with the pile of rubble on the floor. "Would you mind telling me why you lied?"

"Me? Divers?"

"Well, I'm certainly not meaning your grandfather's parrots."

Frankly? Never mind him being that stupid he didn't know, she wasn't about to incriminate herself further by saying, 'Well, I couldn't exactly tell Lyon you were the Cleanser, when you were sodding well standing there, now could I?'

"In what way exactly?" she asked.

He crossed to the sideboard, set out two glasses. A good, or a bad sign?

"Just answer the question, will you?"

Obviously it was the latter. When she was trying to get her hair to sit back down again too.

Well, short of saying she'd gone to Lyon because she not only wanted a life--different from wanting to feel alive--what could she say though? As he stood pouring these drinks, Divers O'Roarke had more confidence than a pack of lions setting about a dead deer. And she? Well, she hadn't wanted to live since Ennis died. But obviously she did. Or she'd never have gone along that cliff path. As for discovering it when her Christmas garlands were on the table and everything? How could she? As for going back along that cliff path ..? Did that inhabit the same realm as a month of Sundays?

"Well, I would have thought it was sort of obvious." She dropped into a chair. "After all, you did warn me the other day about crossing Lyon and after what you said about him shooting that woman--"

"Eirwin?"

She strove to shrug. So that was her predecessor's name? "Right?" Provided that predecessor actually existed. "Well, you see, I thought I better seek him out and get him off me back, before he went and shot—"

"When you can't kill a corpse either?" All right so what she'd said wasn't so clever. What had she thought about dead deers and packs of lions though? As for the way he threw his drink down his throat as if it was the most satisfying thing going? "That corpse suddenly remembers all that. Well, talking lies—"

"Who says it was a lie?"

"Well, the thing is I do." He refilled his glass "Or you'd have damn well told me about Raven's Passage the other day when I asked you."

"Well, I was going to but you see there were things I wanted at the time, like the serv—"

"But you kept it for today and Lyon who I cannot seem to get it through your thick skull, is not a man to cross."

"As I am trying to get through yours that *that's* what I was doing, trying not to cross—"

"All fine, Destiny but I'm not talking Raven's Passage."

Not Raven's Passage? My God, even the fact he'd somehow found Great Aunt Modest's best embossed goblets at the back of the walnut cabinet paled like a dying moon. What other lies had she told here?

"Here."

She eyed what swam into her vision, largely because it all but took her eye out.

"Well? What are you talking about then?"

"Did you lie about Ennis?"

"*Me?*" She almost dropped the goblet. "Lie about Ennis? In what w—?"

"About the things that drive you to have vengeance? About what being with me does to you?"

Her scalp froze. My God, Lyon wasn't the worry here. As sharp a tack as that would surely know why she'd lied. But when her head felt as if it had been stoved in by every conceivable type of hammer going, and some that might have been conceived by a titan, when she'd nearly dropped Great Aunt Modest's goblet--fortunately made of brass--*he asked that*?

An undercover exciseman who was better at this game than her, who, even if he could be trusted, she wasn't going to trust and fall down any slopes over? She should laugh. She did laugh. She tried to anyway.

"My? My? And why do you want to know that? So you can flatter yourself even more than you already do?"

He tilted his jaw. "Why do I want to know?"

Oh God, please don't let him look at everything and nothing here, through the glass of a dark eternity. Don't let her think, across the space of that same eternity, that just maybe ..? Maybe ..? *What the hell was going on here?*

The treacherous perfume of anticipation was not something she could afford to breathe, yet there it was snaking into her pores. Into her. So she struggled to sit, swallow, calm her heart, hear herself think.

And if he said, if he said outright the things she could not ..? Like, *I don't know what's going on here but something is,* when the thought flashed--how clever was he doing this to ensure she didn't go back along that path? Well? When ... that path? That path was something she'd no intentions of? She shrugged.

"Yes, Divers, you tell me. I mean ... " *But what if he wasn't doing it for that?* She passed her tongue over her lips. How could she help it, the way he looked at her? "I mean I ... I'm not going fir--"

He lowered his gaze. "Because you're in this house, after all. I could put you out."

"Obviously." Thank God, the fact she knew this, allowed her to look at him as squarely as he now did her. Imagine if she'd leapt up waving her drawers in the air instead of keeping them firmly about her person that he'd said something more? Something else? About them. About why he needed to know. "So why don't you when the door is there?"

"Lyon."

"*Really?*" Her heart skipped a beat. Please don't tell her he did feel protective. *Then*? When the main things in her life were surely her Christmas garlands? *Then she'd feel bad*. "And? And why's that?"

The floorboards creaked as he walked to the pile of rubble by the fireplace and contemplated the wall.

"Because he feels he has reason to doubt me after that last job."

Her throat dried. What *did* that mean exactly? That she shouldn't feel bad about her garlands? Or more? Far more? Something she'd only rise to hearing and using *if* she did intend going back along that path? And right now ...? The way her breath had tightened ...? And the edge of her seat was something she sat on ...?

He shrugged and took a mouthful of wine. "So if I put you out? Well? That will only increase his suspicions."

"Well, thank God for that. The last thing I'd want is you getting all protective because you were involving yourself with me, like you did with that woman, and you wouldn't want to see me living on the highways and byways, or dead in a ditch."

Because it was. At least now she needn't feel bad about the garlands, about anything. Heavens, weren't moments that seemed to have you in their clasp, more sodding stupid than a fusty bag of beans?

"I'm not getting protective, Destiny. There's no point. Because I believe you're spying for him. So, from now on, you can stay but it will be out of my way. You, in your designated part of the house. Me, in mine. And this drink?" Turning to her he raised his glass. "Finally, this drink is to that."

***

Really?

Well, she never did. That he put down his drink and strode from the room before she could say so too, without wanting to hear about Raven's Passage or last night either.

But maybe it was all of it just as well when his voice, assured as her place in hell, had cut into her spine? Oh? And did she mention, at least she was getting to stay here, which was probably quite nice of him, if you counted such things as nice?

He knew she was spying after all, which probably meant she could now do it with impunity. What a quandary, when she wasn't planning on doing it at all.

When all she wanted to do right now was lie down in a darkened room, there was nothing like giving a girl choices, was there? Look on the bright side. At least it saved her telling him what she'd been doing on that path. Had her head been so panned in by all of this that she'd expected him to say something else there though? It didn't matter how he'd looked at her, what she'd thought might have flickered in his eyes, what had gone down between them last night. What mattered was that she wasn't fifteen any more. It might be for that matter, that her sight was failing her and he hadn't looked anything at all.

Hearing voices outside, she blew out another breath and shifted her gaze to the window. Divers O'Roarke was out there on the lawn. And not just Divers O'Roarke. A shiver scuttled like a mouse from a darkened corner. Divers O'Roarke, Molly *and a woman*. She rose.

Not that it was anything to her that the woman was a grown up version of the child, but what was wrong with *her* that the desire to run out there and rip the golden curls from the woman's head swept all the way from her toes? Because the woman had a better travelling jacket than her? Emerald velvet? Because once, if Destiny had flounced out there with her berry red lips and jewelled hair, there would have been no question about who had the better everything in the eyes of every man in Cornwall? And there'd be no damned talk of her staying in her designated half of the house either—didn't he like her or something?

Or was it because a woman was standing with Divers O'Roarke on the lawn where it swept to the sea? And he? He smiled at *her*. A soft, sweet, carefree smile that would melt ice crystals, even those embedded in the thorniest heart and send them cascading to freedom. Her eyes sank to the back of her head.

This was not going to be.

She did *not* get jealous of other women. She especially did *not* get jealous of frumps like *that*. Only a lot of breath, much more than usual, did seem to be rushing down her nose, as if something fisted her lungs. And she had walked to the window.

"I'm not getting protective, Destiny," he'd said. And maybe, if she'd ignored what had crouched earlier in his cool gaze, she might have believed him? Ignored the thought--my God--that maybe he didn't want drawn to her any more than she did to him, too? And so he pulled this suit of iron invincibility about him and wore it like plate armour. But underneath he was no crusading lion. Just a man stepping out to do battle with life. And what did she really know of his? How had he even gotten out of Cornwall after all? All she knew was that when they were together she forgot so much. He was assured, exciting, dangerous, different to be with.

She shook her head. She didn't know what others might say but in her book it certainly needed clearing.

Keeping to her designated area would work no hardship on her. Would it? In fact some might say this would be easier if he didn't come near her and she didn't go near him, when she was kidding herself to believe that the soul reason she hadn't betrayed him was because it said she wanted to live.

If Divers O'Roarke wasn't interested in Raven's Passage, let her count her blessings. Talking lies, the real problem would have come if he was.

CHAPTER EIGHTEEN

"Your designated area? My, my? Please do tell me, to what do I owe this very great honor of being invited here by the majesty of Doom Bar Hall himself?"

As she swept into the library, with God knew whose books on the shelves and the heap of rubble on the floor, Divers O'Roarke glanced round from his contemplation of the mantelpiece, the grey eyes distant as the North Star--the polar opposite of earlier when she'd thought it would be good to know he didn't feel protective and then he'd told her he didn't in no uncertain terms.

"What do you think?"

"I didn't know I was expected to. I thought what was expected is that I remain out of your way in me—"

"Raven's Passage."

"Oh, right." *Great.* "What about it?"

As if she couldn't guess--that had only taken about four hours, after all--so she might as well. Guess that was.

He thrust his thumbs into his waistcoat pockets. "Unless you want me thinking there was some other reason you went to Lyon earlier, where is it?"

When he knew she was lying too. Had he really called her downstairs from her contemplation of the bedroom ceiling for this? Oh, and counting her blessings. How could she possibly forget about that? When he was the one who had escalated it and was running about with some other woman? Something she had never done. But maybe it had dawned on him their paths were never going to cross? And he didn't like it?

"Well, you seem to think there was anyway, so I really don't see the point of disabusing you of your heartfelt belief."

"Maybe you don't but Lyon will."

"And you expect me to, what? Give a flying proverbial about that when you told me earlier to stay out your way and that me leaving would only increase Lyon's suspicions about you? It was before you were fawning all over that woman out there, mind you, so maybe what you now want is me to go, so she can come in?"

"So you *were* watching?"

"I was looking out the window. Shall we just say she was hard to miss? You were too, before you go thinking I was spying. Anyone would have thought she was great God Almighty, or at the very least, His first cousin."

And anyone would think she was great God O'Blabby, the way she'd come out with that. But so long as she didn't come out with any more, did it matter? And she wouldn't. Dragging her in here like this, when she was well done with it.

He sighed deeply. Oh here it came, he didn't just thnk *she* was spying, he *knew*, no halfpenny short of tuppence that *he* was. She knew too by the exhalation of pure boredom.

"She's Molly's mother. Gil gave her some money to bring Molly here. Seeing as you want to know."

"Hardly." And she'd appreciate it too if he didn't speak to her as if she was an idiot he needed to spare. That coaxing--in fact downright cheeky way--he spoke about parrots and kitchens and things. "What you do in your spare time when you're not out catching smugglers is of no interest to me."

Not if she was cut to pieces and sewn back together again with rusty wire. He could bring the damn woman in if he wanted. Hadn't she thought as much the night he first walked back in here, after all? Well? And he needn't think she cared about it or try to wheedle some other response from her. It wasn't necessary to feel alive. In fact being done with it gave her more time to get on with her cushion covers and things.

Again his gaze lingered on some distant spot. "I imagine she needed the money."

"Really?" She fixed her dullest stare on him. It was hardly difficult. "And I do too that there's plenty ways to earn it.""

"It's not easy leaving an abusive husband."

"You'd know this, would you, nice, little woman that you are?"

"No. But Eirwin was. And she did."

"I see. And you're telling me this, why?" Despite what pounded in her ears like a dirty secret, it was no trouble to speak. "So I'll be nice, take me barricades down and tell you about Raven's Passage? Like I did with Tom Berryman? Which I never should have done, now you're going to work with him in order to arrest him. Hang him in all probability too. Nah, that ship has sailed. Look out the window and you might spot it in the bay."

"I don't make the laws."

"No. But you carry them out."

"You think smuggler and wreckers should go free?"

"Do you, when you were involved with one of them? And then …? Then she got killed. Well? Anyway, who says Tom Berryman's a wrecker?"

"I need something to give Lyon. And you will give me that something, Destiny. *You* will give me it now. Or you know what will happen."

"Hmmm. And pigs will fly round my head when I'm not exactly in a situation where I can afford to let them put their wings away either. Because, let's face it, you're not telling me all this about that woman, either of them, her or Erwin, to assure me you're done playing games about the house. Not when you've set designated areas and you think I'm spying. When you've told me you need me here anyway."

Well?

Or he'd have won first prize in the *best shot in Cornwall* competition for shooting her down over that claim about his spare time. But no, no. Instead he gave her all this cheek and guff.

Equally exactly what *was* she fighting here? What kind of sodding logic was it where she didn't want him knowing she'd lied when he already did? And Lyon could whistle for that proof? Especially when the only way to get that proof was to go near Divers O'Roarke and now she couldn't. Even if she wanted to, she couldn't. She wasn't risking herself any more over him. Why should she?

She shrugged. So? The broom cupboard? The kitchen cold cupboard? She could soon show him something when it came to Raven's Passage. And oh, how shocking, terrible it was, *it* appeared to have sodding well caved in. The moment for any other truth had passed the second Divers O'Roarke raised that glass to his lips and said *designated areas*. Not now. Not ever was it going to come again.

If she'd said she hadn't lied last night? If she hadn't asked him to go first? But he'd had his chance to get off the fence. Instead he'd sat with his backside glued to the wire. She gave another shrug.

"But putting all that aside, Raven's Passage ... seeing as you tell me you want the whole truth and nothing but it ...?"

He raised his head. The dying rays of the slanting autumn sunlight painted his face in such ghostly bands, his eyes stood out like grey sentinels although the tone was as assured as ever.

"What I want is the truth *you* want to give me, no more, no less."

Her heart lurched, down somewhere she'd be winning all manner of explorer competitions to find it in. The way he'd said, '*Lyon*' in answer to her question this morning had sounded like he'd pulled a suit of armour about him. In a hurry too.

So maybe? *Maybe, talking doubts, should she give him the benefit of one*? Last night they had been something to each other, after all. And that feeling, that feeling when she was with him ...?

"Very well." Despite the fact her throat dried to the same status as a sun-dried brandy keg, an empty one, ravaged by a pack of alcoholics she jerked up her chin. "The truth is I lied."

He blinked, edging his gaze sideways. "Lied?"

"Yes. Which you already know. So I can't imagine why you're asking, but if you want me to tell you why I lied, it was because ... because--"

"An explanation ... " His throat tightened. His chest too. Wasn't the drowning pool deep enough that he needed to pour more water in? Have her tell him what, and why? Why the hell was he even asking her? Because he felt bad about the havoc he'd wreaked with that curse? It was, wasn't it? Last night was something he should have dug his grave with a soggy piece of paper rather than let happen. It was plain as that same paper she'd been on her merry way earlier to tittle-tattle to Lyon.

Even if she hadn't *this* was his life. If the world was flat he'd have sailed his ship off the edge and be falling into darkness by now. That's how close to the edge he was. But the world wasn't flat. It was rounded by the fact he could offer her absolutely nothing. Lyon had things on him that went far beyond that last job.

The designated areas were things he never should have done. Not now she faced him up with that glazed, hopeful look, that spoke of glazed, hopeful things that had got him into such a deep hole last night. Wild, untamed things, which she'd always been more at one with than anything on the Earth. He swallowed. Anyway, maybe she hoped for nothing?

"An explanation will not be necessary."

Her eyes sunk to the back of her head. Oh Christ, she did hope. And no Rose to blame for this either. "I see."

So did he, that if he didn't speak he was finished.

"You don't know where the passage is? Fine." Besides she'd had the chance. She'd had the chance earlier to stake her claim. What if she really meant was to betray him to Lyon, whatever the cost, whatever the reason? And this was all an act? She was a Rhodes, for Christ's sake. They'd sell their old, their young, if they thought they could get a few bob for them in the marketplace. "And, after all, it will save you showing me a lot of rubbish in the broom cupboard, or the kitchen. Telling me it's in your designated area."

She stiffened even if she didn't flinch exactly. So he did have the truth of that? Whatever this was to him in the dark, he'd kill it stone dead. If he'd to drain every drop of blood from his body and replace it with stone, he would, although what surged, just smelling her scent, was a deadly white flame, a slow burning need that made him just want to have her.

"Go to Lyon? Not go to Lyon? I suppose for each of us, that's the choice. Now, if you don't mind, *this* is my bit of the house."

After this lucky escape, he'd damn well stick in it too.

CHAPTER NINETEEN

"Good evening, Miss Rhodes."

As the sombre voice spoke from the shadows of the hall, Destiny nearly shot through the roof.

How shocking terrible was this? When what she really wanted was to see how things were in the dining room, she'd to contemplate a sodding, unsavoury stoat right here in Doom Bar Hall? And not the Divers O'Roarke stoat either. If it had been it wouldn't have been anything she couldn't handle. But Lyon-- winning all manner of competitions for looking most like an undertaker and without removing his tricorn either? That was different.

As to how the stoat had gotten in and was lurking in the shadows at the far end of the hall, when there weren't any servants? Well, *that* was probably why.

Lizzie, whatever her faults would never have let him over the doorstep without six pieces of paper saying who his parents were, never mind himself. *And* at least two more bits saying he was prepared to listen to her God-awful sermons. Whatever. She and Lizzie had understood each other that way. Oh, for three seconds of Lizzie now.

"You will pardon my intrusion and the fact I startled you?" he added *graciously*.

"Did you? I must admit it's news to me but then so's many things."

Her reaction to that woman, for example, was surely to do with the fact, she'd just wanted to contemplate the bedroom ceiling. But how could she if she didn't have a ceiling to contemplate? So now, here she was having to contemplate this weasely stoat instead.

She stripped off her gloves. "If you're looking for Divers O'Roarke I do imagine he's about somewhere. Just don't expect me to know where."

His gaze fastened on her. "Then let me tell you. He's out."

"Of course. How could I forget?"

"It's you I came to see."

"Me?" Oh, let her not waste a happy moment guessing why. Two words. Could the first begin with R. and end with S.?

So much for her belief that him being tack-sharp and that he'd know she was making Raven's Passage up and why. But maybe he was mince-thick and that was why he was lurking in the dark of this hall, lit by greying moonbeams, his scent old, bitter rowan berries in the faded air?

"And why's that?"

"Why do you think, Miss Rhodes?"

Were the situation not so dire she'd have died laughing on the floor, the one she suddenly could not remember the most important thing about. When it looked beautiful for example. If it ever had, in fact. Not with the amount of soft-soled dances going on around her.

"Well, since you're here asking me to think, I'd say that earlier is a good candidate, Mr.—?" Gracious. Did she call him Lyon, or what? Nothing at all, seemed the best idea.

"Please ... call me, John."

Right. As in this being a social call. She refrained from falling through the floor. Perhaps Raven's Passage wasn't going to come into it, after all? And all he wanted was to be called John and have a cup of tea and a currant bun?

Although he'd be hard pressed to get that with no servants about the place and sod all food either, perhaps pigs flew?

"And I'd say that earlier *isn't* just a good candidate, it's an excellent one," he added.

That was a pity. "Really?"

"*You* are right, Miss Rhodes. But perhaps you were out looking for me?"

"Me? I mean, I did. I was. Yes. Went to see you, that is," she lied. "But of course, you were here."

"Because I was tired of waiting."

"Right." *The problem being what for*. Hopefully it was that cup of tea because anything else would win first prize in the local *most revolting thought imaginable* competition. Still she had the way to deal with this. She unfastened her coat.

"Well, I'd ask you in—properly, that is--but I'm afraid, as things stand, I wouldn't know which parts of the house are mine to ask you in to."

"And why is that?"

"You mean Divers O'Roarke hasn't told you?"

"He hasn't."

"Yes. And pigs fly all over Cornwall. High in the sky. When we all know he probably has. And if he hasn't--got to you *yet* that is-- he's probably on his way as we speak. It will be to tell you what a liar I am and how he's split the house because of it. Obviously I didn't come to Penvellyn sooner because I had to wait for me opportunity to do so. Anything more would have aroused his suspicions when he caught me talking to you earlier."

"You are going on rather a lot about Divers O'Roarke, Miss Rhodes."

"Only because he is a skunk."

She set her coat on a chair, smoothed her hair back from her face. Actually she wasn't going on about him half as much as she could.

"But you did have something to tell me? It's why I'm here," Lyon said.

Did she? When what she really wanted was to go upstairs and look out her recipe for lavender shortcake too. Maybe find some way of lighting the fire when her nose was pinched by the cold. The distance was there, spread like a long road in front of her. But really, she wasn't getting much chance to go it. Not with the kitchen probably barred to her now the house had been sawn in half. In fact the way this was going, that recipe was about as much as she was going to get.

"Tell me something I don't know."

"I hope so."

Right. Well, she didn't. Did he have a point though? Was she perhaps going on about Divers O'Roarke instead of applying herself to what was important, like finding that recipe? She'd given him his chance. And very good of her it was too, even if she wasn't sure what she'd have done if he'd taken it. Some might say she'd never have gotten Doom Bar Hall for a start. And she was inclined to agree. Maybe for that matter Divers O'Roarke had banned her from half the house in order to spark a reaction in her? In which case she'd be failing in her duty not to give him one, now she'd gone to the wire and he wouldn't come off the fence? Lyon hadn't come all this way to leave empty handed. Had he? He wasn't here for a cup of tea either. And it was time to deal with that fact. Whatever she'd determined earlier, living or dying required a roof over her head. She passed her tongue over her lip.

"Very well, I have nothing much right now beyond what is being said in the village. No. I mean … I mean, I don't just fear that Divers O'Roarke knows you have asked me to spy. He's told me he does and that is why he's now barred me from certain parts of this house. Look, before you say another word, unless it is your assurance that you never told him I am a spy, I *will* get you that information. But it will be far harder now, when you need exact proof. So, let's agree, shall we, to name our prices. Mine is very simple."

Doom Bar Hall. Tasks one, two and ten. If she could not get it from one man she most certainly would from another. The time for prevarication was over. When she fell to earth, as she would, when Divers O'Roarke moved on from this job, who would break her fall?

Certainly *not* the man who didn't own the roof over either of their heads.

CHAPTER TWENTY

Destiny jerked upright in the moonlight. The thud somewhere along the landing would just about waken the dead. Certainly it had woken her. She'd sooner drag the bedclothes over her head and ease back down, than set one foot on the bare boards when the last several days had shown she was as far from being a corpse as whoever had made the noise. Forget how embarrassing it was that Orwell, not content with losing Doom Bar Hall, when he was several sheets to the wind, had only just gone and collapsed on the landing while he was a hundred sheets more *and* knocked Grandmother Tintagel's delftware basin and ewer for six. Between him and Divers O'Roarke the house would be as much as she got, *if* she got it though.

She *had* to go out on that landing. She fished for her dressing gown, threw it over her nightgown, pulled the door open, all in the bitter cold. A candlestick was rolling about the corridor floor. Bending down she grabbed it. For God's sake, the place would go up in flames next then what she'd get was a pile of ashes.

"Sod it, Orwell … For God's—"

"Destiny."

The tide went out on her mind except for one thought. *Divers O'Roarke.* What the hell was Divers O'Roarke doing leaning on Grandmother Tintagel's side table, the one she'd brought from Camborne on her wedding day to Austell Rhodes? And not just leaning. Bent double over it in some kind of agony. Destiny fought not to drop her jaw. Was that sweat, or sea spray beading his generally handsome face? When it wasn't bleached as dead men's bones in the flickering light that was. What the hell was going on here? Oh wait ... how could she forget his poor, broken ribs?

"Divers?"

"There's no need to sound so surprised." He raised his head, exhaled deeply. "I just needed to sit down for a moment."

"Well, there's no chairs here." She set the candle down on the table. Task one? Consider the fact that maybe that curse coming true didn't require her to care for anyone, although those she had cared about had a disconcerting habit of dropping dead. "Where's Gil? And I'll get him to--"

"Why ask when you already know?"

Her throat dried. My God, don't tell her he was dead?

"Yes, Destiny, he's out on the moor. But he's not dead. And neither am I, though it's not for want of trying. You and Lyon. And the little game you're playing."

"Says the man who's playing every dirty little game going."

He dragged his head up, straightened his shoulders, his eyes like drowning pools in the caverns made by the candlelight. "You think?"

"I know."

He loomed, casting a giant shadow over her. "Well here's the thing. I think you are playing games. Or I wouldn't have nearly got my head blown off, now would I?"

She froze as surely as if she'd been dropped into the iced water off Ryland's Point. My God. Nearly got. *But hadn't. Nearly* got. *Nearly.* His head? Not by Lyon, surely?

He stepped past her, just when some might say it was of vital importance that she pick her jaw from the floor too. When that self he'd done his damndest to smash the coffer lid of, that self that had been in his bed ... *that self needed to stay staked through the heart.*

So? Go to her room as he now lurched to his, blow the candle out, sleep, dream. After all, she had named her price to Lyon and Lyon would see that price was met. If Lyon had shot at Divers O'Roarke—well, there wasn't exactly any sign of any blood, was there?

But then how much real sign was there on her that night of drowning agony, of Ennis's limbs like cardboard castles, of her world trodden on by a colossus? She had not been able to function for weeks. Even now could see these images, floating in the huddle of her consciousness, the ones she must shut out, stop, strangle, go to her room, escape from. Not think, *not think for a second,* that she'd any kind of common ground with Divers O'Roarke.

Her throat tightened against the breath screaming for release. Now she was allied with Lyon, some would say to go after Divers O'Roarke could only be over her dead body. And they would be right. It didn't matter what swept and sat like a tsunami in her breast.

She had this.

And that was how she was keeping it too.

***

It was all part of the play. Now he'd lit a candle and seen, wrapped in its dancing light, the wooden edge of the mantelpiece, the mottled ochre of the coal scuttle, felt the sink of the mattress beneath him, Divers O'Roarke lifted his head and himself from his huddled thoughts. He had his eyes on *one thing* and that *thing* was not sitting here, a blanket dragged over his shoulders, like maggot meat.

But a bullet had whizzed past his ears in the moonlight as he'd waded into the swirling icy water to help bring the rowing boat to the shore, and there, that *one thing* was dead. Wounded anyway.

Lyon always made things look good. But tonight? When Divers hadn't even put a toe wrong, never mind a foot?

Tonight he was lucky he hadn't taken a bullet in the head.

There was only one reason Lyon had taken that shot. He thought Divers was the Cleanser and there was no doubt who had offered proof.

He should have known the devil was not, and never would be, someone you could deal with, only someone you thought you could. In that respect he shouldn't even have come back here. Gil was right. With Destiny Rhodes, the only certainty was that there was none. She'd face you with that shuttered stare regardless. And he? In addition to knowing that even under your nose wasn't a safe place to keep a viper, he never should have touched her, then he wouldn't be haunted by her image in the candlelight.

Should he get out of here tonight? Wait till Gil returned and make a run for it with what they had, instead of cobbling together this job, his life? It wasn't like he chose it. No. That too, had been Lyon. But then what? Where could he hide that was far enough? Hated by smugglers and the law alike? He'd be lucky to clear the county before she raised the alarm. The county? He'd be lucky to reach the end of the lawn, the foot of the stairs. And that was before he got to the things Lyon had on him.

No. He couldn't afford to run. Not here. Not now. Not when the thing was to stay here and face her down as if he wasn't fazed. Face Lyon too when that bullet had whizzed past his left ear. Anything less was to say one thing.

He'd sooner it had hit him.

***

As she stood feeling the wind playing havoc with her throat, as well as her cloak, not to mention her hair, Destiny knew one thing. That thing wasn't the usual.

"So, Miss Rhodes?" Lyon's gaze raked the empty rises and falls of the browning landscape. But then anyone could be crawling on their bellies in the spaces there below the wheeling gulls, watching, waiting, listening, to more than the wind's howl, shivering in the blast that cut like a knife. "What do you have for me?"

"After you tried to kill Divers O'Roarke last night, why would you think I'd have anything? Well? I asked you not to make my job harder than it already is. And what did you do?"

Something very like emotion glinted in Lyon's eyes. As if he found her funny. She wasn't funny. But his voice was quieter than the grave. As cold too. "Is that what he told you?"

"It's what I know."

"Hmm. Well, that's very fine you are so knowledgeable. I won't ask how you know that."

"Because I am knowledgeable. More than you know. And you told me to find out. So I did."

"Then you should also have found out that the man is an inveterate liar. It goes with the turf, I am afraid."

"He's not the only one. In fact why not just kill him and be done with it if that's the way you're going to do this? Well? Spare us all the tedious wait. The crawling back and forward to meetings in weather like this, the dangling of Doom Bar Hall like a carrot, when I'm not exactly going to win first prize for doubling as the sodding donkey in the local Nativity play."

Speaking this way was as dangerous as the plunging cliffs that dropped from the edge of her vision into the thrashing waves below. Lyon trying to kill Divers O'Roarke shouldn't matter. In fact, the problem wouldn't just be halved, it would be solved. And whatever was said of her in Penvellyn would be said anyway.

But for some very strange reason she wasn't here because Divers O'Roarke had broken Grandmother Tintagel's bowl and didn't want to own up.

It was far harder to want to see a man dead than she'd thought. Right now anyway. Even one who'd cursed her for nothing. And, some might say, who'd sat on the fence having gone to the wire. But then, others might say she had too.

Looking at her dresses, at Molly's mother, was seeing her old life sitting in a passing coach though, one she didn't want to look in but found herself almost hailing, *when this was her life.*

Just because Divers O'Roarke had been brave enough to let her touch him, it didn't mean a damn thing where the future was concerned.

Of course, some might say it would help matters considerably if she could only get near her lavender shortcake, or cushion covers, the important things. But she couldn't. Her thoughts about the dining room either, for the sea of sheets and ladders. And, so far, so far as she could see anyway, not a blob of paint on any one of the four walls. The ceiling either. But then, they were big walls so maybe she was missing something.

Then there was the fact that, with the exception of what was in the fruit barrels, the various preserves, and some pretty boot-hard bacon hanging in the cold cupboard, there was only what Gil Wryson brought in from the market at Penvellyn to eat. And that wasn't what you would term, much. Were excisemen poor, or something?

It was all beyond distracting, so yes, was it any wonder that Divers O'Roarke, unnerved, on her doorstep was something she couldn't take?

Lyon resumed his perusal of the moorland. "Do you know where I first encountered Divers O'Roarke?"

"Why would I? It's hardly something I'm dying to know."

"Teezer's Travelling Troupers."

"Teezer's Travelling *what*?"

"Yes. Thieves and pickpockets, with some modicum of talent amongst them."

"Are you saying Diver O'Roarke was a—?"

"He was an actor. Quite a good one."

Really? It was the first she'd heard. What a turn up for the books. But then what had become of him when he left Cornwall? How had he even gotten out of Cornwall?

"It made him ideal for what he does," Lyon slithered on.

"Excuse me? Are you saying he stole--?"

"I'm saying he's adaptable and that's why I never had him hung which I could have."

"I see."

She didn't. *Putting a brake on this, remember*? So how Divers O'Roarke got out of Cornwall, whether Lyon could have had him hung, or not, was no concern of hers. Lyon's eyes lingered on her face.

"The woman he was with too." Well, of course she might have known there would be a woman in there somewhere. "Miss Rhodes, I sincerely hope *you* are not playing me."

"Me? That would be good given my feelings about him and how he cursed me for sod all."

"I am not a fly on your particular wall."

Well, wasn't that something to be singularly grateful for. She wouldn't want to have to take Great Aunt Modest's fly-swatter to him. Him slavering over what he might see either. It was bad enough Ennis probably saw these things. Bad enough she thought of them here. *Putting a brake on this, remember?* Now.

"I don't know what goes on between you and Divers O'Roarke—"

"Nothing."

"He is known to be attractive to women."

"I can't think why."

Pray God—task one—especially given the way her head sweated, that more than her face didn't burn and she didn't think *why* right here. Or, on consideration, having lain awake most of the night, she'd know she was kidding herself to think that lying awake was the least she could do, when she couldn't think that. When--all right—she'd had to stop herself more than once—she wouldn't say it was more than that, others might, but she wouldn't--from opening her door, then his, to see he was all right.

"Good." Lyon returned his gaze to the frothing horizon. "But so long as you content yourself with lying about what you do with him—"

"Lying? Me?"

"--and bringing me the proof I need—"

"Who says I won't? I'm just asking–"

"Mathematics, Miss Rhodes."

"I'm really sorry but what has mathematics to do with this?"

"How everything is accounted for in our world."

"Tell me something I don't know. I mean ... *really*?" What did he think? That her world was any different?

"The last few jobs were short, shall we say?"

"Short?" Her scalp prickled. "In what way?"

"What way do you think? I know Divers O'Roarke and that man of his know something about it. I know he has taken gold that was not his to take. And I know he involved himself where he shouldn't. I just need the proof; whether or not he is the Cleanser is, in many ways, irrelevant."

My God. Did this make this better, or worse? Trust Divers O'Roarke to have his fingers in pies. Was that the real reason Lyon had taken a pot shot at him? And killed that woman? Because *he* had more than a finger. He had his whole hand? Along with his sidekick too. *Obviously.*

"And I've told you I will get you that." Because she would now. This was the brake. The brake she needed. Then? *Then she'd get Doom Bar Hall.*

Divers O'Roarke needed her as insurance after all. And no sodding wonder too.

"Good," Lyon said. "You cannot imagine how glad I am to hear it. Especially given how attractive he seems to be to women."

Well, he was. Extraordinarily so with that swaggering air of confidence, assurance and menace, he breathed through his pores, his hypnotic eyes, the way he rolled on like a harrow, flattening everything in his path, which made last night's little episode— *something she shouldn't think about here*. These remarks he'd made about seeing babies getting their brains bashed in, about her not being able to do anything to him that hadn't already been done, either.

My God, Lyon did seem obsessed as a bear with a honey pot about Divers O'Roarke and his many attractions to women though.

One thing *he* certainly wouldn't win was any baskets of apples in the local Penvellyn *handsome men* competition. Unless you liked men who resembled weasels? And spoke as if their tongue slithered about inside their mouths.

Some might say what he would win was first prize *for being a shade more interested in what went on with Divers O'Roarke's private life than was right.* Why was that? Because Divers O'Roarke would win that basket?

They might also add was that the real reason Lyon shot that woman? And should *her* hair stand up over it, or not?

"Just don't send him home a wreck—"

"A wreck? Divers O'Roarke? That'll be a first," he chuckled. "The man wouldn't be afraid of the devil himself walking this way and saying *hello*."

"I mean … What I mean *is* …" Her throat constricted. As for Lyon stepping closer as if he knew exactly what she meant?

"That attack was staged. He knows that. I know that. Anything else is a lie, including however he came home to you. I'm not the man you may think I am that way. Him, now? Given this? Plus his lamentable habit of having his hand where he shouldn't?"

Oh God, not in smuggling pies either. She clasped her cloak tighter against her throat. My God, why think that? Because Lyon was staring intently and his breath was on her face? As if he'd win first prize in the *local graspers'* competition for knowing exactly where Divers O'Roarke had had his hands?

To flinch would be tantamount to spreading oil on her own hand to win first prize in the *picking up burning coals and turning your hand into a flaming fire faggot,* competition. But the fact was, Divers O'Roarke had never shrunk from spilling beans before, despite all the other lies he'd told about being a designer.

My God, why think that either? She swallowed.

"All I can tell you is that Gil Wryson knows where that consignment of goods is now. That one I believe is probably yours. That's it. As to whether something is missing, or going to go missing in the final analysis, I don't know. But Divers O'Roarke—"

She snapped her mouth shut on the words, *is a wreck because you killed a woman who trusted him, who you expected him to lie to and work closely with.* Why go there? Why say it just because she saw it? Why even see it?

Yet the Divers O'Roarke she had once known may have brought the whole house crashing down about her ears, he wasn't that kind of person *then*. The kind to line his pockets, the kind to lose the way, the kind to betray men, at all. In fact he'd been such a sitter at her feet, he'd have won every prize going in the *fawning dog* competition.

"Go on, Miss Rhodes."

Aware of Lyon's intense gaze, she cleared her throat. swallowed. The gale was tearing down it after all. Could she just stop this Divers O'Roarke stuff? Concentrate on winding Lyon round her pinkie nail? She'd made this pact, hadn't she? For one thing too. Doom Bar Hall. Already, having given up on revenge for Ennis, was she going to lose that? The answer was no. Although it did no harm to lay down a few ground rules and after all, given Lyon needed her and she needed him, what was he going to do about it?

"Divers O'Roarke is someone I can only get information about if you don't make it any more difficult than it is. Do we have an agreement, Mr. Lyon? Yes? Or no?"

"Hmm."

"That's not an answer."

"Because I don't like your question."

"I see. Well, I imagine if you only answer questions you like, you must be a man of very few words."

"Indeed, it is one of my finest points, Miss Rhodes, just as your charm is almost certainly yours."

Had a snake just slithered up her spine? She didn't think so but then, before she could check, he reached towards her bare throat and clasped it in his leather-gloved hand--fingered it anyway--his jaw jutting like a hawk's beak.

"But I warn you, you fail me on this matter and this lovely neck of yours is something I will break. Snap in two as if it is of no consequence. Perhaps not right now, perhaps not tomorrow, or next week, but, make no mistake, I will do it. Traitors are something I never let live. And believe me, I want to let you live. We agreed Doom Bar Hall and Doom Bar Hall would be empty without you in it. You and me. It is something I forgot to stipulate—"

"What?"

"Yes. Just as you said, you came with the house, I do too."

CHAPTER TWENTY ONE

"**D**estiny..."

Oh, how lovely and just what she was needing, after that little scene with Lyon. Divers O'Roarke, in her face, in her hall, her lovely hall, that always looked so beautiful at Christmas when she and Orwell stood in its luscious pine-garlanded center, dispensing steaming cups of mulled apple cider—what he didn't dispense to himself anyway--and hot fruit pies—fortunately he wasn't much interested in them--to the servants.

Ashes might be things she rose from on a daily, if not hourly, basis. But to be expected to rise every minute, second, even? How many burnings, shooting downs, could one woman withstand and pretend it didn't matter? She didn't feel them? In this hall. The doom-ridden hall that some might say, was now danker and dowdier than the crypt because there were even less servants to keep it, than there was apple cider to dispense on these Christmases after Orwell had helped himself. And they would be right. One thing this hall wouldn't win was any prizes in the Penvellyn Fair *best hall hereabouts* competition.

'Where were you?' *he* was certain sure to ask.

And, *Oh, you know, having my throat squeezed by Lyon. A consummation not to be wished for. Can you imagine? So now? Seeing as that reptilian mongrel also comes with the place* ... was hardly something she could say here.

Lyon was... *Lyon was*... Well, he might be... *It* might be...

Revolting. A revolting she'd have to bear. Look on the bright side, he wouldn't make her feel alive. And some might say, there was always such a thing as drink to turn to. Hadn't she said it didn't matter who she threw herself on the table to? Talk about sodding roosting chickens.

So? Some might say she'd be most greatly obliged if she could just get to her room and stare at the ceiling for a bit. Her shoulders sagged. She couldn't even conjure a 'well, it's not the sodding parrots,' from their cage. So if that was what he expected, some kind of reaction from her, he could sod off. She was done reacting.

"What?" she asked.

"Been out have you?"

His eyes cold as frosted glass studied her from the dark depths of the hall. As for the cocky chin tilt? The words that were more measured than a yard of the richest silk? This was a man to win first prize for *levelling a gun at her head and pulling the trigger.* When she'd seen him at his very worst last night too.

"Well, I haven't been in."

"So? Where have you been then?"

When she'd give her eye teeth for a lie down, why couldn't he just get out of her face? Really. Truly. She was done. And she'd sooner attach herself to the bridles of the four horsemen of Apocalypse and let them drag her dismembered limbs to the four corners of the earth and back again, than tell him.

"Out."

Tell him he was right about last night too. There was no doubt Lyon meant to kill him, that *this* man wasn't lying about last night, or playing some game with her. And the worst? The very worst? Maybe this was a man to put a gun to her head, there was something in the bitter wind raging through her heart that found that aura of power, of danger about him, even that dark wing of hair across his forehead, horribly attractive, especially given the state he'd been in last night.

How else could she explain the fact that she was struggling to ensure that wind blew no leaves, left no building torn open to the elements? That she wasn't a moth to the flame of life? And that was better than feeling life bleed away from her in drops? When she needed to cement these drops back into her veins? Hard as it was.

Where had it come from, *that* aura, that clung to him like an exotic scent? Teezer's Travelling Troupers? Well?

God, but the path had not been easy for either of them. How she could rage against the heavens for Ennis and Ennis for leaving her. But here? Right now? She just needed to get up these stairs.

He stepped towards her, just as she made for the stairs too. "Where?"

"Places."

"I know you've been places Destiny—"

"Then sodding stop asking me then." Even saying, *aren't you the clever one*, was beyond her, if that was why he was banging on and on at her like this. Well, she was done rising to it. She got up these stairs and she spent her time between now and Lyon moving in, staring at the ceiling. And nothing more he had to say changed that.

His gaze flicked her, something glinting like a diamond in its shadows.

"I see. Lyon? Was it?" He reached his hand towards her, swept the hair back from her face. "Where you got the mark on your throat?"

No, his stomach wasn't going to curdle. She wanted to run to Lyon with her tittle-tattle and that tittle-tattle resulted in him taking her by the throat, that was her affair.

Especially now it also made him feel all manner of secure, knowing the fact she tittle-tattled was what he needed to stay on the straight and narrow and booting her out would only increase Lyon's suspicions. Maybe the heart of a woman beat beneath that crusty shell, breaking her lichened walls didn't give him entry to a place he could live with her. And really, did a heart beat? Maybe he'd been wrong about Rose? Lyon didn't own Doom Bar Hall any more than he did but she'd been prepared to throw herself in with anyone.

"Don't be stupid, Divers. Now why would you imagine he'd want to throttle me?"

"In addition to the fact I don't imagine you squeeze your own throat, do you really want me to answer that?"

"Oh, little do you know the things I do in me spare time."

"And little do you know how much I do."

"Well, what are you asking for then?"

"Why do you think, seeing as you're so knowledgeable?"

After all, Lyon watched his every move and she fed Lyon these moves.

Why shouldn't he be the one putting the food on the plate?

And if she got her throat torn out in the process of running with these titbits to Lyon, what was that to him?

"But a broken vase and however I was last night because he took a pot shot at me, isn't any kind of proof I'm anything other than Divers O'Roarke."

"Tell me about it."

"So, you have just been to him? And he said what? That taking pot shots at me is something he does all the time? All part of the game? So, here's the thing, here's what's going to happen."

"What is?"

"To save me asking Gil to waste his time reporting on all your tiresome, little tete-a-tetes with Lyon, you can ask me what proof you need to say I'm, in fact, the Cleanser. You're right." He smoothed another strand of hair back from her face.

"Proof?"

Christ, but she was delicious when she was beaten, it was almost as well she'd betrayed him and he was done with this, or guilt at having cursed her for nothing and reducing her to this sorry state might cut him off at the knees.

After last night's collapse--shameful in many ways--and this kicking today, when the clock hadn't struck eleven yet, he needed to demonstrate how assured, how in command of the situation he was, though. And that nothing she did could undermine him. Not her closeness, the feel of her skin beneath his fingertips, her soft scent sinking into his senses, her pale throat, tightening in the clasp of the mourning brooch and Lyon's fingerprints, as if the proof was something she didn't want and couldn't take. What level of stupid did she think he was?

"Proof, Destiny," he whispered. "That little thing you're after. That thing you want. Would be lying if you said you didn't. As ever, the choice is yours."

She raised her chin, exhaled sharply.

"Fine. Then how's this?" She grasped his cravat.

The threat he needed to pose here? Where was that exactly? In his dreams? The woman had allied herself with Lyon. What did she think exactly? That being an undercover agent meant he was also some kind of stud? That she could kiss him and he'd think the stars went out—not even one by one on his pride—out completely. But his heart leapfrogged, he couldn't breathe, or think, or anything, for the assault on his senses, his body, the intoxicating feel of her stickpin but soft bones, the scent, the musky scent, of sharp lavender and her, and the heat of her mouth on his. And he needed to. But Christ did he want her.

She drew back as he stood trying to grab the tattered remnants of his control about him.

"*That's* my choice. Now, if you will excuse me, unless you very much want to join me, I have a room to go to."

Her voice, containing every shred of control he damn well strove for, said it was a room he wasn't welcome in either.

CHAPTER TWENTY TWO

"That's what you think."

Having completed task one by reaching the door to her room, opening it too, without missing a beat, *Oh, I don't know, Destiny. Maybe I do want to join you, so we can both be damned to this. What you are. What I am,* were not words she wanted to hear. Although equally, it could have been worse. *He* could have said what she just had, about thinking. He could have said it with regard to having a room to go to, with *please call me John*, Lyon at her back and everything. As for what he had said? A cocky, cheap poke.

Clasping the door handle, she cleared her throat. "The dining room is looking just the same by the way. Yes. I looked in it earlier. And I have to say, that despite all your fine talk, it was quite disappointing. But some things just are."

Then she shut the door firmly behind her. Of course, how the dining room would look at Christmas she'd no idea, with sodding John sitting at the table and that. But at least she could think about it now she'd gotten Diver O'Roarke out her face.

Bending down she eased off a boot. When it came to shedding light, Divers O'Roarke liked to leave no-one in the dark. In fact he'd give Christ Almighty a game for his crucifixion nails that way. It would be a close run thing who could illuminate the most bits of the world. *When it suited him.* There just now? Offering proof about the Cleanser? What did he think? That the back of her head had pink ribbons up the back and tied nicely to hide the fact she'd no brains?

She hoped he'd liked that kiss. It was the last he was getting. She edged off the other boot. Maybe, for that matter, she should go to a solicitor about being conned out of the house and then those doing the conning—Lyon--saying they came with it?

Right now though?

Right now when some might say there were other reasons she hadn't wanted that proof? And she didn't want them to be right? Bed and ceiling beckoned. Doom Bar Hall was within her grasp. And when it was and Divers O'Roarke had stopped getting in her face, one thing she wasn't going to do was let Lyon's words work on her like this.

And not the ones about coming with the house either.

***

"*C*hrist!"

"*Shit!* I mean … Yes, Divers? Is that you?"

Some might say that was obvious but then they weren't about to win any parsnips in the county *just been caught with your hand in the apple barrel* competition. So, task one. Forget the candlestick skittering round the landing floorboards, the boiling wax coating her bare toes in the darkness. This was war and she must wage it. .

The mound that had been in the bed, *his* bed in *his* room, hadn't been him at all. A trick of the light. Not a mound at all, in fact. And so she'd gone downstairs, padded silently along the thin ribbon of moonlight, past the silent portraits of Sir Grimscott Rhodes and his wife Bodinnar, knowing *he* still hadn't come in, despite the fact midnight had died two hours previously.

It was the biggest amount of inconsideration she had ever seen in anybody because then? Then, just as she was imagining him dead, his brains blown out, or worse and them all gathered round, singing dirges, in he'd waltzed, large as life. Right in the front door, as she reached the foot of the stairs too—a place she never should have been, with her *is this it, or not,* thoughts and her heart pounding like a judge's mallet about what she'd do if it was. Because life was never black and white. Life was to be lived. *However. Whatever.*

So now, having dropped the candlestick in her efforts to leap up the stairs two at a time, on tiptoes, so as not to make a sound ...*now she stared harder at her door.*

Because now the stairs creaked as he sprung up them. She didn't need to look to know his first move was to pick up the candlestick, any more than she needed to know that some might say the candlestick was like a leadership baton. Who ever got to it first had the upper hand. When a second ago, some might add, he'd been as startled to see her as she was when he came in the door. As if he'd thought she was a ghost caught there on the staircase in her white gown.

Equally, in his line of work his back must be in constant danger. It was probably why he was so edgy about everything ... because he never knew where the assassin lurked, where they kept their knives. Hers now?

"Burnt your toes, have you?" he said.

Option one. When Lyon had obviously heeded her demand not to shoot his head off? Was there one? His head, yes, obviously there was his head, or it wouldn't have a mouth that had just spoken. Which brought her to ...

Option two She stared harder at her door. Some might say it was preferable.

"Does it look like it? If you must know I was going to me room."

"And I'm the Queen of Sheba." He set the candlestick down on the side table. "But maybe it was another look at the dining room you were after?"

"I might. If there was something worth looking at."

"What do you want to know, Destiny? How much Lyon missed me by tonight? What I did as the Cleanser? Or is it, that all this grief over Ennis is just a distraction, a burial you had to stage for yourself when what you'd sooner feel is alive with me, right here, right now? And that's what you're doing out here?"

Option three? Despite the fact it might involve taking his throat out? Which some might say was a bad idea, him being an agent of the Crown and all. Which brought her to ...

Option four. Which she would say could prove to be her undoing ...

"You should be so lucky." No. Option four might be a mistake too far. Unless she could keep her mind on her dinner plates? "Now if you will excuse me?"

Obviously not, or his hand wouldn't descend on the door, not to push it open either when she really needed to win every prize going in the *pushing the door open* competition.

She dragged her gaze up, met the dark curve of his eyelashes on his cheekbones, the scent of rough moorland and sand-stretched beaches. Another world. All of it. Powerful, evocative.

Option four ...

Whatever else she did tonight, *if* she was not going in her room alone, *if* there was only one way out of being caught like this—*snooping*--the dinner plates had better prove to be the most interesting things she'd ever seen and would ever see again, when really, in terms of options, she knew one thing.

Options five and six, like seven, eight and nine, were things she was out of.

She was a Rhodes and when Rhodes' were all about living life to the hilt, should he be worried about the fact that now she'd turned around, her mouth was short inches from his when he was standing too close for comfort? How distressing to note, that as he felt the brush of her nightgown against his legs, he *was* worried but pulling away didn't come into this.

It *had* thrown him seeing Destiny Rhodes on the staircase—he wanted to blame Rose making him jumpy, making him think it was her—but it didn't justify the primal urge that had swept as he'd slammed his hand against the door.

Now Destiny Rhodes stood there her back against that door, moonlight icing her face, now he felt the serrated edge of her breath against his lips, now he heard the steady drum of her heart, felt the press of her breasts against him, it was nice to think he knew what her game was and it wasn't the snap they played as children which she'd always won. But right now? He didn't know. Why the hell she was spying downstairs instead of raking about in his room, had failed to take the proof he'd offered, either. Especially if Lyon had threatened her. Destiny Rhodes liked to paint her heart blacker than the night sky. It was the reason he'd been so ready to believe Rose about Chancery, *about everything*.

One thing though, was if she thought she had him at a disadvantage because here she was, pressed between him and the door, she was mistaken. After all, she wasn't the first woman he'd bedded undercover, so it was nothing, to meet her coolly salacious stare with one of his own, to press even closer too, press his mouth to her soft throat, her neck.

"You know, Destiny, I can tell Lyon tales too. That we've been together. Doesn't that worry you?"

"Just don't make me care for you," she said. "That's all I ask."

That was when the silence of snow fell on his breath, his everything.

CHAPTER TWENTY THREE

The low drone worked into Destiny's consciousness so she struggled to keep her eyes closed and cling to the blackness of sleep. Was it morning? It couldn't be, let alone a *good* one and not just because some inconsiderate sod was winning prizes for droning on about it, just outside the bedroom door. They were clinking crockery too—Great Aunt Modest's best china cups, in all probability. *Of all things.* After she'd meant to keep her eyes firmly fixed on them last night too.

Well, she hadn't. *Of all things either.*

How could she? Spend half the night locked in his embrace, kissing him either, when, at the very least she'd needed some sleep, after inconsiderately being kept up till two in the morning, never mind this stopping now before she was ironed flat?

"Look, Divers ... " Gil Wryson's voice ghosted through the closed door.

"No, you look ... " Divers O'Roarke's gravelly undertone followed.

"I am looking. Looking hard, man. But I never expected to come back here to find you with *her*."

Really? Well, she didn't either. Who did Gil expect to come back and find his precious Divers with though? The Mona Lisa? Not much sodding chance in the wilds of Cornwall. She sat up.

"Fetching her tea, too. A lying snake. Now, I know," Gil droned on, "*I know I have no business—*"

He could say that again.

"You don't."

"But you saved my life. I will always owe you—"

"And I will always thank you today as ever, for going on with things the other night. But you're mistaken if you thought I was tempted."

Who by? Her? Someone other than her? Or not by her at all? Wasn't that something to remember the next time when she ooh'd and ah'd in ecstasy? The sod had probably had more women in his line of work than she'd had Christmas dinners, served on Great Aunt Modest's plates—certainly now. Certainly he'd seemed pretty tempted by *her*. Last night anyway. But maybe, when it came to being tempted, what she should be asking herself here was *by what*?

Some might say things were to be learned and she should yank the sheet loose, wrap it around herself and go and do just that--at the door. But then it might depend on what she listened to there.

Hand Lyon the proof and there couldn't be any more of this. What there would be was Lyon right here in Doom Bar Hall. God Almighty though, when there was no getting away from this, what exactly was she prolonging? Her misery? If she'd kept her mind on Great Aunt Modest's plates perhaps? But she hadn't exactly won any prizes for doing that. How could she? Ennis hadn't kissed her all night long like that. So even now, what flooded thoughtwise, what flooded, more than thoughtwise, dried her throat. But ultimately she couldn't ever go to a place where she couldn't breathe because she didn't have someone in her life. Once was enough.

She looked round. Somehow she'd sat up, hadn't she? There wasn't much point in sitting here lamenting the general state of her life because that state wasn't going away any time soon. She edged the sheet loose and wrapped it round herself. Then she eased off the bed. Even if wild horses careered through the door and dragged her away, she couldn't afford not to listen at it. It might be she heard nothing. She tiptoed forward, taking care to avoid a creaking board. Hesitation was for the faint hearted, after all. Gil was speaking. And not, what some might say, was very nicely at that.

"Sir, you can lie to yourself about her, the snake *she* is—"

"Who says I'm lying?"

Obviously. It was something she knew already. The news would have been if he wasn't. And she'd seriously been worried last night about caring for him?

"All right, but even if you weren't going to take any of that consignment for yourself the other night and you're not going to warn Berryman, or any of the—"

"I've told you, all that is behind--"

"Because ... Sir, all right, why do you think I'm saying this? I'm with you on this. You know that. I understand Berryman's not a bad man. He's not a wrecker And he keeps a squad of grandchildren. A daughter who's a cripple too. People who all depend on him."

What the blazes was going on here? *Berryma*n? Why the hell would Divers O'Roarke warn Berryman? Unless he was lying to Gil about what he did, or not really working for Lyon at all? She pressed closer. What, with the thickness of the door and the fact they stood on the other side of it, it was difficult to make out what was being said but she did her best.

"And that was why you went with sorry tales to Lyon, was it?"

"I told you why I did that. See sense when he's on to you. To *us*. Why the hell else would he damn well nearly blast your head off? He *knows*. He just doesn't have proof. You need, you *must*, give him what he wants. That's this gang, pure and simple. The sooner, the better."

"You think that's not exactly what I'm doing? That I don't have reason to now?"

"Come on, man. The other leg rings when you pull it."

"Because I'm with her? You somehow think I'm going to help Berryman?" Divers O'Roarke's tone notched down to icy waters but she didn't mistake the words.

"Sir, I've lined, *you've* lined your pockets, on occasion. But with a snake, like her on the loo—"

"Think very carefully what you're saying here."

Some might say that people who listened at doors never heard any good of themselves. But really, since it was no more than what was being said in Penvellyn, did it matter? Especially when she was also hearing all this too. *Lined his pockets*? Well, knock her down with one of Lizzie's feather dusters. *How could he be doing that?*

"All right, so lined maybe isn't the right word?"

But then again, how could he not? Was that why he was after Raven's Passage? Knocking bloody great holes in the wall to find it too?

"And I know we, neither of us, meant it or that money would have been spent," Gil went on.

"I'm glad you think so."

She was too. It meant there might be something left to give Lyon.

"Don't think we both don't know how a man can get drawn into this world. Get involved with these people. Look the other way. Find it hard to stay clean. Stay away from the thrill of doing something illegal as they do, like … like handing back a consignment that's short, because it's more trouble to explain why it's short and man, the bag of gold is in *your* hand and you're being asked to get in deeper. But *this* is not the occasion. Christ, why can't you *just* see that with a snake like her on the loose?"

Drawn into this world? Well, she never. Destiny pressed harder against the door, so she drank its essence through her pores and the secret words being whispered on the other side. She'd hear better if they'd speak up but she couldn't very well ask them to.

"Well, maybe that's so. I don't deny it. The fact is I'm with her precisely because this is not the occasion. And only a blind man wouldn't see she's in league with Lyon. All for the sake of a house. Because that's Destiny Rhodes, for you. So, you might even call it insurance. No more, no less, when she's exactly what you say. So she goes to Lyon as I know she's done—"

"So this is what? Insurance you keep your nose clean? Is that what you're saying?"

"Give me the tray."

My God, but obviously he hadn't answered so maybe she wasn't? Maybe he was with her because he was drawn to her?

"Christ, it is, isn't it?"

"I said—"

"And that curse ... that curse makes you safe. So you don't even have that to fear."

"Chance would be a fine thing. The sacrifice I'm making here. Now, the tray. Thank you."

The handle turned. Maybe Destiny had crept across the floor, now she streaked faster than if she was a comet entering the local *best person dash* competition by mistake, crash landed in the bed, rearranged herself on the pillows, eyes shut, hand strategically placed beside her left cheek, breath squeezing through the peepholes in her throat, her lungs, her *eyelids*. After what she'd just heard, was it any wonder? No wonder that her heart hammered with such force, he must hear it too.

The insurance wasn't just that Lyon was on to him. It was what Lyon was on to him about and what *he* was doing about that.

Soft footsteps padded towards her. The rattle of crockery said the tray had been placed on the bedside table. She didn't move. She daren't although her throat was scalded dry, her breath scaling such dizzy heights—largely at her own folly--she might be flying. Did he look at her? If he did she must pray he found her attractive, although paradoxically, if he did, given how alive he made her feel, given it was easier walking a mile barefoot on broken glass, was that wise? Everything she cared about, remember? *And she was starting to care.* By the tiniest degrees and inches. And she couldn't. Not that it was a tit for tat competition or anything but he'd agreed she was a snake.

"You might as well stop pretending you never heard that."

Christ, he wouldn't have driven by mistake over that cliff like Ennis, would he? Because he'd never have been in the sodding coach.

"That's rich." She flicked an eye open. "With me *deaf as a post ears*."

But maybe he would have been in the coach? Spilt what he had to Gil, hadn't he, knowing she was in here? As for where this information left her ...?

He sat down on the edge of the bed. "Well then, would you like some tea before you go to see Lyon with all that tittle-tattle you have for him today? It's there if you do."

What she'd like, what she'd really, really like, settling her gaze on his greatcoat gracing his shoulders like an embrace, the triangle of golden skin that peeped out? One thing and one thing only. Never to have heard what she damn well had. But she had heard it. She hadn't denied it either.

So now? There was only one thing she could do here when she was meeting Lyon later this morning and that wasn't just to wipe every trace and memory of last night from her mind either. She sat up.

"Not if you made it. I mean I wouldn't want to drop dead before I got there because you put something in it." She tugged the sheet free and rose from the bed. "Especially as you probably want me to. Go to Lyon, that is, although, let's face it, I'm sure you'd be happy if I did the other thing too."

Then, despite the fact it was technically hers, she walked from the room.

***

Divers O'Roarke stared at the floor, then he flicked his gaze over the ceiling, before settling it on the tea pot, the backs of his eye-lids and the floor.

He wasn't dying to have her--that was the last thing he'd do--just as she hadn't gone to Lyon the other day to beg him to spare his life. On that he staked that same life.

So why think otherwise because last night, yet again she'd wanted him?

He shook his head largely to clear it. She was his insurance here. No more. No less.

All he needed to do was see this and sit quiet. And when he could soon discredit her with Lyon, feed her falsehoods, do whatever it took to finish this job, he'd be damned to thinking she was anything other than what Gil said. A poisonous snake at that.

So why do it?

***

All right, so she'd left the room in such a hurry, she'd have won the golden ribbon in the *fastest woman in Cornwall* competition. Left it is such a hurry she was standing here in a leaky old coat, muffler, boots, hat, skirt and would also win the wooden spoon for first prize in the *whatever she could cobble together and go out in at short notice* competition. In a torrential downpour too, having no time to think either. *But now she had.* Did people think she was a helpless cabbage, or what? Hadn't she thought about keeping that appointment with Lyon given the last thing she needed was him turning up at Doom Bar Hall and thinking she was fair game for winning the *squeezed throat* competition?

"Miss Rhodes? You have what is required?" Lyon's middle name was obviously *desperate* because he rounded on her before she reached the path. But she did. She did have what was required. "As opposed to hauling me all this way for nothing, like yesterday?"

She also had a runny nose, advanced shortage of breath as she wheezed through the bracken and feet wet enough to put in her bath and save the need for any water.

Why hadn't she just played along that night Divers O'Roarke offered her to run things for him? Showed off her obvious talent in design by polishing up a few of Aunt Elowen's old horse brasses and hanging them in the powder room. She and him might be sharing a tentative friendship by now, fired by their mutual love and adoration of design.

All right, he wasn't, technically speaking, going to win any prizes in the actual house and garden design stakes, what with him being a smuggler and that. But just think of how conflicted he'd have been feeling by now, had she only kept her cards tight against her chest, instead of letting her blabby big mouth rule the roost.

Think of how surprised he'd have been, coming in to find her maybe rearranging the dining room, how a golden glance could have been exchanged as he acknowledged her great taste in such matters and thought she wasn't so bad really. Just the kind of apple you'd want in your barrel.

"And don't think to cross me either." Lyon eyed the dwindling horizon as she reached the path, her coat skirt soaking to her knees to add to her misery. "Not when I can smell him on you."

And so friendship led to love, it led to Doom Bar Hall.

Look on the bright side though. It wouldn't be news to this sodding stoat when Divers O'Roarke told him. Maybe he'd even leave her throat alone?

"Well, I had some trouble myself getting here this morning. But yes, yes I do," she gasped.

"Well? Are you going to tell me what it is? Or are we going to stand here all afternoon too?"

"Us?" She exhaled sharply trying to catch her breath. She probably even smiled a little even if she'd be fair game for winning the *squeezed throat* competition, *not* as the person having their throat squeezed either. The sodding cheek of the sodding man. But she was too far in to take issue with it. This was about the *sacrifice* the sneaky O'Roarke sod was making here, in order to stay on the straight and narrow.

Last night? The tangle of ecstasy, what they had been to each other, the images that crashed like waves in her brain, the places he had taken her to, they didn't any of them, mean a bloody thing.

She'd given Divers O'Roarke his chance. He hadn't taken it. At least she understood one thing now. Why.

So, these other stupid, *stupid,* thoughts, the ones that might otherwise have been well-nigh panning her head in? About how she could have played this differently--when she and Orwell and Chancery had done terrible things to him as children? About how he'd this stash, he could lift and escape this whole situation with either? Why waste her energy even suggesting it, just because, when he'd kissed her, nothing else had mattered? No. The sod would rather use her as his insurance. Have her trailing back and forward like this in sodding weather Noah would have been right at home in. Water dripping down her back, her front, her nose, her hair.

So, what she was going to do here was swallow the cold, choking lump of marble in her throat, drag another breath to the furthest corners of her lungs, fasten her gaze on the smack bobbing out in the bay. Christmas was coming. What other way was she going to get her garlands? Not even that stitch in her side would stop her. Lyon *not* squeezing her throat and listening intently to all she had to say would be its own reward for now.

"Well, as I say, I just had some trouble, so what I could do with getting, is back, before he sees I've gone. But yes ... he told me he is the Cleanser," she panted.

Lyon's gaze dug holes in her face. "And *you* didn't think to say? Sooner that is?"

"Well, how could I, when I didn't know? Didn't he tell me he was a smuggler, after all? Then obviously, that he was an undercover exciseman? What's one more progression?"

"Hopefully the one where you provide actual proof." She begged his pardon but perhaps him listening intently to all she had to say was yet to come? "But perhaps you are going to tell me words are cheap and saying is never proof and that was why you were sleeping with him?"

"Not exactly." *What kind of thing was that to say*? Certainly it was not the kind of thing to suggest that something, that some might say deserved a medal for government service, was noble and self-sacrificing. "When you're taking the words out me mouth, why should I?"

His ice-cold breath hit her face. "If I am taking the words out of your mouth, it is because I told you yesterday that whether or not he is the Cleanser, is in many ways irrelevant. I also told you other things."

"What? When you nearly broke my throat?"

"Do not exaggerate."

"I'm not. I'm merely saying—"

"Not good enough Miss Rhodes," he snarled to match his name. Stomped up and down a bit too. "This is not what I came here to hear."

"Well, what did you come here for then?"

Well really? Plainly *not* listening intently to all she had to say, about the gold, about what Divers O'Roarke had hidden, or he'd shut the proverbial up and stop bumping his gums to no good end. But maybe he just liked the sound of his own voice? *Or he wasn't the only one gum-bumping around here?*

"That remains to be seen," he muttered. "But let me tell you this one thing."

"What?"

He jammed his tricorn back on his head. Here it was *finally*. The reward she sought for now.

"I can see why he likes you."

"Who?"

"Don't pretend you don't know. If there is one thing I cannot abide, next to a traitor, it is a pretender. Who do you think?"

What? Divers O'Roarke? It was why he'd made her tea this morning too, no doubt, with fairy bells on. Such big, fancy ones she smothered the laughter that rose in her throat.

For that matter, what she'd overheard could be fanciful as her flying to the Moon and back. Something he hoped she'd overhear and come running here, so she looked no end of stupid while he was somewhere else all together. He'd said as much about tittle-tattle. So maybe it was as well she wasn't getting her own reward?

But what if he hadn't? What if he'd made that tea and then Gil Wryson got in the way? Never liked looking a fool, had Divers O'Roarke. And who could blame him, the amount of times she, Chancery and Orwell had made him look just that. Her scalp prickled. The sharp tang of the sea caught her throat. Last night? Last night had been very different. An endless pleasure and treasure. And here she was betraying him because what else was there for her to do?

Sometimes in life you had to get in the leaky boat, to see if you wanted to sink, or swim.

And she had.

Look at it that way. Gone to the wire she had.

Rising from ashes, even if her eyes prickled was her specialty after all.

As she made her way back along the bleak cliff path, she knew one thing. It was also Sir Tredwynne's.

CHAPTER TWENTY FOUR

"I say Destiny, old girl, would you mind telling me exactly what it is you are you up to?"

"Me?" Destiny stopped her rummage in the broom cupboard beneath the staircase, the dark, cobwebby one that crawled into an emptier shell than her and smelled like an ancient cask. But then that might have been because Orwell was in the vicinity. "Apart from wishing you would stop calling me old and girl? Something that would not have been necessary if you hadn't lost the house, that's what I'm doing."

She tossed a moldering shoe aside. Unless Gil Wryson had buried Sir Tredwynne in the garden, dumped him in the sea, the cupboard seemed the most likely, if not the only place, he could have been left to rot. Although some might say the thought of such an action would once have fried her veins, what was that to her now, so long as she found him? She could not do this without him. And frankly, she *had* to now. She'd stood in the leaky tub and there was no other way.

"So? What are you looking for exactly?" Orwell's voice dripped a honeyed helpfulness she didn't need, as if finally, he really didn't like seeing her on her hands and knees in the dust like this. At least it didn't ooze booze. Sober? When the clock on the hall table had just chimed three. Well, she never. He never either.

"Sir Tred … Oh never mind. Got him."

A metal leg, then a gauntlet then, well, *then what she was looking for*. She snatched it up, held it to her breast.

"Destiny, old girl, I hope you do not mind me asking but exactly what the blazes do you want with that? I mean I know you like to repair—"

"None of your sodding business." She scrambled to her feet, brushing the dust off her skirt. "So why don't you just go out and get drunk? Because me? I have things, important things to do."

***

Destiny's eyes were open before she knew it. Or was she so sodding tired, she just spent all night staring into the inky darkness? Five weeks to Christmas now. Time yet to raise a glass from the steaming punch bowl in the hall and library anyway, the dining room was still under wraps, to thread her garlands along the mantelpiece. At least she sodding hoped so. The bed creaked as Divers O'Roarke pushed the covers aside.

"Where are you going?"

Icy moonlight silvered his face, glittering on the tips of his exquisite eye-lashes and his blatant disregard, his attempted blatant disregard for all she offered him, on his distrust of everything she was. That thing she felt at all times, against her cheek, her lips, her body. Because whatever about him, whatever he thought, felt, business was business. She understood that now. A dangerous one perhaps, but business nonetheless. Somewhere outside an owl hooted.

"Now then Destiny, don't pretend you don't know. It's hardly becoming, especially when you were probably listening to me earlier."

She yawned. "And don't you pretend you don't get something out of the fact I'm not becoming. Every night in fact. You won't mind if I go back sleep. I mean if you want to go out in the cold and the dark, that's entirely your affair, I'm sure."

He didn't speak, just rose from the bed. Thank God she was meant to be sleepy. Ennis never had quite that width of bicep, that narrowness of hip, that---*quite a lot actually*, especially for someone who was meant to be averting her eyes and for whom business was also business and who was going to wrangle Doom Bar Hall out of this. Finally. Her way too.

It would not happen if she let her gaze drift to the perfect nakedness of the man who had just left her bed. Only if she painted herself in colors she had always worn to sheer perfection. For God's sake, Divers O'Roarke was just a man and after tonight he was a man she would be done with. There was no room for anything else here just because some might say he had rather nice buttocks and was sort of half decent in bed. All right he was very decent. Indecent actually. But that did not a lifetime make. She wasn't exactly going to win the local *happy ever after* competition with him.

It hardly mattered there were times he came home, shaking, pouring a drink from the bottle, making out he was in complete control when she sat up, getting in to bed with her as if there was no tomorrow.

As she also knew, all things were temporary, even the raw, heart bleed bite of grief. She'd already stood at the graveside of one man she'd loved. And once was quite enough. It was what had allowed her heart to ignore all these times. Ignore her guilt too, over what she'd told Lyon.

Twelve o'clock. The clock on the landing had just solemnly chimed the witching house. By one o'clock, the silent, mossy smuggling paths that led up onto the moor would be awash with the murmur of bracken, the owl light sparkle of forgotten stars, blurred by the men the night came to chase, in the sky the moon hanging like a silver orb.

She sighed. Provided she kept to her plan, by three o'clock this would all be over.

To her satisfaction.

Finally.

The door clicked shut and taking a deep breath, she rose from the bed.

***

Never had Divers been so glad of his low brogue, the softly spoken Irish that was second nature to him as in the moment when he rounded on Gil Wryson.

"What do you mean, *Sir, leave it?*" Do you really think I'm stupid enough, when we're so nearly there? Job done?"

But, having stood in the ice-cold swirling tide, feeling the starving lather eat his boots, his stockings, his toes, for the last perishing half hour and having struggled against air cold and sharp as steel, to drag a breath into his frozen lungs, felt his nose run with every conceivable thing a nose could run with, wiped icy sweat from his brow, *Sir, leave it,* were not words he wanted to hear. Words he'd once picked Gil off the starving streets of London, alone, dirty, starving, despite the gold fob watch in his pocket, to hear *ever*, either. Gil's eyes glittered with black despair.

"Sir, I know. That's why I want you to give me the barrel. Just give me the barrel. That's it. Easy. Easy. And just let me put it with the rest."

Fury sparked along Divers frozen veins. Brandy, wine, tea, lace. Every tooth of hell, when Lyon next showed up, as it was written in Divers' stars he would, he wouldn't find so much as a missing drip, thread, leaf. There would be no more wrinkling his nose around Divers for the infinitesimal stink of rat, as he'd been doing since Divers came back to work. Why not just let this go? Let Gil roll the barrel through the marram grass to the cart, the bones of which stood out in the moonlight like a dead man's? Well?

"Do you think me so dishonest I'm incapable. Is that it?"

He wasn't letting it go without saying his piece though. How could he? Were the nostrils of all of them--Tom Berryman and his crew, dotted about the shoreline and the frothing brine--afflicted by that same stench? One that was more powerful than the night cold, festering seaweed and all that was decay? When he wasn't, *he wasn't that rat.* A different one perhaps, as Berryman and his family would see before the week was out. But not *that* one.

"Sir ... " Gil's breath stung his cheek. "I don't anything."

"That's a first. I must say. A man who doesn't think." Divers grimaced, dragged the keg closer. "Because *I* think. I think all the time."

And what he thought, glancing at Berryman, was, *he* wasn't any different. Why not just take this barrel, take that trunk of lace? Put them with the rest. The ones he and Gil had secreted. Add to the gold that was stashed too? Get the hell out of this life of deceit and lies now? Destiny Rhodes wasn't the insurance he needed. Or sweat wouldn't slick his palms. Not just tonight. Every night he did this, then went home to a woman he shouldn't touch but had to touch and couldn't seem to damn well stop touching either, not if someone handed him a bent daffodil stalk and said, 'Stop it, or dig your grave with that.' That's how poisonous this whole situation was too him although he'd kept his outward cool about it because there were times when he had been suited to this work, was good at his job, before Eirwin, before he'd been left for dead, before he'd been drawn into worlds he never should have entered, had to see things he never should have seen always, *always* to keep his cover, break the ring.

What he needed to do now was beat down any thoughts about heading off with this cask into the star-lit yonder and get to the end of things. Hand up Berryman, his brother, son. Leave three families with no man to fend for them. One with five orphaned children in it and a woman who couldn't walk. To know him was death sure enough.

"And I told you it was a mistake to come here. *Let it go, man.*" Gil tugged harder. So did Divers. Yes, he did need to let it go but why the hell should he just *because Gil said so?*

"Why?"

"Because you keep looking at Berryman."

"Maybe that's because a cat can look at a king. Thought of that, have you?"

"But he's not a king. He's someone you must take down and stop giving Destiny Rhodes wrong information about."

"I don't necessarily do that. Not when, after some consideration, I saw it saved me setting up tiresome meetings with Lyon."

"Sir …"

"All right, *once*," he panted. "I thought about it once. Then I thought that sending Lyon on wild goose chases would show I have something to hide. When I don't. Although no doubt you think I shouldn't even have done that. Now let go of the damned keg."

"And why's that?"

The voice cut bullet holes in his spine, knocking out his breath, nearly stopping his heart. But not quite. He dragged up his chin. Lyon, his eyes like ice chips in the moonlight, with his little ring of men, was *probably to be expected.* Wasn't he in for the surprise of his life though? Divers perused Lyon as the seconds crawled by, then held up his hands. Lyon was an exciseman. And Divers? Divers was a smuggler who'd just been caught. All in the game. Even if he hadn't known Lyon was going to pounce tonight.

Behind him curses laced the bitter air. Cold metal dented Divers' temple where Lyon's pistol pressed.

"So you can take it to wherever it is you all take it?" Lyon's voice was a low, throated growl. "Is that it, Mr. … ?"

Divers set his jaw, stood with as much icy calm as he could muster. In truth with the wind tearing at his hair and water swirling around his ankles, it wasn't difficult. "O'Roarke."

"Except that's not what you do. Now, is it, Mr. O'Roarke?"

"If you say so."

Here they went. It always had to look good, convincing. The play tonight was a little before curtain up time but who was Divers to argue? For that matter Destiny Rhodes may have informed on him. For that matter, Lyon may have all the information he needed on this ring *now*. Whichever it was, Divers hands were clean. So lily-white, he fought not to laugh. If this let him finish up earlier here, wasn't he the lucky one? Had he really thought about stealing that barrel in order to finish up sooner? Relief flooded. What a mistake that would have been.

"I do say so. And to answer my question, Mr. O'Roarke, or rather add to it, should we ask her?"

"Her?" Now he did laugh. "What the hell are you talking about? *Her*?"

"This." Lyon stood back as two of his men dragged a squirming figure forward in as far as it was possible to drag that particular figure forward, backwards, or even sideways, without being spat at, threatened, kicked. "What we'd call caught bonnie, *snooping*, on the far side of Heffin's Bank."

"I'm glad you think so even if no sodding brain is what it shows you have. Now you tell your men to get their self-satisfied, smug—"

"But you're here, aren't you?" Lyon snarled.

"Obviously I'm here but not for him. Are you serious? In fact I came to tell—"

"So maybe you'd like to be reunited?"

"Not especially." Because Divers didn't. He may have shot a hand out as she smacked against his chest, his heart had sunk to his boots. What the hell was she even doing here--on Heffin's Bank at that, the most obvious place anyone could be seen on? She was with Lyon? With Lyon surely?

"So you say." Lyon's voice was deadlier than he'd ever heard it. "So? Tell me *what*, Miss Rhodes? When you've already told me everything?"

"Me?"

"That my own exciseman is the Cleanser, that I should keep an eye out for his betrayal tonight."

"The Cleanser?" While it almost killed him, Divers allowed himself to live. To speak too. After all, was any of this so unexpected? Except perhaps the fact Lyon had just given the entire game away? Yes. Perhaps that was unexpected.

To give into the urge to run his tongue over his suddenly calcified lips was to show the alarm coating them. "That's a very serious allegation. Even for a man like you. You better be sure you can back it up. Even my own man here, will tell you, it's a lie. As for being an exciseman, any man here who believes—"

"I don't need proof." Lyon raised his pistol. "A man like me? Are you being ridiculous? A man like me just has to say. And no-one questions it. Not even these men here."

"Well, I'm questioning it because if you're basing it on her say so, her say so, is lies. It's all she knows. All she's capable of. She's a snake. Believe me, if anyone knows that, it's me."

Thank Christ he'd never been a gentleman. The pang of guilt he suffered as he grabbed her wrist and dragged her squirming body from his, might have been much larger otherwise. As it was, it wasn't even a pang. A pinprick. Anything.

To think he had had this woman in his bed not two hours ago. Thank Christ it hadn't meant a thing. Thank Christ his brain was iced as the Moon above his head. Thank Christ for every woman he'd ever bedded undercover.

As for Lyon? The man no-one questioned? How true. Remembering Eirwin, the game Divers had been forced to play since, his mind actually swirled in the red curtain enveloping it. It would all be for nothing if he now admitted how sweetly Eirwin had drawn him into that world because he had cared for her even if he had never loved her. She had risked everything for him. It was the start of his fall. And even now a bit of him admitted he hadn't just kept Destiny Rhodes under his nose, in his bed as insurance. Some stupid, errant, certifiable part of him, that part of him that hated what he'd done cursing her that night, thinking now it might have been for nothing, was trying to keep her safe. Himself too. *Everything she cared about, remember*? When this was what she was?

Why not just admit it?

The click as Lyon cocked his pistol was unmistakable. It even froze Destiny Rhodes to the spot, the wind whipping her hair, cloak, the bony wrist his fingers clenched, *everything*.

"And yet, she wants you," Lyon said.

"Her? Now isn't that the funniest thing I've heard in quite a while when what she wants is Doom Bar Hall. She doesn't care what hell she'd go down to, to get it. Yours. Mine. Gil's there. The dog's if need be. The kind of woman she is didn't care who she offered herself to just so long as she won Doom Bar Hall back off the table."

Hell's shrunken teeth. Divers wanted to add that he meant it but terror iced his scalp, freezing his laughter to his mouth. Back, forwards, the pistol went. Him. Her. Him. Her. Slowly, with perfect deliberation. Christ Almighty, Lyon wasn't going to shoot them both, surely? Eirwin was one thing. A poor man's wife. But Destiny Rhodes? A name that held all beneath its sway, even now, *whatever* he said about her.

Unless, talking sways, Lyon was beneath hers?

"And yet, she never offered herself to me." Lyon dragged a breath, looking at neither of them. "So? Miss Rhodes? Why do you want him?"

"Me?" Destiny Rhodes jerked up her chin. "Is there some other way to say you're being ridiculous? A complete and utter cretin? Well? Is that what you want to hear? Hmmm? I thought not. So? Where do you want me to start? With the fact I always have? But you see, it wasn't ladylike of me to say so, whatever he says about me."

"*What?* What the hell do you think you're doing?" Divers spun her round, glared into her hotly glazed eyes. An act. All of it an act. Even the way she thrust herself against him, leapt as if she wanted to eat him. Small wonder he shouted the words. "You know and I know you've never liked me. Ever. *Ever.* What is it? Do you want to get me damn well killed, is that it? Because of Ennis? Christ. Well, don't tempt me. Don't tempt me to--"

"Grant that a girl can change her mind, Divers."

"No, don't touch me."

"Can choose you. Yes. Because you made me."

He tried stopping her but she stood on tiptoe so her lips were inches from his before he could stop them. Her frosted breath mingled with his, her lips moist crimson in the moonlight. Hot, honeyed, succulent as her eyes, her manner, when life wasn't even sweet, was it?

"I made you nothing. All these years the belle of the county. You never needed to act then. But now? Christ, you want to take your turn on the stage in Drury Lane."

"If you ask me to. I'll do whatever."

"Then damn well, let go of me now. Do you hear? Get your lying, betraying, hands--"

"And still you want him? Stand aside," Lyon snarled.

"Fine. Then I will."

"Thank Christ for that," Divers muttered.

Now, just maybe, it would be possible to get out of this mess. How, he'd no idea but he clutched the bitter straw of hope. When death ..? Since that last job ..?

"Yes. I am nothing if not obedient. Something neither of you have ever really understood about me." Divers' heart sunk further down his boots as she went on, her eyes glittering in the moonlight. "In fact, I don't know that a lot of people have. To answer your question, seeing as Divers doesn't want to, although I never would have thought he'd win any prizes for being coy and retiring, he would for being good in bed. Not that I have any idea what you're like, *John*. No. But a woman doesn't have to, to know whether she might like--"

The noise ricocheted around the rocks, the foaming beach, sending the night birds screeching to the sky. Divers' whole life flew towards him on a slowing bullet. He saw his father riding through the long grass in the meadows at Connaught House. His mother, Kitty, her red hair tumbling down her back, walking barefoot along the terrace in the drowse of summer bees. And *Rose* ... Finally Rose.

In that second Rose, her eyes like black clouds, her mouth, a torn handkerchief, put out her hand to him, taking him home to the white walls of Connaught House, to everything that was in them, from the tumble of Latin books on the shelf behind the door, to the smell of tipsy apples stewing in the copper pot. To all that was his. Destiny Rhodes sank to her knees, then she sank into the sand. Her cheek thudded off the ground, sending grains spinning everywhere.

The candle of generosity that flamed inside him extinguished the fury at her treachery. In fact it extinguished everything—even the fact she'd called Lyon *John*-- except the ice cold agony in his brain. She had stepped in front of him. Why the hell had she stepped in front of him and taken what was meant for him? So now? Now she lay there. A dark stain, a dying cloak, water swirling around her. He thudded onto to his own knees trying desperately to gather her up, everything washing past and around him, wheeling above his head, like birds in slow motion. Dead? His breath tore. She couldn't be dead. But her flesh was cold, shrunken beneath his fingertips, her body like ice as he dragged it against him.

"Destiny ... Christ, girl, come on, speak, *speak to me*," the words also tore, ripped by the wind from his throat as he shouted them. But this wasn't happening. It wasn't happening. Connaught House? How the hell could he be there one minute and here the next? "No ... It's all right. You're all right. You're not Eirwin. It's all right. It's going to be all right." He pressed his mouth to her hair.

"Jesus ... man ... You've killed her." Gil leapt up, his eyes raked by specters.

"On that you're wrong, if that is what you think." Lyon's voice shook. "What I've done is rid the county of—"

"Oh, I'm sure you *think* you have, old chap, but I am afraid I rather agree with Mr. Wryson here that you have killed her—*my God*--whether you meant to is, of course, debatable."

Astonishment raked what tiny bit there was left of Divers scalp to rake. Orwell Rhodes, dapper in his perpetual cream coat and green neck-tie, moonlight glittering on the silver handle of his cane, and whatever laced his eyes, fell on his knees beside Divers, his face somber as a tomb.

"I've no doubt that Mr. O'Roarke is who you were aiming for. But, from where I'm sitting, I have to say that your aim is none too good. And so you've shot her dead. My sister. My God. How could you do this?"

"He hasn't." Divers held her limp body closer, fighting what tore at his lungs. "She's not dead—"

"Well, she's not moving that's for sure, old chap. But, thank the Lord, there are penalties. Yes, even here in this God forsaken place, for this sort of thing. My sister. You've killed my sister." Orwell pressed his fingertips to the drops that ran like quicksilver from his eyes.

"Mr. Rhodes, she killed her—"

"He's right." Had Divers ever thought to see the day he would see eye to eye with Orwell but Destiny Rhodes was lifeless against his chest. There was a first for everything, including the fact his tongue felt like nails in his mouth. But it was the least he could do now. "This is murder." There was a first for letting go too of a cover that was already blown. What the hell had she done this for? Nothing, if he let this go. He couldn't let it go. Her body maybe for now but not this. Never this. Somehow he struggled to his feet, tossed the hair back from his face. "You, men ... You know who I really am. You know we wear the same uniform. This is twice now this man has murdered a woman simply because she was with me. Because he could. Because you let him away with it the first time. And me? I had to pretend I didn't wear your uniform. But I do. And I'm done pretending. I'm stripping him of his command. Arrest him."

"A good try but you wouldn't dare."

"But I do dare. Just as you've dared twice now. I dare I'll see you on the gallows too."

"Not when it becomes known who you really are. *What* you really are."

"I'm Divers O'Roarke, once of Connaught House in Cork. Try as you might, turn up what you like, you won't find any more than that."

"Oh, I think the record will show—"

"Now take him." He flicked his gaze to the excisemen, dark in their corded coats in the sliver of moonlight, eased a frozen breath. Dares also needed a certain level of calm. He *was* second-in-command. Being that wasn't worth a chipped farthing if no-one obeyed him.

If he leapt at this man with the black fury that was boiling in his veins, the desolation that scalded them dry, as Christ was his witness, he'd do no good if Lyon levelled that pistol on him and he'd been no good to Eirwin. "Not that it should matter but this woman has connections here. You can't go around shooting those that do."

"Well said, old chap." Orwell pressed Destiny's lifeless hand to his chest. "Well said."

"I'm not your chap and I'm not old. Now ... " Ignoring the nerve ticking in his cheek, he glared at the man closest. "Do it."

By Christ he'd never been so desperate to see anyone obey him in his life. Destiny Rhodes had her uses, Orwell did too, although the pleasure any of that might once have given him festered like poison in his veins. He couldn't look as Lyon surrendered his pistol, was hand-cuffed, led away, each sound searing itself into his senses, until there was only the quiet rise and fall of the waves and maybe what breath was left in his lungs.

And then there he was standing on the shore as men he'd come to know were hustled past him by men he knew better. At his feet kegs bobbed at crazy angles, the sound echoing in his heart. This was his life going down here, because whatever he was, or wasn't, whichever way he looked at it, he'd gotten involved. It didn't matter he'd never touched what he'd taken. The fact was he had it. He'd got involved with Destiny Rhodes too. He had to, to feel like this.

Jesus Christ. Now what? Apart from closing his eyes, drawing another breath into his tortured lungs, flicking his eyes back open, trying not to stagger into the waves and vent his agony to the heavens, to the horizon, to the sky that wouldn't hear him. *Now what?*

A voice spoke, a familiar voice that cut into what was left of his senses,

"Has that sodding stoat gone yet?"

***

Destiny Rhodes. How the hell could it be, not just Destiny Rhodes, but Destiny Rhodes sitting up? "Oh, for any's sake Divers, please stop trying to win first prize in the *oh, how amazed am I* competition, by letting your jaw lie about the sand like that--and help me up." She held out her hand. "You didn't seriously think I'd take a bullet for you. Now, did you?"

He didn't. He didn't anything for the shock that thudded through him, driving his breath to the four corners of his being. Destiny Rhodes ... Destiny Rhodes was alive. Not just alive, alive and holding court in that *matter of fact, I'll just open me mouth* way. How the bloody hell was that when he'd just seen her die?

His mind reeled but he clasped her hand. Christ, he didn't for one moment imagine she'd go to all these lengths for him either. Time was all she'd bought and what would be the point of spending herself on that? For him? He hardly needed it. Orwell dropped his funereal expression as if it was a hot coal.

"Destiny, old girl ... "

"Well, it's not me sodding namesake. For God's sake, Orwell, who invited you to the party?"

"I ... I saw you go out. I thought ... I thought you were mad but you did it."

"I did. Yes. Sir Tredwynne's breastplate does have its uses. But that doesn't explain why you followed me."

"Because I knew you had the old chap's breastplate. I knew you were up to something. And then ... then I could see Divers here needed a bit of help."

"Well, while I didn't take a bullet, I did do this for you, Divers. Lyon was going to kill you. Come hell, or high water he had you in his sights. He knew you and Gil were on the take. But now, now you can take charge of this, clear your name. I've bought you the chance while he's locked up."

"Bought me the chance?" Oh, how quickly did he go from one thing to another? But what was he missing here? The fact she'd squawked once too often and felt obliged to row backwards? That she *had* told Lyon he was the Cleanser? "Jesus, Destiny, while I'd like to thank you for the stunt you've just pulled off, how the hell is that buying anything when he finds out you're alive? And comes after you? Well?" He gestured hopelessly. Her gaze, confident in the moonlight, met his.

"Oh, it's quite simple. In fact I'm surprised a man of your undercover capabilities hasn't thought of it. I will just claim one thing, in addition to Doom Bar Hall, which you will give me. Yes. Don't you see? I was only ... "

Wounded? Was that the word her lips died on? But then she glanced down at what coated her moonlit fingers. A crimson, seeping stain that crept as if from an ancient crypt, onto the stomach of her gown.

Blood.

Hers.

CHAPTER TWENTY FIVE

Never mind tiresome. Or impossible. Lyon couldn't have shot her beneath the edge of the breastplate? With Doom Bar Hall in her sights too? What kind of justice was that? She hadn't felt a thing. Yet, now she did. A slow sinking of her blood to subterranean levels she hadn't known existed. When she'd *had* to do this.

So Divers O'Roarke, his equally boundless aura of power, his ceaselessly handsome body, and all the things she tried so hard to hate him for, never troubled anyone here again. So that she was free, not just of him, of Lyon, from this situation that would otherwise have bound her to him, in chains.

Because she didn't hate *him*. She just couldn't, wouldn't, love him. Someone as cursed as her—how else could she have been shot?—should let their heart be empty. And hers was. What was more she'd done a not very nice thing saying he was the Cleanser, even if he was.

Down. Down. Down.

All the way to dusty death. While she'd died a thousand times before, she'd never really died. Not so all she could see was the retreating threads on the breast of Divers O'Roarke's coat. Soft, weaving beneath her fingertips, laced by damp and smelling of the ocean. Going now, replaced by the thud of his heart against her ear as her head bumped against his chest. "Christ, man ... " Replaced by his blurry voice too, the drip, drip of water around her in the strangely roofed darkness. "What the hell is this place?"

Well, what the hell was it? The passage to hell? She tried raising her head, failed.

"Oh, I imagine it's what you've been looking for, old chap." Orwell's voice? Was that Orwell's voice? Or a muddy echo? She couldn't tell, only that her teeth chattered. "For some of the time anyway. But let's just say it's the quickest way of getting her to the house now. I'm not going to stand on ceremony about that. She's my sister and she's wounded."

"You mean she did know of … ?"

"No, no. Not guilty. She believed Raven's Passage was the stuff of legend. In many ways it is. The gold business? That's legend."

What? Only her heart hammered so loudly, had she misheard?

"And how the hell do you know it's not legend? What the hell were you really doing on that beach tonight?"

"What do you think, old chap? That I'm really the drunk everyone thinks me? No. The answer is quite simple. Ridiculously simple. Because I'm the one you're all looking for. I'm the Cleanser."

***

The Cleanser? That was what she'd heard anyway. My God. When she'd said it was Divers O'Roarke? How could it not be Divers O'Roarke? No wonder her whole body juddered as he eased her onto the mattress in her bedroom and her breath caught. How had she even come to be in her room? She tried to speak but nothing came.

"Easy, girl. Not just now. I've got you. Do you hear? Bring the lamp, Gil."

"Sir … you're not …"

Not what? She wanted to know but how could she when everything had black edges, her teeth were making a funny noise and Orwell …? Orwell was the Cleanser. And he'd told Divers. Why? Because he knew what? That Divers might turn a blind eye? Unless? Unless, there was some other more sinister reason Orwell had told him? My God. A lot of good he'd be to her then. As for her noble sacrifice? As for getting Doom Bar Hall if Lyon got free? As for *anything*? If she could stop juddering she'd know but she couldn't. As to why she was juddering?

"*Now* Gil. It's all right, Destiny. You're all right."

Never mind her, what about Great Grandmother Endelienta's sewing box as he upended it, raking through the contents? The clatter as it hit the boards showed the most shocking lack of respect for its age and welfare. She tried saying so but who was she to argue when she couldn't speak? And she'd done this awful, awful thing? This thing that made her shake harder--did the bed frame rattle? This thing she could of course deny.

"I need you to hold still."

"W-what d-d-do you t-t-t-think I'm trying to do? Judder uncontrollably for the g-g-g-good of m-m-me health?"

Ignoring her he bent closer, so the dark wing of hair fell over his brow. "I'm going to look at this."

Not when the farthing dropped that Lyon had told he truth on that beach. But maybe that was why he snatched the scissors? So he could stick her with them before she could say what a lie, shocking and unprecedented told by people who didn't like her, it was. But should she? The struggle, the struggle, when she was going down through black clouds, as if she was a marionette whose strings had been cut and these clouds were rushing up to meet her was too much.

Down, down.

She hit the bottom of the well even as she struggled to surface. She had done a terrible thing betraying him to Lyon. And still, here he was trying to save her. Well, he couldn't. She didn't need his salvation. She was going to Ennis. It was all she wanted now. And so very easy when she thought of every cliff edge she had ever stood on in these past two years. And, oh God, there had been many. But Orwell was the Cleanser. She needed Divers O'Roarke to sod off now before a different net closed about him.

She knew exactly how to get him to do it too.

After all, tell him the truth and she wouldn't see him for dust.

"D-Divers ... P-please listen. I h-have something t-t-to t-t-ell you. On that b-beach, L-Lyon w-wasn't lying. A-About m-m-me an-an-and ... H-he was telling t-t-the truth ... "

"Not just now, girl, he's not capable. So ..?" Dragging his gaze and his fingertips from her face, he grasped the scisssors. "What you said back there in Raven's Passage, Orwell, is it something I should worry about? Or not?"

Maybe his throat had tightened, his hands were trembling--no wonder given that nightmare journey off that beach, not to mention that startling revelation, step one, *was still step one here*. He ran the scissor blade through the candle flame.

"What? Christ, man, you're not seriously going to slice her up?" Orwell ran his fingers through his hair. "We *need* to get a doctor."

"Divers knows what he's doing." Gil set the candlestick on the bedside table.

Christ, he only hoped, given what glazed his palms. "But to answer your question, I could, of course, make the wrong incision."

He wouldn't but as he cut into her bodice, it did no harm to say. Orwell was the Cleanser. The scores it settled, the slates it wiped forever clean, *were* almost too good to be true. And things that were, generally weren't. But here he was and he wasn't going any time soon either. How could he? As it was he'd no idea if he could save her. So he needed to know the hunter had not become the hunted.

"D-Divers ... No. L-listen, w-whatever you s-say, I did ... I've done an awful t-thing. Such an awful t-thing to ..."

"Well, I am the Cleanser. Good God, yes. But that doesn't mean I'm anything to be feared, old chap. That's just balderdash. Do I look like anyone to be feared? No. Surely you see we just had to do something here about you excisemen snooping about wrecking our trade. And really, if you want to know the truth—*I'd be a damn site happier if you'd just let me ride for the physician.*"

Another snip. Now to get the breastplate off. "Worrying you, am I?"

"Yes! I mean no. I mean ... Well." Orwell took out a handkerchief and mopped his brow. "You're not exactly inspiring me with confidence, old chap. And Havelock lives ... *Havelock lives not a quarter hour's ride away.* I could go—"

"We don't doubt that you could, sir." Gil now set a basin of water down in the candlelight. "The question is who else lives not a quarter hour's ride away I'd say, if you don't mind me saying. The question is who you might fetch."

"Me? Old chap? You think that I--while my sister lies dying-- would take the opportunity to turn you both over to the scum of the county?"

"In a word? Yes. Actually." Divers flicked his gaze sideways. The hell, was there no end to the bits of a woman's gown? The breastplate was welded to the chemise and the chemise was welded to her skin. He needed to see what he was dealing with. As things stood he'd no idea how bad this was, apart from the fact his fingers were sticky and she turned paler by the second. As for the hot, sweet smell burning incense-like in his nostrils? That wasn't just blood. It was death.

"Not when she's my sister. When she's—" Orwell dug in his pocket, for what Divers had no idea. But then again ..? He raised his head.

"I'm hardly going to kill her. But if you kill me—. Just think about it a moment, will you?"

"Then help her. *Just help her.*"

He paused. "In case you haven't noticed it's what I am trying to do. I'd do it better if you'd be quiet and take this." He edged the breastplate free.

"Very well. But she didn't do all this for you to stay here. Don't you see that? You should be at the jail, taking charge. Lyon thinks you are the Cleanser—"

"And don't think I need reminding why that probably is."

"D-D-Divers ... Y-you you m-must."

"I don't need reminding that you preferred she thought it was me either."

"I could have told her. I accept it." Orwell took the bloodied breastplate Divers handed him. "I should have. But then what? You know what a damnable loose cannon she is when she gets going—"

"But as for me going right now ...?" He peeled the last piece of chemise back. At last. At last he was through the sodden silk. As for what he saw? Was it better or worse than he expected? He hauled a breath into his screaming lungs.

"I h-have d-done a terrible t-thing to y-you. The m-most terible t-thing." Right on cue she caught his hand. The level of tenderness that rose in his gut, swamped everything else.

"That's not possible, girl."

"Yes. It is. B-because I did. I did it. I b-betrayed y-you. I betrayed y-you to Lyon. I t-told him y-you were the C-Cleanser. And I need ... I just n-need your ..."

He swallowed. What? His forgiveness? She had taken a bullet for him. She could have it with bells on. Sodding ones at that. Now he saw how shrunken, how haggard, how pale she was, what the hell else could he do here but give it? Lyon could just as easily have shot her in the head. So yes. Yes, he gave it.

He parted his lips. *But maybe that was what she wanted Lyon to do?* Bloody hell, the thought thudded, raking his scalp with shock, along with the thought it was something he understood. And he did. He understood. Only too well he understood. *Everything.* He leaned closer.

"And I don't forgive you if that's what you want to hear—"

"But, you--you m-must—. Ennis. E-Ennis is waiting. H-he is waiting f-for me."

Well, wasn't that too bad? So whatever Divers *must* he wasn't doing it. Not when what *he must* was get out of here and how the fecking hell could he do that if she died here on this bed? It was the most ridiculous thing. Forgive her indeed. ulous thing. Forgive her indeed. WAll so she could go to Ennis? Who hadn't even damn well troubled himself to secure her future?

But it wasn't just that, was it, that made him speak?

"No. No, he's not. And I'm the one who makes you feel alive. Not bloody Ennis. So if that's what you want my forgiveness for, so you can go to wherever little heaven you think you can have with him and sit about on clouds, playing golden harps all day long, I won't give it. Do you hear me?"

"But I'm n-not going t-to make—"

"Not while there's still breath in my body. Because that's not forgiveness. That's giving in. That's letting you go to Ennis when I'm not going to, when *I* want you to live which Rose, which Eirwin, which Ennis never got the chance to do, because of the trail, the trail of breadcrumbs that leads back to the first night I ever walked in this house, all these years ago. You are going to make it. So you stop all that rubbish you're spouting like a broken watering can—"

"It's n-not rubbish."

"Because I'm not letting you go. Do you understand? And what I need, what I need you to do is press this till Havelock's here, all right? Because Orwell's right. Yes he is. And it's all of it all right. Just hold this handkerchief here, okay." He raked in his pocket. "Can you do that? Keep the pressure on till Havelock's here? I want your word. You do not let go. I want you here till I come back. Then we'll talk forgiveness. It's the only way to have mine."

Because it was.

The wound? All right the wound seeped blood, was possibly not as deep as it might have been and yes, the sweet smell mingled with the sickly candlelight. Yes, her teeth were chattering. But a quarter hour's ride? A half hour all told? Provided Havelock was there? She'd be all right. He had no choice if he wanted her to live. And he did. He could not lose her. What? To Ennis?

Orwell stepped forward. "I can do it for her, old chap."

Hardly reassuring. In fact she really must be in a bad way because the wonder was she didn't say so. But for him to do anything else was ridiculous. Orwell Rhodes had not been on that beach by chance. If *he* didn't take charge it would be *his* head on a platter. Wasn't it bad enough that in some ways, his heart already was? When that moment when she'd fallen on the sand reverberated like a gunshot in his mind?

Equally maybe she was stunned by the thought she couldn't waltz off with Ennis with his blessing? And that was why her gaze flickered to the side?

"Then you keep her alive till I come back. Do you hear that, Destiny?"

Calm and measured. Calm and measured. Although surprise rippled at how he had risen to this with a passion. All the more reason to add, "What's more. Just think, I'll also see you get Doom Bar Hall."

Now that. *That* was something he should have put on the table sooner, the obedience with which her fingers brushed the handkerchief.

He snagged another breath. Now to reach the door and more importantly the handle. He turned.

Rose.

Damn it all to the furthest reaches of hell. He hadn't imagined her in weeks. He didn't imagine her now. Just the words, the words Destiny Rhodes had said that night, before he'd said what he had.

'You're not seriously blaming Chancery, are you, for what is her doing? Whatever is being said, mainly by her, I never egged him on. How could you think I'm that bad?'

Was that what Rose needed so badly to put right though? What, all along had been staring him in the face? What the man he'd once been would have seen far sooner? It was only the one he'd become who couldn't afford to, even as he'd wanted to. The thing he already knew.

The thing about him and who was for him really.

God, but he was kidding himself about why he needed this woman to live. Truly. Utterly, kidding himself. About why it had cut to his bones about Ennis too.

And that was when he fought to calm his hammering heart because he also knew, he couldn't leave here. Not right now. Not when he could remove that bullet and he could stitch that wound. He could be the one to save her.

But whether he could give Rose what she really wanted was another thing altogether, the places his head was in right now and the things he was being asked to forgive.

CHAPTER TWENTY SIX

Destiny was not expecting heaven exactly, which was why surprise rippled. She was there, despite causing all these men to shoot each other and themselves. And she was not alone in the billowing white, the softness of clouds—amazing as a spring day. On the lonely streets of her heart she walked, she'd known the baby was a girl. She'd even chosen a name. And now Evadne wasn't standing on every corner, always out of reach, no matter how Destiny strove to reach her, followed her down the dark and cavernous places of her mind. No, her hand, hot with a child's clamminess, sat in Destiny's. And they laughed. How they laughed. So the sound sat warm in Destiny's heart, the forlorn places she'd forgotten existed. Was it any wonder she sighed?

How beautiful was death, not to have to struggle any more. To be here finally lying here in Divers O'Roarke's arms, his breath warm on her forehead.

Divers O'Roarke?

Destiny flicked an eye open, shut, then open again. Why was Divers O'Roarke still here? Dressed if nothing else? Forget the fact there was but one answer--because *she* wasn't in heaven. Why the hell would she be in heaven, after all? Because she floated? Spun on like a snowflake. For just that second as he looked into her eyes and she looked into his. What else was there to do? She groaned. No. Starting with the hot pincers that someone had been sewn inside her skin, to the dry snake that circled her tongue, this was utter hell. Was it any wonder that, from head to toe, she couldn't stop shaking? And when she tried to speak she'd have won first prize in the *no-one had taught her* competition? Yes. Forget heaven. After last night and him knowing she'd done awful things to him, please just let her die now.

"Please just tell me that you've been to Penvellyn."

She tried to speak. But obviously she didn't do it very well, or warm brandy wouldn't spice her tongue.

"Easy. Here."

It wouldn't spill out of the corners of her mouth and down her cheeks either because she couldn't sit up to drink it. Was that why he was still here? She couldn't even sodding feed herself? Oh Christ, she hoped so. After what she'd done to him, anything else would finish her. She coughed.

As for why *she* was still here? Maybe even hell didn't want her? It was not outwith the bounds of possibility. She coughed again, so her eyes watered.

"Please. Just tell me—"

"What?" He reached across her to set the glass down. "And miss all your raving about Evadne?"

Oh Christ, how could she? So? She wasn't imagining that wet and cold and sea-sprayed as he'd been, it was still the warmth in his blood that had kept her teeth from chattering in the middle of the night, while the breath was ragged in her throat and she'd shook from head to toe? When he could have let her go? She'd talked bags of prize rubbish to him too. But maybe *that* was why he was still here? So he could hear her talk some more? Evadne? Even the name was stupid to her now. It wasn't the only thing. She turned her face to the side, flicked her eyes shut.

"Divers ... I ... "

"So? Who is she, Destiny?"

"Well, she's not one of Grandfather Austell's parrots. I'll tell you that."

Such a cheap way to talk about Evadne. But what the hell was she meant to say when she couldn't even punch the pillow to her satisfaction? Turn over and hug it to her head for the hot pincers in her side either? A side *he'd* removed a bullet from, deftly, carefully, his knuckles brushing her skin as he'd stitched it up again, when he could have left her to it after what she'd done. Well? '*Evadne is the life your curse took from me. That curse you rashly and misguidedly uttered. Don't you know? Because you didn't like me.*' Not that many people did, so she didn't blame him.

The last thing she ever wanted was to win someone's pity, in the local, *let's all pity her* competition. Them wearing their guilt like a beggar's badge on their sleeve either, so they'd sit here and keep her company when she'd betrayed them something rotten. This wasn't about pity. Truth to tell, it was hard, with her body feeling as panned in as her head, to know what this was about.

But last night it had been about Doom Bar Hall. About her settling this to her satisfaction, which many might say, she hadn't done or she wouldn't exactly be lying here, beating everyone else hands down in the *dying swan* competition. So really, the sooner he went and dealt with Lyon, the better.

She'd live. She always did. Look at last night. When she'd wanted finally to go to Ennis, who had stopped her? What way was that to carry on exactly? Certainly not in a way that filled her heart with the joy of *them* being together now, or any time soon.

Although it well-nigh killed her she ran her tongue over her lips. Then she turned her head to face him--something that killed her full-nigh funnily enough, except she wasn't laughing.

Well, he went to Penvellyn, he took charge, Lyon got sent to London. She got Doom Bar Hall back for her services in saving a crown agent. She put up her Christmas garlands. That crown agent moved on. All in a day's work to him.

And her? Maybe he did make her feel alive—all right, he did or she wouldn't be looking now at all the bits of his face she still hadn't kissed--some might say feeling dead was preferable when all this mess resulted. And she would be one of them. There were things that could never be put back. Betrayal was certainly one. Task one? Let him go now. He was going to. And last night? Last night it was Ennis she'd wanted. Some bits of a heart could not be given away.

"I'll also tell you I never did this for to sit here talking *Evadne* to you. Lyon means to kill you, you know? He knows you were involved on that last job."

"I know why you did this."

Would he just take his sodding fingertips out of her sodding hair? Last night, when she'd opened her eyes and seen him there was one thing. But this?

"Well, good for you. He never needed me to tell him. Consignments have been short. Why do you think he killed Eirwin? So, what I need, what you need, is to go to Penvellyn and--"

"And you do realize, before you go further, I have a problem in terms of what to say about Orwell?"

"Orwell?"

He glanced down at her. "The Cleanser, in case you've forgotten."

"Right." *Great.* As if her head wasn't already so panned in, it was probably flatter than a battered bit of bacon on top, he took out the frying pan and finished the job. Why stop at *great*? Why not add *great* God Almighty. "*Orwell*?" Who'd only gone and lost Doom Bar Hall in the first place? And now was going to do it all over again, when she'd gone to such pains to secure it, that right now she couldn't rise from the sodding bed? "And that's why you're still here? Because of sodding Orwell? Well, thank God I hadn't seriously thought it was because I was knocking on death's door. I might otherwise have failed to recover. What? Because Orwell's me brother, you ..." she broke off.

But maybe it was?

He just struggled to say it. So there were things he thought she'd guess. And this was one. Because if he handed Orwell up, how would that stand between them? So this was on her to say so?

No wonder her eyes felt as if they'd sunk so far into the back of her head, she'd never see out of them again and her mouth was drier than last year's dust.

As if all that wasn't bad enough, the door flew open.

Talk of the devil and that devil always appeared.

As Divers O'Roarke tore his gaze from her expression, not quite as unreadable as worn Sanskrit, but not far off of it, he only knew he needed to make his the same. He snapped his mouth--which had opened in the hope of discussing this little problem-- shut. He also leapt off the bed.

Gil. *And* Orwell. Well, well? To what did he owe the dubious pleasure? When he was *what* exactly? Dallying with a traitoress because earlier she'd talked rather nicely—for her anyway--of things that had undermined him? And she'd been, not just strangely beguiling in her trembling, haggard beauty. She'd been quite cowed. For her anyway too.

Well, at least Lyon wasn't here, making things all manner of worse for him. He had the floor. As a man who'd tried, ye gods and their miniscule fishes, to explain his present dilemma, at that. Although he'd have liked her to understand a bit more of that dilemma, business was business.

He held up his hands. "All right, so you've come to drag me to Penvellyn jail to deal with Mr. Lyon? Let me save you the time by saying I'm ready and willing to come."

Because? Well? He'd have to now. It didn't mean he couldn't still ask for a moment here, talk to her first. Although equally, given how her soft, trembling body had worked on him in ways he'd never expected last night, maybe he should just leave now? How the world had passed from him in that moment when she first hit the sand, how he'd known fear, real fear for the first time last night, too. Business *was* business though. He'd made a good start. Maybe he had saved her, it was always going to be Ennis first with her. Why look a bigger fool than he already was? She'd done things to him but he'd done things to her too. Evadne? Evadne was one. And really, he had misjudged her for weeks, thinking she ran to Lyon when it wasn't with what he'd thought.

"Well, thank God for that." Gil's face wasn't just earnest it was white. "Have you not looked out the window, man? We need to go. You need to go. *Now.*"

Orwell's face was studied as a tomb. "And you need to play the dying swan, old girl."

"Pardon me, but what do you think I'm doing? Lying here for the good of me health, in which case I'm making a sodding muck of it?" she croaked.

Divers lowered his hands. Look out the window? No. He hadn't looked out the window. As to why he needed to?

"There's soldiers out there," Orwell added.

"*What?*" The bed creaked as she strove to sit up.

"They've got the place surrounded. No. Don't get up." Orwell gestured at her to lie back down. "Divers, you must go. You must go at once. I don't know what's up, whether Lyon, worryingly, has talked his way out of jail because—"

"*What?*"

She said it again as Divers crossed to the window. But then facing Christmas without her pine cone garlands and other things she'd flung herself on the table to keep, was probably bad enough. Facing it in jail was another matter, especially when, sure enough, the late afternoon drizzle was being brightened. And not by the sun peeping through the clouds either. The cheaply dyed uniforms were no trick of the eye, scarlet drops of blood in rusting foliage either. The Brown Besses, maximum range, or rather, best range for inflicting damage—hopefully on the house—fifty yards. Did he need an inch tape to measure the distance to the tumbledown wall they glinted above to know they could be fired with confidence, when this was what he did for a living? As for where the soldiers had been mustered from and why they were here ...? All the things he measured in an instant...?

"I told you, sir, we both did, you had to take charge. And now--"

"Whatever we said is of no importance, Gil," Orwell said. "What is, is that you and Divers leave here now before it's too late. Go by the passage. There's a boat. I took the precaution of leaving it on the beach there when you wouldn't leave last night."

"Divers." Gil yanked him back from the window. "There's no time. They're not surrounding the house fully armed, to parley, take up your offer of a cup of tea, with some fruit cake made by me thrown in. We need to get out of here *now*. Come on. This is over."

Well, yes, he could see that. Over in every sense of the word. More over than the life of a ten day old corpse. Should he just say he was too astonished trying to swallow what knotted his throat, to say so though?

Had him, didn't they, these damned Rhodes in every way?

So now? Like it, or not, he was going to have to start that new life. What the hell else could he do? Stand here and be killed in cold blood? What was it she'd said? *Don't make me care for you*? Chance would have been a fine thing. And he was still cursed.

Coat. Hat. He donned one, jammed the other on his head, brushed aside her mounting platitudes, whatever they were, as he shoved his pistol into his belt. He didn't even know what she said for what was ringing in his ears--the sounding bell of doom--and the way his heart dropped like a stone to his boots. Whatever Rose had whispered last night, he knew one thing.

That was goodbye to the woman who had cost him everything.

Because she had.

As he pulled his hat down over his eyes, he said so too.

"Whatever else you think, of you, of me, of us," he added. "I broke your fall last night."

Then he walked out the door.

***

The door shut, not a moment too soon--in fact a moment earlier might have been nice--but at least, now the door had shut, she could sink back on the bed. Not that she wanted to betray a weakness or anything, but when her head had just been panned in, how could she help it?

How dare he? Say she'd cost him everything he owned. A fine thanks for all she'd done for him. When, if everything she'd heard was to be believed—and some would say that it was--even the clothes on his back, did not appear to be *owned*. Certainly they were not *owned* by him. Everything about him was lies—the only things he did own. And, if he had become one with the smugglers, the chances were he'd lined the pockets he didn't own, with goods that weren't his either.

Honestly, the sodding cheek of some people knew no bounds and would win every *sodding cheek competition* going. As for that sodding guff about breaking her fall? Please don't tell her that in addition to raving about Evadne, she had shot her blabby big mouth off about how no-one ever did, while she was delirious? It was an odd thing to have said, standing there with that aura of power about him, so handsome, there she was again, looking at the bits of his face she hadn't kissed, remembering the bits she had.

Well fortunately, he was gone now, all she need do was arrange herself like a corpse on the pillow and wait. It would hardly be difficult. As it was her neck felt like it belonged to a giraffe with a broken one.

Orwell squared his insubstantial shoulders. "I say, are you ready for this, old girl? We'll be singing Christmas songs in no time. *'Bring ye the wassail bowl over here.'*"

"*Own?*" The word spilled from her mouth before she could stop it, when she'd meant to forget about it too. "What did he mean by *own?*"

"Destiny, whatever he meant is of no importance to us. Not now, old girl. Not when Lyon's men are ... " he broke off, his words arrested by the hammering at the front door. "Well, you can hear what they are ... "

"And why did you tell me things were being said about him when they probably weren't? Him being the Cleanser, so ... so I ... I only went and cost him his cover, didn't I? With Lyon on his heels. That's what he meant by *own.*"

These words fell too, despite her sterling efforts to nail her mouth shut and win the *dying swan* competition. But so long as no more words peppered the bed sheets, this was fine. And they wouldn't—task one. If she'd to stuff the pillow in her blabby mouth to clog her throat, tightening in ways she couldn't understand, they wouldn't.

"Look, old girl. Desperate times and all that. Now, come on. We still—*you still*, need to pull this off after all you said on that beach."

"Desperate times?" She tried plumping the pillow. "The only thing you've ever been desperate for in your life, so far as I've ever been able to see, is your next drink."

"A trifle harsh, I think."

"Harsh? You don't know the half of it. As for you thinking? When did you ever in your whole life think about more than *where* your next drink was—"

"*If* you don't mind me saying, that is."

"I do mind and I do say. And I will say this as well. *Did you lose Doom Bar Hall on purpose that night?*"

My God. She had never thought so before. Why do it now? Because Divers O'Roarke had gone, swaggered out the door, without a backwards glance, thinking the worst of her and *that* was a fire she couldn't rise from? Her throat, her voice, heart, blood, bones, were ashes at the thought. Of course she didn't feel quite well, but how could they be ashes? Because a man had gone? A man she didn't need? Didn't want? Didn't love? Surely? Couldn't let herself, even if she did feel any of these things? A man who had nothing? While she sat here with what? Doom Bar sodding Hall?

In that second she tore the covers off herself.

"Destiny …"

"No, don't bother answering me, Orwell. You just have."

"I am answering you."

"No. No, you're not."

"Well, obviously I was drunk and it may well be, that knowing, or more importantly, *seeing* him there, that night—"

"He told me he was the Cleanser. Why did he do that? Because he knew damn fine I was going to betray him?"

"Well, you are something of a clipe, old girl."

As if she needed him to tell her that. That battering at the door either. Somehow she grasped at the breath tearing her throat to pieces and swung her feet to the floor.

"I say, what are you doing?" Orwell demanded.

"What does it look like? I'm getting up."

"Jesus Christ, *no*. You can't. *You can't get up.* Now you listen to me." He snatched hold of her arm. "Someone had to stand up for our rights. Our rights *here.*"

"What rights? Smuggling ones?"

"What other ones can there be? This is how the world works here. For you, me, everyone here. Don't pretend you haven't dipped your cask. However I lost Doom Bar Hall. I have it back now guaranteed." He dragged her closer, dragged her so she'd to dig her heels in for purchase.

Guaranteed? My God. What she had wanted since the sorry evening it had been lost. And all she had to do was arrange herself on the bed and pretend to die like a graceful swan. She could do that. She would do that but the noise as her hand glanced off his jaw ricocheted around the room's sallow walls. The words, 'And I'll never lose it again,' petered into oblivion. The same one Divers O'Roarke would peter into if she didn't get her boots on and go after him because these soldiers weren't real soldiers, they were Orwell's militia. The real menace was someone else. She could get her boots on, couldn't she? Task one. Only her lungs had emptied of breath and her side couldn't be worse if a medieval torturer had just strapped her to a table and was giving it special attention with hot pincers.

"Jesus, old girl, are you mad? No. Don't answer that. Because it's clear you are. No. Don't push me away. Let's not forget, this man, no, listen—"

"Get your hands off me, Orwell, we're done."

"This man I've given an out to, incidentally, once cursed us. All these years ago."

"Just the once?" She tightened her jaw. "Oh, really, I'm surprised given everything we did to him, to Rose, on a daily basis—"

"He cursed you, me, Chancery. You most of all. *Think* how different your life would now be if he hadn't uttered these damnable words. When Chancery loved Rose. Wanted to marry her, for God's sake. That Divers O'Roarke didn't know is no damned excuse."

"I am thinking. And I'm thinking we are the life we live. Its graces and its pain. And while we may not always have any control over it, we can control what we do about it. But if you want to believe in a load of old gypsy mutterings and superstition and hold it responsible for the fact you can't walk past a drink, without feeling obliged to down and then drown in it, that's your choice. This is mine."

Because suddenly it was.

CHAPTER TWENTY SEVEN

Reaching the windswept shore Divers O'Roarke knew one thing. Maybe Destiny Rhodes had done him a favor by holing the boat beneath him, so he'd no choice but to swim for the shore; when he was swimming there he was well shot of her, of the Rhodes. Surely?

As he inched through the cracks in the rock overhung by dead bracken and withered tufts of marram grass, he saw it, the only thing he wanted to see, oiled by moonlight. Not Destiny Rhodes, not Rose, not that damned mausoleum standing like a skull on the cliff top. He saw the rowing boat Orwell had promised, a shapeless hulk, draped in tarpaulins and nets.

"Hurry, man." Gil's voice was just the match for the howling gale. "We need to launch it. Then … I don't know about you, but I need to get out of here."

The tarpaulin was oily beneath Divers fingers. "Oh, I'll be joining you. Push. We can get to everything else later."

Things like the mess he'd made in other words. As it was, he was just about holding this together. Square one was a place he wasn't unaccustomed to occupying. Thinking about it now, about getting to square two, could prove his undoing. He might stay a stranger to square two, after all. Forget the perils of clambering aboard this rickety boat in a frothing sea, he'd damn all to his name. The sand slapped around his ankles. At least the fecking boat wasn't holed, had oars and was stocked. If they could make it around the coast in it, they'd have a fighting chance. He'd been in worse, hadn't he? And they did have some stolen goods. Not touching them now wasn't an option.

He dug his heels in harder. Gil tossed the hair out of his eyes.

"Don't worry about it, sir, we'll be all right. So long as we get out of here."

"That depends on where you're going, don't you think?"

The press of cold steel against his temple, snap of a twig underfoot, click of a pistol being cocked iced his spine. Then there was the voice. The one he heard in his worst nightmares. *Lyon.*

"Hell, now, Mr. O'Roarke? Hell isn't the place to be all right in, unless you've done a deal with the devil. But then, maybe you have? Certainly you've broken any we had."

Divers swallowed. His gaze skittered sideways. Hell's teeth, but he should have gone to Penvellyn, should have taken charge while he'd had the chance. Now that chance was as much dust as he was soon going to be. And for what? Christ Almighty, he had cursed himself. And there was nothing except the moon and the cold stars overheard to save him. How could he have longed for such wrathful vengeance? He was done. Him and Gil. And all because of Destiny Rhodes. A stupid passion not to have just let her die and go to her sodding Ennis as she'd asked him to. Why hadn't he? Because in his heart he'd never moved past being the boy she didn't want? It didn't matter how he touched her, what he did.

"Now, let go of the boat. Both of you." Lyon's voice was ice cold. "I mean it, I may be alone but I will shoot first one and then the other and claim self defense, if you don't. That's it. The only options which are open to you both."

"But ... "

Divers' throat tightened. It was like Gil to try and save this as Gil had tried to save so much because of the one time he hadn't even been able to save himself. The thought forced him to speak.

"Leave Gil out of this, will you? Although really, I don't know quite what I'm meant to have done. I didn't think that being absent when I'm undercover merits being shot."

"Oh, you know perfectly what you've done. Who you are, really are—"

"Chance would be a fine thing."

He couldn't help it. He sighed. He probably rolled his eyes too. Here it was again, The old sweet song. What he was. When it was things he wasn't. A man who had lost his way perhaps? But that was it. Show him the man who hadn't. He'd show you the man who hadn't lived. It was the price of the game, wasn't it? No more. No less. But this? This, if he couldn't stop it, this could be the finish. And how was he going to stop it? He was armed, yes, but his pistol was stuck in his belt. As for Gil? Gil had never been any bloody good at this bit of the game.

"You always were a cocky bastard. But don't make the mistake of thinking I don't know. You're not innocent. Even if you're not the Cleanser, you're hardly lily-white."

"Lily White? No. That's true. I was never *her*. Everyone else maybe—"

"You see? Cocky. Now let go of the boat and step aside, or this bullet, this bullet I've been keeping for you since that day my pocket was picked by Teezer's Travelling Troupers, is going to wind up in what there is of your brain."

"Nice to know you think I have--"

"And this one will end up in yours."

The voice was low and throaty. The voice had always been capable of making ribbons of a man's gut. But in this instance Divers' throat and breath were the things in tatters. Destiny Rhodes. What the hell was Destiny Rhodes doing here? Not that he wasn't that tiny bit glad to see her. Where was the end to her stupidity? In her state Lyon would overpower her in seconds and all Divers' saving of her would be for nothing. The saving that meant the cold steel of a gun was now jammed against his temple.

"Destiny ... "

"I mean it, Divers. If I have to, I will kill him."

"I'm sorry, old chap, but I'm afraid she does," Orwell spoke above the waves thrashing against the rocks. "I tried to stop her. I'm sure as you know yourself; you might as well try holding the tide there back with a fishing net. A torn one at that."

"I can't begin to tell you what that vote of confidence means to me. *Now,* put the gun down."

The click as she cocked the pistol matched the click in Divers' throat. Maybe Lyon's too for that matter. Divers' heart thudded above the crashing waves, the wind tearing his tear. Icy drips of sweat beaded his forehead.

"So? You are alive, Miss Rhodes?" Lyon said. "Your brother did say as much."

"You sound disappointed. But ask yourself, why don't you, would a corpse be standing here with a gun to your head? Ready to pull the trigger too? Well? And let's just leave Orwell out of this, shall we? He's no brother of mine, not any more. And you did shoot me actually. That was no lie."

"So Mr. Rhodes said. And I would like to leave him out of this but it's just that he has bargained for Doom Bar Hall."

"Doom Bar Hall?"

"Yes."

Here it was. The fly in any ointment, no matter how sweet, or soothing. The one thing she'd never part with in a million years. She was a Rhodes. And a Rhodes could never, ever be without their crumbling staff and anchor, their once palatial palace, upon which crawled the flies of doom. Maybe he had gone to places he shouldn't have gone with her? And so he'd said what he had about what she'd cost him? But he was done for sure enough. Lyon might as well hand him the shovel to dig his own grave now.

"You really think I care about Doom Bar Hall?"

"Do I think you have a certain affinity for it? Yes. Yes I do. Perhaps you just didn't have that affinity with me in it, but--"

"*Drop the gun*. Now, I say. And I'm not for hanging about either."

Divers flicked his gaze to the side, masked the shiver that stole up his spine. So that was what she'd traded? Her? And Lyon? And now? Now Lyon laid a different card on the table, Divers knew one thing. When it came to guns and dropping, *hers* would be lying on the sand. It didn't matter what she said. Not now Pandora's box was open.

"Very well." Astonishment rippled as Lyon's gun thudded onto the sand. "But I know ... I know my words have weight. Besides, shoot me and you will have to dispose of the body, or face having every exciseman in the country and every bailiff and magistrate hunt you down. You will hang. It is that simple. So really, Miss Rhodes, don't you think we should come to some—"

"That's where you're wrong. No-one found Raven's Passage in thirty years of looking. So they're not going to find me. Divers, get in the boat. Now."

"Aid his escape and the law will come looking. You know this. I know this."

"Goodness. And I will start trembling in me boots. You know, already I fear my heart has missed all of twenty five beats. Divers, do as I ask. You too, Gil. Go on."

Gil's look of surprise, of exaltation even, was tempered by what thudded through Divers. Lyon was right. He would never let this go. He'd hunt them to the four corners of the earth and he'd arrest her. If he went he'd be leaving her to that fate. Unless? Unless this wasn't bluff. Unless ..?

"And don't take all night," she added. "Stand about debating it either."

Gil was fast but Lyon was faster. He bent for the gun lying on the sand. But Destiny Rhodes was faster than any. In one movement she kicked it aside and rounded *him*, so there she was in Divers' line of vision, the primed pistol jammed just above Lyon's left eye, her face, a ghost ship in the moonlight, an inky patch on the waist of her gown. Christ, the bloody wound must have opened.

"The boat, Divers."

"Destiny ..."

"*Now*. I won't tell you again. I'm fine. I swear it. I'm absolutely perfect ... "

Sinking onto the sand, in this perishing cold too, the gun still leveled on Lyon, was what she was. With a churning in his gut he knew he must reach it but even before that, he must reach *her*. Whatever he'd said about her and what she'd cost him, was nothing suddenly to what it would cost him, *if* he didn't break her fall, didn't save her. Christ, she'd haunt him for a start and already the ghosts he carried were bad enough. Could he take *her* barging into his thoughts?

But it wasn't just that that made him leap forward when what anyone in their right mind would be leaping for was the gun, or the boat. How could she have got so far beneath his skin she was trapped there? And he was trapped because of it? Or was it that she'd always been there, living in some part of himself? A part his old self could acknowledge, but what he'd become couldn't let in? So he'd had to keep her separate? Whatever? In this dangerous game he'd played with her, knowing her touch was death. He loved her. He always had from her imperfect heart, to her dauntless bones, because she wasn't all imperfect or dauntless, was she?.

He just had had to wrestle that bit of himself to the ground. Sleeping with the enemy was never easy and she had been the enemy. It was why, even last night, he'd been tempted to run. He must have made her care for him a little to now be this cursed that he stood on the edge of losing everything. Her above all else. He eased the gun from her quivering fingers, hooked his arm around her waist.

"Please, D-Divers ... l-let me go, let me go, I'm fine. I swear it."

"Not in a month of Sundays, Saturdays too, girl."

"Divers ... "

"I'm not doing it."

Whatever she'd done, she'd done to save him. And he damn well should have taken charge while he had the chance, but somehow that teeth of hell business of Evadne had totally undercut him. How the hell was he meant to leave a woman who dreamt in these terms of torture? Christ, these moments last night when she'd been a trembling wreck had totally undercut him because these moments had shown him the woman she was beneath her rock-hard front. And ever since he'd stepped, besieged, into this howling maelstrom, he'd been struggling, to hold to a life he didn't want, not to grab the one he could have, *because there was no life there.*

Even now, dragging her so close, her soft, but sharp, bones melted into his, *there was no life. Not there, not anywhere.* The maelstrom was one he walked in alone. He was the architect of his own destruction and that building, slowly crumbling, had caved in about him. All he knew was he couldn't let her go, here now.

Looking back on every cut, every gibe, every wound, every flicker of her eyelids, since that first night he'd clapped eyes on her, a boy of eight, peeping out from his step mother's shadow, dwarfed by the one *she'd* cast, in the darkened recesses of that accursed house, he hadn't been able to do that. It hadn't mattered he'd let her go, it didn't matter he'd walked away, that he'd never been anything in her life and seeing her again, was the last thing on Earth he'd expected. She'd been there with her shuttered face, haunting his dreams.

"Divers ... " Her breath snagged the back of her throat. Jesus Christ, don't tell him it was her last. Or, if not, it wasn't far from it. "Divers ... Please ... The boat ... the boat, now ... "

"Well, isn't this nice? The nicest thing I've ever seen. And given my line of work, that's quite a great deal."

He froze. *Lyon*. How could he have forgotten Lyon and the gun he'd had? Especially now that gun, silvered by moonlight, was pointed at them.

"**A**rgue, argue, argue." As Lyon stepped forward, Destiny's heart lurched. "Do you know how much of an old married couple you sound? *Divers this, Destiny that*. Of course I knew from the start there was something between you. I just wondered when you were going to get round to running away together, as I know Mr. O'Roarke here wanted to do with Eirwin St. James on that last little job he messed up."

"Really?" Destiny spoke with a confidence she was oceans away from feeling. *Messed up* were not words she wanted to hear here when her side was dying on her. But if she didn't speak, she never would. "And you somehow think this is of interest to me because ... well, why? No-one ever wanted to run away with you, is that it?"

"I considered you, Miss Rhodes—"

"Really? In your dreams was it?"

"--despite the sharp tongued bitch you are. Uh—" Divers O'Roarke lunged forward. "Stay exactly where you are, or I'll shoot her where she stands."

"Look, it's me you want not her. Let her go and I will come with you. I *swear* it. Look, I'll even do this." Leaning forward he set the pistol slowly down on the sand. "There. Just … just … "

"Divers? What the hell—?" *Had he done that for? Given away their insurance?* "When I went to all that sodding trouble to get that? How could you? Are you mad?"

"To hang for treason, theft?" Lyon didn't move. "Possibly he is. Because that's what's going to happen. Even nobler, don't you think, Miss Rhodes, which is why, really when it comes to throwing yourself in with a man, you should have a little more care and consideration?"

"I'll have what I sodding well want. And that won't be you, you prune-faced—"

"*Destiny*. Much as I share your sentiments, now is not the time—"

"Then when is the time? Because I'm telling you now. You can't … you can't give yourself up. I won't … I won't let you."

Actually she could. She easily could. In fact shock waves rocketed to her core to see how easily she could and it would be an end to everything. But that was her, wasn't it, push things as far as she could, because she could rise again and in that second she was done with all these things, every fall she had taken, every storm she had walked in, every harsh word she'd uttered, uncaring shrug, always so easy to hand out when there was always tomorrow and nothing could break you. In that second she rose from the ash that was everything she'd given Ennis—dead, gone, he couldn't break her fall. But this was life and maybe this man could? Why else would she cling to him when her side . . . her side plainly had eight spent arrows dying in it. Staring her in the face, wasn't it, what she felt for him? And it was all right. Time to live again.

He clasped the sides of her face.

"Listen to me."

"I'm trying to but not when it's things I don't want to hear … Not when there's something I need to tell you."

"Go home. Go home, Destiny, right now, because whatever it is there's no other way."

He bent his head. The kiss was fierce, sweet; the kiss was everything to cling to. She could not be left with nothing here. *She could not be left.* What went through her despite everything, the blood trickling between her fingers, the gun pointed at her breast, the wind tearing at her hair, the water lapping at her feet, even the sweat that inched down her cold skin in the moonlight, *was life.* And not just that, it was everything she craved now, forever and so simple. How could she choose anything else?

"Divers … I'm not letting you go. Not with him. Last night? Last night you saved me. Saved me when you could have let me go. When I was ready to go. Before I realized, me and Ennis, these were golden clouds you spoke of."

"Step aside, Miss Rhodes. When you're told, now. You are allying yourself with a man who is a traitor to the uniform he wears. A breaker of the law he swore to uphold. And, when it comes to mathematics, a thief. A man headed for the gallows."

"Destiny, old girl …"

"Destiny, do what they say." Divers O'Roarke's fingertips traced her cheeks. His eyes were lit by stars in the moonlight as they met hers, the smile the sweetest she'd ever seen and one she wished she never had, as she tried to speak. She had never felt his fingertips quite like this on her face either. "I swear it. I'll be all right. Do you hear me? Listen. Listen I swear I'll be all right."

"You're absolutely right, in more ways than one, man." In that second Gil Wryson spoke. "Drop the gun," he said to Lyon.

Destiny swallowed the gulp.

"I mean it," Gil went on. "I have two guns here, one pointed at the back of your head, Mr. Lyon, *sir*, and another at you, Mr. Rhodes. Make no mistake, I will use them too. So if you, either of you, think you can outfox me, you're mistaken. Nice and slowly. I don't want to hear argument or dissent. Do it now. Then put your hands behind your backs."

"Ah, the weevil crawls out from the biscuit, Mr. Wryson. I was wondering how long it would take for you speak."

"About half as long as it will take for me to blow your brains out and splatter them all over that rock there if you don't shut up and do what I say."

"Gil …" Divers O'Roarke murmured.

"I mean it. Do you think it's anything to me to see this bastard in hell? The hold he's always had on you? Don't kid yourself you're the only one, because that's how people like him operate. That's what they do. He got away with Eirwin. He's not getting away with this. Do it." He tightened his grip on the pistol that was jammed against Lyon's left temple. "Now. Or so help me God, I won't care what gibbet I swing from. As for you Mr. Rhodes, make one move and you're dead."

Destiny snagged another frosted breath. My God, was it possible they were getting out of here? Well, Divers O'Roarke and Gil Wryson were. Herself now? Gil Wryson had never liked her. In fact he so little liked her, some might say, the wonder was he didn't have a pistol trained on her head, ready to add her brains to Lyon's *if* Lyon didn't put down the gun, and there was nothing to say he would. This was the man who had blown Eirwin to bits. There was nothing to say he wasn't about to win the prize for best shot in the Penvellyn Fair competition, by adding to his tally. Certainly not the breath tearing in her throat, the pincers ripping at her side.

"Very well." Lyon edged down. His eyes gleamed as if it either killed him, or he was looking for the way to take this back. "I am at your disposal."

"Divers, get the guns, both of them."

"Gil … "

"Whatever else you do, man, *get them*."

She grabbed what breath she could from the moonlit air as he reached forward. The shingle would not be a good resting place, after all. But she had this, surely? Even if she felt as if death had invaded her veins. One thing she was sure of through her blurring vision? Gil Wryson would never allow her on that boat.

"Easy." Divers O'Roarke clutched her closer. "I've got them. But I can't get in that boat. I can't do it."

"Divers … I … You … You have to," she murmured.

"Are you both crazy? How the hell am I meant to go? What? And leave you here to his tender mercies?"

"Take her with us then." Gil tossed the hair out of his eyes. "The hell, I'm not going to argue so long as we get the hell out of here in one piece, so long as you keep the gun on him while I tie his hands. You know she's the one for you."

"Divers ... "

Oh, God, how awful to have to make what might be the biggest decision in her life largely because she seeped blood and could do with a seat--task one. And yet, it wasn't so crazy—task two—to look at him in the moonlight and see reflected there all the things she wanted. Why else had she come all this way? Everything and nothing was what stood before her. The fall she must take in the hope he would break it. Let him go and what would she have? A load of old plates and some pine cone garlands? It was hardly going to win first prize in *the living life* competition. Imagine getting to be a hundred and that was what she had to show for it? All because the idea of ever falling again filled her with terror? Wasn't it terror not to be able to breathe if she wasn't with him? She had risked everything after alll and he'd saved her.

"Destiny." His breath tore. "I can't. You come with me, girl and nothing is what you'll ever have, I have *nothing* to give you."

Everything? Nothing? Everything? Nothing? How true it was. In that second did she need to sit down to make that decision? The wind tearing at her hair, at his, the sea washing round their feet, the midnight gulls screaming overhead? Were these things going to make it for her?

"That's still enough for me. Divers, I'm not letting you go. Nothing is what I'll have staying here because there's *nothing* I want. Nothing. It's you, or it's nothing. And perhaps it always was. I just couldn't see it because I will trample on what can be trampled on. And I'm not sure I'm good at what it all does to me. But I'm not choosing nothing. I'm choosing everything. I'm coming with you because you see the clouds? Well sometimes clouds are silver. Now, help me in the boat."

"Destiny ... Old girl, are you mad?" Orwell's eyes, raked her, like skeletal ships passing into another world, one she was done with. "You can't go with him I've secured Doom Bar Hall. *Our* home, I ... I told you ..."

"*Your* home, Orwell. And one I wish you luck of, joy, everything you could want in it. Divers, the boat. I think I sodding love you, just so as you know and I think you better sodding love me back because I really can't stand here all sodding night, nigh unto and slowly bleeding to sodding death. I need to sit down. Mr. Wryson, you can tie Mr. Lyon's hands once I'm seated."

"With pleas—"

"Oh, it's not quite nothing you're going to, Miss Rhodes, as I'm sure Mr. Wryson here will tell you, although it is nothing much." Lyon's voice was dry. "Yes. True love, eh? Why you'd run off with a man who has broken the law and will be hunted in every corner of this kingdom."

She drew herself up. "Well, so long as it's not every corner of the Earth, it's none of your business."

"Perhaps? If that is the fool you want to make of yourself, so be it." He shrugged.

"I don't see what's funny."

"Me neither, Miss Rhodes. There is no need to tie my hands, Mr. Wryson. It's an indignity I can do without."

"Oh, I'll be the judge of—"

"Whatever you think, I'm not the villain you all believe."

"Oh, you're a villain all right." Gil jerked Lyon's hands behind his back.

"On the contrary. I am an admirer of love's sheer folly. Of a woman choosing a traitor and thief, despite everything and the fact my men will be here any minute, so you can tie my hands and those of Mr. Rhodes to your heart's content. That is why I'm going to give you half an hour."

"Half an hour?" Divers O'Roarke narrowed his eyes. "We'll have a damned sight more than half an—"

"Hour's head start. Then, believe me, I will come after you and I will hunt you down like the dogs you are. Whatever else you think of me, Mr. O'Roarke, I am a great believer in fair play."

CHAPTER TWENTY EIGHT

I think I sodding love you, just so as you know.
With the water's edge lapping at his boots and the wind tearing at his hair, he turned and grasped her, looked down into her face, silvered by starlight. Yes, they had half an hour but it was worth taking this crazy minute to knock it down to twenty nine.

"So, Destiny, do you mean what you said?"

"What? About the fact I know places here? Don't worry about that or him," she murmured. "He wouldn't even know which haystack to start looking for that particular needle in. We'll get away. I promise."

"Not that. What you said about me?"

"Oh that? You're asking me that here? Now?"

"Do you love me, Destiny?"

If he stared at her with bemused eyes in the moonlight he didn't care.

"What do you think?" Maybe her throat tightened but her pale lips managed a smile. "I mean, I don't attest to the rest of you but your confidence is not half bad for starters. I mean … I don't think you have any idea how hard it is sleeping with someone for the sole purpose of keeping them safe. Talking of which, don't take my advice or anything, you never do, but if I were you I'd tie his nibs up with my brother and leave them both in Raven's Passage. They'll get out eventually and it will give us more time. Thirty minutes?

Thirty minutes isn't long, especially if you're going to waste five of it on this sodding nonsense."

"Good idea, Destiny. One of your better ones if you don't mind me saying."

"Thank you, Divers. I think, all things considered, we make a not too shabby team. We might even win a prize some day."

"Then let's do it."

So he did what she suggested, while she clambered aboard the bobbing boat.

Love? The rock beneath the crumbling stone. The frailty and strength of human nature, human passion, because if somebody like her could see beneath the cracks, to love somebody like him, if he could love her through these same fissures for that matter, see her strength and her endurance, even in the chasms she'd fallen into, could set to the side everything she'd done, then there was that other great thing, the hope that beat in his heart like a bird's wings, *that this could work.* So long as they didn't drown on their own folly here.

He stepped into the stern of the boat, the cold biting so hard now, even through the wool of his coat it ate him raw, nose, fingers, breath. As for her? He glanced down at the sooty line of her eyelashes and settled down beside her. As for her, he hadn't the least idea apart from the fact her teeth were chattering. But dare he forget, he'd been ready to hand himself over to Lyon to see her go free?

Love? What he was in apparently. And it was all right. Hell, it was more all right than anything he'd ever felt in his life before. Scary? Scary as hell? And yet, so damned right, it was almost a moment for celebration. She could have chosen Doom Bar Hall. With, or without Lyon in it. She hadn't. She could have chosen the past. Him too. Dare he forget that either?

She'd said she liked his confidence. It was time to be that man again. Sort of anyway.

"Let's go. By the stars," he murmured to Gil.

Start as he meant to go on, now? With a confidence he had not felt in weeks. It was time. Somehow they would find a way out of this. Prove Lyon wrong. The sole reason he'd let them go.

"Did I tell you, how very romantic this is? No. Truly." As he gazed down at her, she smiled at him faintly and whispered, "By the stars and down the coast, there's places there we can at least stop safely. Clouds of silver now."

As muddy dawn fingered the horizon and Gil eased the boat another creaking foot through the frothing waves, the words circled like gulls in Divers' head, bleak except for one thing—the feel of Destiny Rhodes' faintly shivering body against his and her eyes, the stars he'd now guide himself by. His Destiny.

Where they were headed, he didn't know. But one thing he did.

"I love you, girl. And you better believe I'll do it till these same stars we're heading for, go out."

The End

Splendor by Shehanne Moore

He hates to lose. Especially to a man who's not.

One move to win ten thousand guineas in a chess competition. One move to marry her fiancé. Another to face the most merciless man in London across a pair of duelling pistols. For Splendor, former skivvy to the London's premiere jewel thieves, it's all in a day's work. But when one wrong move leads to another, can she win and keep her heart intact against the one man in London with the potential to bring her down? Especially in a chess game where the new wager is ten thousand guineas against one night with her.

The Endgame to end all Endgames

One move to pay back his ex-mistress. One move to show the world he doesn't give a damn he's been beaten in every way. The ton's most ruthless heartbreaker, bitter, divorcee, Kendall Winterborne, Earl of Stillmore's, pet hates are kitchen maids, marriage and losing. Knowing Splendor has entered a male chess competition under false pretences, he's in the perfect position to extort her help, regardless of the fact she's engaged to someone else. He just doesn't bank on having to face up to his pet hates. Certainly not over the kind of skivvy who ruined his father and set him on this course.

As one move leads to another, one thing's for certain though. His next move better be fast if he wants to keep the Cinderella he's fallen for. But the clock is ticking. When it strikes twelve, which man will she choose?

London Jewel Thieves.
Available from Amazon

Loving Lady Lazuli by Shehanne Moore

A woman not even the ghost of Sapphire can haunt. A man who knows exactly who she is.

Only one man in England can identify her. Unfortunately he's living next door.

Ten years ago sixteen year old Sapphire, the greatest jewel thief England has ever known, ruined Lord Devorlane Hawley's life by planting a stolen necklace on him. Now she's dead and buried, all Cassidy Armstrong wants is the chance to prove she was never that girl.

But her new neighbor is hell-bent on revenge and his word can bring her down. So when he asks her to be his mistress, or leave the county with a price on her head, Sapphire, who hates being owned, must decide…

What's left for a woman with nowhere else to go, but to stay exactly where she is?

And hope, that when it comes to neighbors Devorlane Hawley won't prove to be the one from hell.

London Jewel Thieves.

Available from Amazon

His Judas Bride by Shehanne Moore

Desiring her could be murder.

To love, honor, and betray…

To get back her son, she will stop at nothing…

Dire circumstances have forced Kara McGurkie to forget she's a woman. Dire circumstances force her to swear to love and honor, to help destroy a clan, when it means getting back her son. But when dire circumstances force her to seduce her fiancé's brother on the eve of the wedding, will the dark secrets she holds and her greatest desire be enough to save her from his powerful allure?

To save his people, neither will he…

Since his wife's murder, Callm McDunnagh, the Black Wolf of Lochalpin, ruthlessly guards heart and glen from dangerous intruders. But from the moment he first sees Kara he knows he must possess her, even though surrendering to his passion may prove the most dangerous risk of all.

She has nothing left to fear except love itself…

Now only Kara can decide what passion can save or destroy, and who will finally learn the truth of the words… *Till death do us part.*

Available from Amazon

The Unraveling of Lady Fury by Shehanne Moore

Genoa 1820
Rule One: There will be no kissing. Rule two: You will be fully clothed at all times...

Widowed Lady Fury Shelton hasn't lost everything—yet. As long as she produces the heir to the Beaumont dukedom, she just might be able to keep her position. And her secrets. But when the callously irresistible Captain James "Flint" Blackmoore sails back into her life, Lady Fury panics. She must find a way to protect herself—and her future—from the man she'd rather see rotting in hell than sleeping in her bed. If she must bed him to keep her secrets, so be it. But she doesn't have to like it. A set of firm rules for the bedroom will ensure that nothing goes awry. Because above all else, she must stop herself from wanting the one thing that Flint can never give her. His heart.

Ex-privateer Flint Blackmoore has never been good at following the rules. Now, once again embroiled in a situation with the aptly named Lady Fury, he has no idea why he doesn't simply do the wise thing and walk away. He knows he's playing with fire, and that getting involved with her again is more dangerous than anything on the high seas. But he can't understand why she's so determined to hate him. He isn't sure if the secret she keeps will make things harder—or easier—for him, but as the battle in the bedroom heats up, he knows at least one thing. Those silly rules of hers will have to go…

Available from Amazon

Other books from Black Wolf

The Eyes of Grace O'Malley by John Quinn

State ... Security ... *Secrets ...*

Scotland 1972. A turbulent place - miners' strikes, blackouts, Clyde shipyard workers defying the British Government, oil discovered in the North Sea and the long and deadly arms of conflict in Ireland reaching across the Irish Sea.

Farrell Golden is a bright working class kid from Dundee with an Irish heritage. But he hasn't always paid it much attention. Thanks to his family he's made it to the University of Edinburgh against the odds. But does he want to stay there?

There's beer and there's women - in particular a beautiful ethereal English girl called Maggie. She's out of the London stockbroker belt but she's not all that she seems. Then there's an Irish girl who is somehow familiar ...

Roisin O'Malley's not like any trainee teacher Farrell's ever seen. What is she getting away from in Edinburgh? What are her family's links to the Troubles? What of her ex-boyfriend?

At a Bloody Sunday protest march Farrell sees Roisin in trouble and goes to help. He's knocked unconscious. When he wakens up he finds he's stepped down a rabbit hole of Irish history, family ties and state security. Is there a way back? Should he have paid more attention to the family heritage? Who is Roisin O'Malley really.

Available from Amazon

Printed in Poland
by Amazon Fulfillment
Poland Sp. z o.o., Wrocław